Cait's warm body was curled around Tyler.

Gentle, soft hands stroked the damp hair away from his face. The clean, flowery scent of her skin enveloped him. It was so foreign to the life he had led for so long that it stunned him. A rough yearning uncoiled from the dark, cold emptiness inside him.

"Cait," he muttered. His hand was heavy. Clumsy. Somehow he managed to lift it high enough to touch her cheek.

"I don't want you to be hurt anymore," she whispered with a sob in her voice. Her fingers closed around his hand.

"Used to it." His eyelids closed drunkenly. In the harsh light, his thick lashes made dark crescents on his too-pale skin. He muttered something she didn't catch, and his hand fell away.

Cait bit her lip. She cradled him against her and tried not to think of the pain that had put deep lines in his face and silver in his hair....

Dear Reader,

I'm really excited about the books I'm bringing you this month. I think every one of them is a winner. Marilyn Pappano checks in with *Somebody's Lady,* the sequel to her ultra-popular *Somebody's Baby.* Lawyers Zachary Adams and Beth Gibson met as adversaries in that first book, but this time they're on the same side of a difficult case, one that tests all their professional skills as they work side by side. Of course, emotions have a habit of coming to the surface in such situations, and this one is no exception. Can "city" and "country" meet and make a match? If you know Marilyn's talents, you'll know this book is a must read.

Paula Detmer Riggs will also put you through an emotional wringer in another must read: *Paroled!* When Tyler McClane got out of prison, all he wanted was to forget his ex-wife's unjust charges, charges that had destroyed his career and torn his daughter from him. But Caitlin Fielding wasn't about to leave the past alone, not when she knew her sister had wrongly sent a man to prison—with her own unwitting help! Not when a little girl's future happiness depended on setting things straight with her daddy. I don't want to tell you any more, because you should experience this wonderful book for yourself.

To complete the month, we have Mary Anne Wilson's *Echoes of Roses,* a beautifully wrought story of a man who's the idol of millions, but wants only one woman, a woman with a secret she's sure he'll never understand. And welcome new author Sally Tyler Hayes. In *Whose Child Is This?* she has written a stunning debut book filled with characters who will touch your heart.

Next month, we have a very special book from Joyce McGill, but that's all I'm going to say for now. I hope you'll join me then to hear all about it.

Yours,

Leslie Wainger
Senior Editor and Editorial Coordinator

PAULA DETMER RIGGS

Paroled!

SILHOUETTE·INTIMATE·MOMENTS®

Published by Silhouette Books New York

America's Publisher of Contemporary Romance

SILHOUETTE BOOKS
300 East 42nd St., New York, N.Y. 10017

PAROLED!

ISBN: 0-373-07440-9

First Silhouette Books printing July 1992

Printed in the U.S.A.

Books by Paula Detmer Riggs

Silhouette Intimate Moments

Beautiful Dreamer #183
Fantasy Man #226
Suspicious Minds #250
Desperate Measures #283
Full Circle #303
Tender Offer #314
A Lasting Promise #344
Forgotten Dream #364
Paroled! #440

Silhouette Desire

Rough Passage #633

Silhouette Books

Silhouette Summer Sizzlers 1992
"Night of the Dark Moon"

PAULA DETMER RIGGS

discovers material for her writing in her varied life experiences. During her first five years of marriage to a naval officer, she lived in nineteen different locations on the West Coast, gaining familiarity with places as diverse as San Diego and Seattle. While working at a historical site in San Diego, she wrote, directed and narrated fashion shows and became fascinated with the early history of California.

She writes romances because "I think we all need an escape from the high-tech pressures that face us every day, and I believe in happy endings. Isn't that why we keep trying, in spite of all the roadblocks and disappointments along the way?"

Chapter 1

The screams started around midnight. Caitlin Fielding had been deep in sleep. Now wide-awake, she was sitting on the side of her daughter Kelsey's bed, trying to calm the screaming child.

"Kelsey! Wake up. Now!" she ordered in voice loud enough to penetrate the deepest dream state. Kelsey's eyelids fluttered open, but her eyes were unfocused.

"It's just a dream, sweetie," Cait soothed. "A bad dream."

"M-mama Cait?" The child's voice was thick with confusion.

Soon to be nine, Kelsey Caitlin McClane had known Cait for most of those years as her adored aunt and her mother's older sister. And then, almost a year ago, Crystal Fielding McClane had been killed when her candy-apple-red Porsche had gone out of control on a rain-slicked San Francisco hill.

Kelsey was Cait's child now, legally adopted after Crystal's will had given her custody. They were a family, just the two of them.

"Yes, baby. I'm here. Everything's going to be all right."

As a practicing child psychologist, Cait had been increasingly aware of the telltale signs of distress in her daughter. Mood swings. Tantrums. Sulks. And now nightmares.

Still cradling Kelsey's shaking body against hers, Cait settled against the headboard. Instantly Kelsey twined her thin arms around Cait's waist and pressed close like a frightened nestling huddling for warmth against a dangerous world.

Beneath Kelsey's soft flannel jammies, her heart pounded hard enough to shake her small body, and her fair skin had a porcelainlike transparency, revealing fine blue veins close to the surface.

"Do you want to talk about your dream?" Cait was careful to keep her tone calm and nonthreatening.

Kelsey shook her head. A small whimper escaped her throat, and her fingers clung even tighter.

"Is there some little thing that's bothering you? Something we should talk out before it gets to be a big, awful thing?"

Kelsey's throat worked as she swallowed a sob. "Mama Cait, is . . . is my daddy really in prison?"

So that's it, Cait thought. The past coming back to haunt both of them.

"Yes, Kelsey, he is. Your mommy and I explained that to you after the trial, remember?"

After Dr. Tyler McClane had been led away in handcuffs and shackles, sentenced to six years in the California State Penitentiary at Vacaville for felony molestation of a minor.

The judge had been particularly rough on him because of his status as a pediatric surgeon, and because the child he'd been convicted of abusing was his own daughter. That had been four years ago. For all Cait knew, he was still in prison. He certainly deserved to be.

Kelsey raised her head and looked up at Cait. Her eyes, a rare shade of smoky topaz, were swollen and shadowed.

"Mama Cait?"

"Yes, sweetie?"

"Why is my daddy in prison?"

Cait took a slow, even breath. She'd known that sooner or later this would come up. She had hoped it would be later.

"When you were five, your daddy did things to you that he shouldn't have done. Remember when you and I and your mommy went to talk to the nice policemen and Mr. Lamont, the man who asked you questions in court? After that, the judge and jury decided that Daddy had to be punished, so they sent him to prison as part of that punishment. Remember? We talked about that a lot, too."

Cait made herself speak calmly, even though her stomach was quivering. Just thinking about Tyler McClane made her sick inside.

"Sarah's stepdaddy said that prison is an awful place where they put bad people. People get killed there."

"Sometimes, but that's not your fault. Your daddy is in prison because he hurt you."

"But...but maybe if I hadn't told the judge those things, he wouldn't've had to go to that awful place."

Cait's fingers trembled as they gently cupped the little girl's chin. "Kelsey, listen to me," she declared firmly. "You did absolutely the right thing when you told the truth about your daddy. It's always right to tell the truth, no matter what happens. And none of this is your fault. Not what your daddy did. Not the trial. Not the prison."

Kelsey sat up and began playing with the top button of Cait's nightshirt. Her eyes were downcast, revealing glistening tears clotting her eyelashes.

"I...I saw this TV show at Sarah's house the last time I slept over." The thin little voice was barely above a whisper, and Caitlin had to lean forward to make out the words.

"What was the show about?"

"About telling the truth and what happens sometimes if you don't."

"And that...upset you?"

Kelsey's face crumpled. Tears streamed down her face.

"I didn't want to l-lie. My Sunday school teacher always said it was wrong, and Daddy told me once when I told a fib that it would make people not trust me, but I was so s-scared. I wanted to be with Mommy."

Lie? Cait went still. With the instinct of a trained therapist, she kept her expression blank, but she felt the blood draining from her face. She had trouble breathing normally.

"What did you lie about, sweetie?"

"D-daddy."

Cait felt chilled through and through. All of a sudden she couldn't seem to get enough air into her lungs. Careful, she cautioned herself. Don't put words into her mouth.

"You told the judge that you were afraid of your daddy. Was that the truth?" Her voice was calm. Only another therapist would hear the sudden panic she was concealing.

Kelsey shook her head very slowly, as though she were afraid of Cait's reaction.

"You weren't afraid of your daddy?"

Again Kelsey shook her head. "I was never scared of him, but he . . . he wasn't home very much. Mostly he worked at the hospital, making other little boys and girls better when they got sick. Once, when I had a bad temperature and couldn't sleep, he told me stories, and he used to sing to me sometimes. I liked that a lot."

Cait inhaled slowly, willing the air to fill her starved lungs. "Think very carefully, Kels. Did your daddy ever touch you in ways that scared you or hurt you?"

Kelsey shook her head.

"Did he ever do things when he tucked you in at night that made you feel funny inside?"

"Uh-uh."

"Never? Not even once?"

"Uh-uh. Mostly he wasn't there when I went to bed. Sometimes, though, he kissed me on my bangs and tucked the covers in tight, so I wouldn't fall out."

"Then why did you tell the judge that Daddy did bad things to you?"

Kelsey dropped her gaze and chewed her lip.

"Kels? Why did you say those things if they weren't true?"

"'Cause Mommy said I had to." Her voice was subdued, almost inaudible.

"Mommy told you to lie?" Cait asked without a hint of inflection in her voice.

"Uh-huh."

"Do you know why Mommy told you to lie about your daddy?"

Kelsey's throat worked as she swallowed a sob. "'Cause of the divorce."

"Your mommy and daddy's divorce?"

Kelsey bobbed her head dejectedly. "M-mommy said he didn't l-love me and that's why I had to tell the judge that he did bad things, so me and her could be together always and always."

Kelsey clung to her, thin legs drawn into the fetal position against Cait's midriff. Tears wet Cait's neck. Kelsey's shudders shook her, as well.

"It's okay, baby. Cry it out." Cait gathered her closer and began to rock her with the age-old rhythm that all mothers seem to know instinctively. Gradually the child's sobs subsided to an occasional whimper. Still Cait held her, her own gaze unfocused now and glazed with shock.

Sometime later the distant shrill of a siren gradually sliced into the turmoil in Cait's tired brain, drawing her gaze to the impenetrable blackness beyond the windowpanes.

Outside, Sacramento was settling uneasily into another sweltering summer night. Sheltered by the old house's thick walls, the cheerful room lovingly decorated for a happy child suddenly seemed filled with ghosts.

Crystal Fielding McClane, brittle and beautiful, as always.

And Tyler McClane. Darkly powerful, ambitious, the man Cait had hated for four years.

There had been many nights since the trial when she'd lain awake, suffering from tormenting regret. Regret that she had once trusted him. Regret that she had ever introduced him to her younger sister.

Cait had been a psychotherapy intern at Stanford Medical and he'd been a surgical resident specializing in pediatrics when they had literally bumped into each other in the staff lounge.

Tyler had apologized and offered to refill the coffee cup his clumsiness had sent flying from her hand. After that, it had seemed the most natural thing in the world for them to sit together. Over stale doughnuts, the two normally private people found that they had surprisingly a lot to talk about.

Surprising, because she and Tyler couldn't have been more different. Her background was middle-class and genteel. His was hardscrabble blue collar. She'd always lived in Marin County, an upper-middle-class suburb of San Francisco. He'd grown up on a scrub ranch near Placerville in the Sierra Nevada foothills. She'd gone to school on the money from her trust fund. He'd borrowed and scrimped and worked two jobs as a wrangler every summer to pay for his.

When Cait had first noticed the reserved resident, he'd still been range tough, even after years of college and medical school. Endless summers of hard labor under the omnipresent California sun had layered his skin with color until it had taken on a burnished bronze stain. His thick hair, streaked a half-dozen shades of blond by that brutal sun, always looked as though it were permanently wind whipped.

A healer with the body of a rodeo champion and a rawboned face right out of a rough-and-tumble western movie, that had been Tyler.

Normally impervious to handsome men, she had never tired of looking at him, especially when his sensitive gray eyes burned as he talked about his plans for the future. He intended to make a difference in the world of suffering children. It was the only thing he'd ever wanted, the only thing that mattered. Cait had believed every word that he'd said. Then.

Her vision blurred suddenly as she gently wiped Kelsey's hot cheeks with the lacy edge of the sheet. Kelsey whimpered. Her swollen eyelids were closed, her breathing heavy with exhaustion and thick with unshed tears.

"Sleep, baby," Cait whispered. "Mama Cait is here. I'll always be here."

Kelsey settled more firmly against her. Cait's throat stung from a need to cry, a need she couldn't gratify. She had three degrees, including a doctorate in clinical psychology, a dozen citations from various child abuse foundations and a gratifyingly long list of successes with her small patients.

Yet suddenly she felt as helpless as the child in her arms. She had to do something, anything, to ease Kelsey's suffering.

And Tyler, a voice prodded. Don't forget his suffering.

The shadows shifted and darkened until the memory of Tyler McClane's tormented eyes bored into hers. Caitlin squeezed her eyelids tight, but the memories remained.

It was so long ago. It was yesterday.

Kelsey had been five. Precocious. Mischievous. An adorable chatterbox. She had been living in the Bay Area where Tyler was a junior partner in a prestigious surgical corporation and Crystal cultivated the "right" people to advance her husband's career.

Their marriage had been rocky from the start, but they had both doted on their little imp. Her Aunt Cait, too, had delighted in spoiling her on the few occasions when Kelsey had visited Sacramento. And then, shortly after the divorce suit was raised, everything had changed.

Kelsey began to throw tantrums. Her playmates' mothers complained that she was becoming a bully. Crystal asked for Cait's help.

"You're a shrink, Caitie. You know what makes kids tick. God knows, I don't. Kelsey is driving me bats with her whining and screaming and kicking."

So Cait had had a quiet talk with the child. It took several tries and a large measure of patience before Kelsey had begun to talk.

Her daddy was hurting her, she'd said with a haunted look in her big gray eyes. He was doing things that made her feel bad. To Cait's horror, she realized that Kelsey was speaking the unspeakable.

When Cait had confronted her sister, Crystal had burst into tears and admitted, through her sobs, that the child was telling the truth.

"You don't know him, Caitie. He's not really the nice guy he pretends to be around you. He's...he's so cold, like all his feelings are all frozen up inside."

It had been storming that terrible night when Cait had confronted Tyler, Kelsey's halting accusations and Crystal's corroboration still fresh in her mind.

"How could you do such a thing?" she had raged in white-lipped disgust. Tyler had turned ashen, his gray eyes nearly black with pain.

"I wouldn't hurt my daughter, Cait, I swear. This is all Crystal's doing, to make sure I don't get custody. You have to believe me."

If it had been a choice between Crystal's accusations and his denial, Cait would have been inclined to believe him. After all, since childhood Crys had been known to twist the truth for her own purposes.

As for Tyler, he loved children. He'd devoted his life to caring for them. Cait had seen him with his patients, seen the way they responded to him. She'd seen him with Kelsey. For all his reserve and toughness, he clearly adored his only child.

But Kelsey had been too young to carry off such a deception. Or so Cait had believed with all her heart. Trained to discern truth from lies, reality from fantasy, she had seen only truth in Kelsey's eyes, heard only truth in her wavering voice, sensed only truth in her body language.

Cait had taken action without hesitation. She'd gone with Crystal to file charges against Tyler. She'd supported both Crys and Kelsey through the police interview, the medical tests, the district attorney's questioning.

When Tyler was brought to trial, Cait took a leave of absence and moved in with her sister and niece. Both depended on her. Both turned to her. She had been their rock.

On the stand, sitting on two telephone books so that she could reach the microphone, Kelsey had testified to despicable things that had made Tyler's face grow whiter and whiter and Cait's stomach knot.

Looking beautiful and tormented in designer linen and silk, Crystal had tearfully corroborated her daughter's story.

Cait had seen the belief in the eyes of the jurors and known it was reflected in her own.

Tyler had seen it, too.

Now Cait slumped against the headboard, and her arms tightened protectively around his daughter.

Her gaze shifted to Kelsey's latest school photograph on the bureau. Kelsey's resemblance to her father had grown stronger over the years. Her thick wheat-blond hair curled rebelliously at the ends the way Tyler's had when he'd forgotten to get a haircut. Her gray eyes, so like his in color and expression, were framed with the same dark blond lashes. Her stubborn chin was a dainty version of her father's strong jaw.

But the delicate, almost ethereal bone structure had come from the Fielding side of the family. And her laugh, too, carried the same infectious lilt that characterized Cait's.

Nowadays, however, Kelsey's expression was usually solemn. The corners of her mouth were touched with sadness. The eyes that should be filled with childish sweetness were older than her years. Much older.

What about Tyler? Cait wondered. What would she see in his eyes now?

Even though there had been no medical evidence of abuse of any kind, the jury of seven women and five men had taken less than three hours to agree on a verdict of guilty.

"There's something particularly heinous in a pediatric surgeon victimizing his own daughter," the foreman had later declared with righteous indignation to the press.

Moving slowly, she eased Kelsey from her lap. The little girl whimpered but didn't waken. With gentle fingers, Cait wiped the last of the tears from Kelsey's cheeks.

"No matter what, I'll make everything right for you," Cait whispered. "I promise." But the suffering eyes she saw in her mind belonged to Tyler McClane. The only man she had ever loved.

The dinner hour was long past. The streetlights had been on for hours. The North Sacramento Mental Health Clinic was closed. Doctors, nurses, receptionists, bookkeepers—all had gone home. Every office was empty—except one.

Cait was still in her book-lined retreat on the second floor. Her friend and colleague, Dr. Hazel O'Connor, was there as well, curled into a chair opposite the desk.

On the sunny side of forty, Hazel had a freckled face, a happy-go-lucky smile and naturally curly auburn hair worn in a slapdash tangle that made her look like Little Orphan Annie most of the time. But her mind was the keenest Cait had ever encountered, and her heart the kindest.

The pizza Cait had ordered lay cold and uneaten in the soggy box. Cait's soda had grown warm at her elbow. Hazel had taken only a few sips of hers.

For the past hour Hazel had listened without interrupting as Cait poured out the story of the trial and Kelsey's present emotional distress.

"So that's why I called you in," Cait finished in a tired voice. "Kelsey needs treatment, and I can't treat her."

"Have you talked with her teacher?"

"Actually, Mrs. Eddington called *me* a few weeks ago. She said Kels couldn't seem to concentrate, and when she did try, she couldn't seem to retain anything she heard. That's when I started to suspect a problem of some kind."

Hazel nodded before saying in her slow, deliberate way, "From what you've told me, I suspect she's suffering from delayed posttraumatic stress, exacerbated by repressed guilt. That TV show sounded like the perfect catalyst to release the lid on a pot of simmering emotions already close to boiling over."

"I agree."

Cait slumped in her chair. Beneath her summer tan, her muscles were knotted with tension. Across town, the sitter would have Kelsey snugged into bed under her own special quilt. Would she get through tonight without sobbing herself awake? Or would she toss and turn, transforming her blankets into a constricting cocoon?

It was a night for bad dreams, that was for sure. Rain sheeted down in torrents, and the wind drove the drops into the windowpanes like hailstones.

"I knew my sister was selfish," Cait admitted with a heavy sigh. "Even vindictive at times, but I was sure she wouldn't use her own child as a weapon."

Hazel poked at the congealing pizza before giving her head a slight shake. "I'm not certain Kelsey truly understands what happened to her father, but it sounds as though she knows it's her fault, whatever happened."

"In a way it is," Cait murmured in a dispirited tone. "She did lie. To me, to the social worker and to the police. To the jury."

"True. No doubt that's part of what's tearing her apart. After all, she's an unusually bright child with a vivid imagination and a strong conscience. Right now she's punishing herself because she knows she did wrong. In fact, it's highly probable that in a child's convoluted way, she also blames herself for her mother's death."

Cait nodded. Such things were common among troubled children. "She wasn't very talkative this morning, but from the few things she did say, it looks like she's absolutely convinced that Tyler hates her."

"A logical assumption for a child to make, especially since she seems to hate herself so much for lying."

Cait stared at the silver picture frame proudly displaying Kelsey's latest school photograph in a place of honor on her desk. "I was so certain she was mourning Crystal. Fourteen years of experience, and I didn't even suspect anything like this."

Hazel smiled slightly, as though she'd been expecting such a comment sooner or later. "You're Kelsey's mother in every way that counts, Cait. Your objectivity is shot."

Cait stared at the raindrops bleeding down the windowpane. Outside, the wind tore at a newly planted sapling that bent but refused to break. Would that be Kelsey? she wondered. Or would the force of the guilt she was feeling destroy her?

"I keep thinking what it must have been like for Tyler all these years, knowing he's innocent and that no one believed him. Years and years locked in a cage." She turned to face her friend. "God help me, Hazel, I helped put him there. I'm as much to blame as Kelsey. More. I'm supposed to be a professional, an expert in behavior problems and childhood trauma. I did my thesis on the symptoms and lingering effects of sexual abuse on children, for heaven's sake. I should have seen through her story. I should have believed Tyler."

Cait crossed her arms over her breasts and tried to rub some warmth into her body. She hadn't felt warm since she'd walked out of Kelsey's room at a quarter past two last night.

"You did what you did out of love," Hazel said with quiet conviction. "No one can blame you for that."

"I can. I do!"

Hazel didn't answer. When Cait glanced up to see why not, she discovered a look of genuine anger on her friend's face. "What about the DA? The judge? The jury? Do you really think you're smarter than all of them combined?"

Hurt, Cait opened her mouth to reply, but Hazel didn't give her a chance. "You were just one of a considerable number of intelligent, caring people who had to weigh any doubts they might have against the consequences to countless other little girls if *Dr.* Tyler McClane just happened to be guilty."

"Only he wasn't!"

"But he could have been! Think what you'd be feeling if you'd somehow managed to get him off and then found out that he *was* guilty. Then what?"

Cait sank back in her chair and picked at a scratch on the edge of the desk with a slender finger. "I knew their marriage was in trouble. Tyler was working day and night to build up his practice, and Crys was bored. I think she asked him for a divorce to shake him up. Instead, he seemed almost relieved."

Cait's mind summoned an image of Tyler's increasingly tense features. Every time she had visited, he had seemed preoccupied, even curt.

"He told her he would give her everything," she continued in a flat tone. "The house, the cars, the membership in the tennis club. But he wanted joint custody. I thought it was a reasonable request. I was trying to convince Crys when all this just . . . blew up. I should have seen through Crys's lies then."

"Stop beating on yourself," Hazel chided. "You know that in cases like this it's always better to err on the side of the child. *Always.* You're not responsible for what happened."

"Perhaps not, but I *am* responsible for what I do about it now."

"True."

Cait glanced impatiently around her familiar, comfortable office, as though the answers were somehow written on the walls. "I have to do something, talk to the authorities, something, anything to help him."

"Yes, and as soon as possible." Hazel took a sip of soda and narrowed her eyes in concentration. "What did you say the prosecutor's name was? Lamar?"

"Lamont. Jackson Lamont. You must have seen him on TV. He's been on all the local talk shows, preaching his get-tough-on-criminals philosophy."

Hazel grimaced. "I've seen him. An up-and-coming politician if I've ever seen one. Contradictory as it sounds, though, he seems sincere."

Cait sighed. "Let's hope he's fair. Even if he isn't, no matter what Jack Lamont wants or thinks, we have to help Tyler get a new trial, or whatever the procedure is in cases like this."

"We will," Hazel assured her. "But first we have to decide what to do about Kelsey."

Cait was grateful to have something concrete to occupy her thoughts. All day, between patients, at lunch, on her coffee break, she had found herself alternately thinking about Tyler and grieving over her mistake. At odd moments she'd even found herself struggling to formulate the words of apology she owed him.

She pulled a yellow tablet toward her and began making a list. It was an old habit that helped focus her mind.

"Initiate intensive therapy, of course." She glanced up and said with a tense half smile, "By the way, I'm officially asking you to take her on as a patient."

Both noticed that her tone was brisk and professional now. So was Hazel's as she answered, "I'm officially accepting."

Cait relaxed slightly as Hazel went on, "My initial plan would be to address the issue of her father's feelings toward her. Do you know where he is?"

Cait drew a sharp breath. "The last I heard he was in Vacaville, working as an orderly at the prison hospital." Emptying bedpans, cleaning up vomit, taking orders when he had been used to giving them, she thought. That had to be unutterably humiliating for a man as proud of Tyler.

"The judge forbade him from ever seeing or contacting Crystal or Kelsey again," she added softly. "And, of course, he lost his license to practice medicine. After Crystal's death, he signed the paper relinquishing custody to me. That was the last time I heard from him."

Hazel shoved her soda can aside and rested her forearms on the desk. Cait gathered up the uneaten pizza and stuffed it, box and all, into the trash basket. Outside, the storm beat relentlessly on the tile roof.

Hugging herself, she stood up and went to the window. Instead of the storm, however, she saw Tyler's haggard face when the marshall had slipped the cold steel shackles over his wrists.

He had turned to look at her then. Only her. Stunned, she had seen a terrible, bitter anguish burning in his gray eyes. And then the pain had been replaced with icy hatred before he had allowed himself to be led away.

"I wonder what he's like after so many years behind bars," she mused aloud. Muted by the cold glass only inches from her mouth, her voice sounded hollow.

"Is he a fighter?"

Cait glanced up. Hazel was watching her calmly, but there was a sharp glint of curiosity between her lashes.

"If you mean physically, I don't know, although I do now he was pretty tough when I knew him. And…and he's all and built like a wrestler, which helps."

"And emotionally? What kind of a man is he?"

"Self-contained. A loner. The kind of man who has to now you for a long time before he's willing to risk his riendship."

"*Were* you friends?"

"Yes, we were friends." For five wonderful months.

"Were you lovers?" The question was quiet, nonthreatning, but Cait's heart began to race and her mouth went ry.

"No. We never even kissed," she said with a defensive dge to her voice. No one had believed that ten years ago. Why should Hazel believe it now?

"You were also terribly in love with him," Hazel said with a sympathetic smile.

Beneath the silk of her tailored blouse, Cait's shoulders drooped. She was too tired and too upset to try to fool her riend. "Yes, I was in love with him." Such an inadequate vord for the maelstrom of emotions she had felt when she'd been twenty-six, she thought. And yet, the only one that vould do.

"Did he love you?"

"No. At least, he never said so, but…" She shrugged and ell silent. Talking about that time was painful, even now.

"But what?"

Cait's gaze shifted to the wall where her diplomas were rranged alongside a carefully framed display of former patients' artwork. Studying them one by one helped ground er in the here and now.

"Tyler was different from the other residents, quieter, nore intense, really focused on what he was doing." She brought her gaze back to Hazel's, but her eyes were fixated n images of the past.

"Sometimes the others acted more like, oh, I don't know, nischievous little boys, I guess. Ragging each other, flirtng with the candy stripers, things like that. But not Tyler. As soon as he put on that starched white coat, he was a

doctor, as though nothing else mattered. I respected that.''
She blinked, and Hazel's face came into focus again. ''Am
I making any sense?''

Hazel nodded. ''Sounds like he took himself and his re-
sponsibilities very seriously.''

''Tyler was a very serious man. Maybe that's why I found
him so interesting.''

''And did he find you interesting?''

''He seemed to.'' Cait's smile was crooked and just a bit
self-conscious. ''At least, he laughed at my jokes.''

Hazel snorted. ''I've heard your jokes, Cait. If he
laughed, he *must* have been interested in you.''

Cait's smile faded. ''He trusted me, that much I do
know,'' she said softly. ''With his hopes, with his dreams,
things he'd never told anyone else. Do you know how special that made me feel?''

Hazel nodded but wisely remained silent.

''I had this very active fantasy going, you know. How he
would suddenly come to me and confess that he, too, was
harboring thoughts of, well, undying love, I guess. He
would kiss me breathless and then ask me to marry him.''
Cait felt her face flood with heat.

''What happened?''

''I introduced him to my little sister.'' Cait stared down at
her hands. She wore no rings. Never had. ''Crys took one
look and had to have him.''

''Just like that?''

''That's the way she was. All of her life, she'd gotten
everything she'd ever wanted just by looking adorable and
batting her big blue eyes.''

Cait's eyes were a plain sparrow brown, and her hair was
almost the same color, with a mind of its own when it came
to style. Crystal's, on the other hand, had been a shimmering thick platinum that had been the envy of all her
friends—and Cait, too.

It had taken Cait years and some hard work in therapy to
conquer the jealousy her sister had aroused in her almost
from the cradle. But she knew now that Crystal's surface

appeal would have faded in time, leaving her only a pale shadow, without personality or wit.

Hazel's expression turned thoughtful. "She *was* beautiful, Cait. And, from what I remember from the one time we met, dripping sex appeal, in a classy sort of way."

A fleeting smile erased some of the tension from Cait's face. "Oh, Crys was classy, all right. Mother insisted that we both grow up to be perfect ladies."

Hazel grinned. "I guess your mom would have had a fit if she'd lived long enough to see you climbing trees with Kelsey."

"Lord, would she!" Cait explained softly.

Hazel's expression sobered. "I take it Crystal got Tyler."

"Yes, she got him," Cait said with a humorless chuckle. "She told me she would. I didn't believe her—until the day she asked me to be maid of honor at their wedding."

"You didn't!"

Cait waved a hand in a dramatic gesture. "Sure I did. A Fielding faces life with her chin up and a smile on her face. I was charming and pleasant and oh so polite—until they left the reception to begin their honeymoon. And then I went into the ladies' room and threw up."

Hazel looked amused and sympathetic at the same time. "An understandable reaction."

"I threw up every day for a month, and then I decided to stop loving the man and get on with my life. Eight months later, after I'd finished my internship, I moved here and began building my practice. By that time Kelsey had been born."

Sudden understanding flashed in Hazel's eyes. "I see."

"Yes, so did I. My little sister had used the oldest trick in the book."

"Perhaps, but it takes two to conceive a child."

"You're right," Cait declared flatly. "It takes two. I think that's what hurt the most."

She drew a shaky breath. She'd made a mistake, taking this trip down memory lane. If Hazel hadn't needed to know Kelsey's background, she would have left the memories sealed up tight, the way they'd been for so long.

"So," she said to her friend, "you're the therapist, and I'll leave the therapy to you. But I want to help in any way I can."

"I expect you to. Even so, this isn't going to be easy. Sounds like there's a lot of hurting going on in your little girl."

"Whatever you want me to do, I'll do. Anything."

"Of course, Tyler McClane is the key to relieving Kelsey's guilt," Hazel said, as though continuing a conversation with herself. "If she can be made to believe he doesn't hate her or blame her for lying, she'll gradually stop blaming herself. For that, we absolutely have to have the father's help."

"I agree."

"I realize he can't contact her directly, but perhaps we could get permission from the court to read her a letter that he's written."

"A letter saying what?"

Hazel rubbed her temple. "First of all, that he doesn't hate her. And that he doesn't blame her for what happened to him. Something along those lines, anyway." She glanced toward the storm. "The question is, where is he?"

In hell, Cait thought with a rush of guilt. "First thing tomorrow, I'll start making calls," she promised. "I'll start with his attorney. Dante's his name, I think. I seem to remember that the guy's right here in the city."

"Who, McClane's attorney?"

Cait nodded. "They were old friends, I think. Crys said they grew up together."

Hazel leaned forward, her expression intense. "As soon as we find out where he is, one of us has to go to see him. Under the circumstances, I think it should be me."

Yes, Cait cried silently. You go. You face him. I can't. Dear God, I can't. Not after so many years. Not after so much pain.

"No," she said, slowly getting to her feet. "I'll go. I don't think I could live with myself if I didn't."

Chapter 2

California Route 49 stretched like an angry sidewinder through the foothills of the Sierra Nevada. Dangerously narrow in places, the old road linked the historic mother lode communities founded during the gold rush of 1849.

Cait had always loved traveling the picturesque highway, especially in the fall, when the leaves were changing color. Now, however, in late afternoon on the Saturday before Thanksgiving, the trees were bare.

The small town of Sutter Creek was her destination. According to Jess Dante, Tyler had been paroled there in March. Eight months ago, she thought. And living only sixty miles away.

Denied the reinstatement of his medical license and forced to register as a sex offender, he was working as a bartender in a place called the Lucky Horseshoe Saloon. According to Dante, it was the only job he had been able to find.

"It's a bikers' bar, mostly," the kid at the town's only service station told her. "Three blocks east, on the left. Just look for the hogs parked outside."

Cait's startled look had elicited a grin before the teenager had added, "Bikes, you know, like in Harleys."

Sutter Creek was too small to have a wrong side, but the street Cait was driving along was shabbier than most. The pavement was badly patched. Sidewalks were nonexistent.

In Sacramento this neighborhood would be listed on real estate maps as "in transition." From neglected to downright seedy, Cait decided as she downshifted to navigate a particularly nasty pothole in front of an abandoned auto body shop.

She found the Lucky Horseshoe at the end of the block. The building was a two-story cement boxlike structure that had once been painted white. The roof was corrugated steel in sad need of repair. Long streaks of rust ran down the facade like tears. A large sheet-metal horseshoe hung over the door. Once bright red, the block letters were so sun faded that she had to squint to make them out.

Lined up in the parking lot next to the building were the motorcycles she had been warned to expect. There were at least a dozen, perhaps more—huge, mean-looking contraptions overloaded with chrome. Saturday evening must be a busy time at the Lucky Horseshoe, she thought as she pulled into the first available parking space.

She killed the engine but made no move to get out. In spite of the outward calm that had become second nature to her after so many years as a therapist, she was quaking badly inside. Too many years had passed. Too many words had been said. Or perhaps left unsaid.

Tyler had never been an easygoing man. He'd been too intense, too focused, too driven. His stride, his quick, masculine gestures, his economy with words, had signaled an underlying impatience that had often flared into temper.

Not that he was a prima donna, she was forced to admit. Far from it. Of all the residents she'd known, he had worked the longest hours, devoted the most energy, cared the most.

A lump rose in her throat. She swallowed, and it eased. But the sick taste of regret remained. If things had been different . . .

But they aren't, she reminded herself as she jerked open the car door. The time for Tyler and her was past. They had both seen to that, she thought as she stepped from the car.

Gravel crunched under her feet. A wild wind snatched at her skirt and tore at the neat French twist that she always wore when she wanted to feel especially professional.

Head down against the wind, she made her way past the Harleys to the door. As soon as she walked in, she felt her defenses go up.

The interior was dimly lit. The air was blue with cigarette smoke and smelled of stale beer and sweat. Two pool tables took up one end of the long narrow room. An ornate, nineteenth-century bar complete with brass rail and flyspecked mirror took up the other.

Booths upholstered in dingy red vinyl lined both sides of the entrance. In the center of the long room, scarred wooden tables were arranged in a ragged circle around a small dance floor presently packed with burly rough-edged men and hard-looking women.

Instead of chaps and Stetsons, however, these would-be cowboys wore black leather and tattoos. Their women wore skintight jeans and equally tight spandex tops.

As Cait hovered by the door, waiting for her eyes to adjust to the artificial night, several of the women sitting around the tables glanced her way. In moments it seemed that every eye was on her. Not only was she out of her element, but she was conspicuously so in her best cashmere suit and expensive pumps.

Clutching her purse tightly, she jerked her gaze toward the bar. Through the smoky haze she saw that every stool was filled—by working cowboys, this time. Muscular male backs formed a wall of plaid, obscuring her view of the man behind the bar.

According to the woman on the phone, however, Tyler was working. "Yeah, Ty always works weekends," the slightly nasal voice had volunteered. "You a friend?"

Cait had hedged. Not because she wanted to be coy, but because she simply didn't know what Tyler and she were to each other now.

Taking another deep breath, she craned her neck for a better look at the man drawing schooners of beer and pouring shots of cheap whiskey.

Sinewy and lean, with long legs and muscular arms, he was wearing a faded blue shirt and black jeans worn to gray at the pockets and in the creases across the front.

The years hadn't been kind. His thick hair was now more silver than blond, and his cheeks were hollowed into a new gauntness. The web-fine network of lines surrounding his eyes made him look older than his forty-one years.

In her mind's eye she saw him dressed in prison denim, losing his humanity day after day until his smoke-gray eyes had turned to slivered ice and his once-sensuous mouth had taken on that bitter line.

Cait felt the blood drain from her face. Her heart was already beating faster than it should. Now it faltered, then began racing again.

Her bottom bumped the door. Without realizing it, she had taken a step toward escape. A warning twanged in her head. *Get out while you can!*

But Cait had run away only once in her life, fleeing from the pain of Tyler's marriage. She had vowed never to be that cowardly again.

Drawing a steadying breath, she slipped into an empty booth to her right. As soon as the crowd thinned, she would find a quiet moment to approach Tyler.

Several seconds later, however, she realized that quiet was a luxury at the Lucky Horseshoe. Country rock pounded from the jukebox and reverberated against the nicotine-stained ceiling. Conversation droned like angry bees. Couples crowding the small dance floor called to one another. Others concentrated on their drinking, keeping the saloon's lone waitress in constant motion.

Five minutes passed before the harried woman with platinum curls and black roots found time to take Cait's order. Her face was young, but the faded blue eyes beneath overplucked eyebrows seemed ancient. The badge on her cheap red blouse said "Angie."

"Sorry to make you wait, honey," she said. It was the same weary voice that Cait had heard on the phone. "Gladys called in sick again today, and me and Ty are workin' the place alone."

Cait instinctively glanced toward the bar. Tyler was drawing another beer. Each movement stretched the fabric of his shirt over wiry muscles and sinew. Under the worn cotton his shoulders seemed wider, his chest broader. That was often the case with men confined for long periods. Exercise and weight training were sometimes the only outlets for their pent-up energy. For a man of Tyler's stamina and vitality, that might not have been enough.

"Uh, I'll have Beaujolais," Cait said with a smile the waitress didn't return. "Whatever you have open will do."

"We got white or red, take your pick." Angie's pencil poised over the pad.

"Red, please."

Angie scribbled the order, slapped down a white cocktail napkin and walked away. Cait glanced toward the bar once more.

Tyler was now leaning against the counter, talking to an older man wearing a sweat-stained Stetson. Mostly he listened, she noted. She noted, too, that there was a wound-tight tenseness about him that was new.

She told herself that it was too dark where she was sitting for him to see her clearly. Still, she sank into the shadows and tried to make herself as inconspicuous as possible.

A loud burst of laughter erupted to her left, drawing her gaze. A giant of a man with a greasy ponytail and the flush of drunkenness on his unshaved face pounded the table with a massive fist, clearly enjoying his own joke.

Cait hastily looked away, but not before she'd caught the lascivious glint of sexual interest in the small, mean eyes aimed directly at her.

Terrific, Cait. Just what you need right now, she thought, glancing at the dial of her gold watch. It was nearly five. How long did bikers party on a Saturday afternoon? she wondered.

The music stopped. Another song began. Someone shouted an obscenity. A woman's laugh shrilled.

Across the room from booth number six, Tyler McClane listened to stockman Rand Harding's description of his latest problems with tourists hiking through his south pasture.

At the same time, force of habit kept his gaze sweeping the room for potential trouble. The place was nearly full and had been since noon. It was the usual mix—bikers, wranglers from nearby ranches, one or two tourists, like the two ladies at the end of the bar.

Right now the mood was happy. Several of the wranglers were quietly getting drunk. When they'd had enough, he would know it. So would they. There were one or two of the bikers that he would have to watch, particularly their leader, Big Mike Bronsky. Sober, he was run-of-the-mill mean. Drunk, he was dangerous. Tyler had had a bellyful of bullies like him in prison.

"Hey, cowboy, got a light?" one of the lady tourists called over the din.

Tyler fished into the watch pocket of his jeans for the matches every bartender learns to carry and silently lit her cigarette.

As she leaned forward, her blouse gaped open, revealing the rounded globes of generous breasts. Rather than inciting him, however, the invitation made him realize just how long it had been since he'd felt the sharp, urgent ache for a woman.

"Real interesting place you have here," she said with a gleam of interest in her overly made-up eyes. "Are you the owner, honey?"

"Nope, just the hired help."

"Can my friend and I buy you a drink?"

"Thanks. I don't drink."

A crusty old man at the bar looked up from his empty glass to shout, "Hey, Ty. Pull me another. I'm 'bout to die of the dust in here."

Tyler excused himself to draw Ben Hadley another draft. Ben grunted his thanks before taking a long thirsty drink. "You pour a mean draft, son."

"Part of the job, Ben."

Hadley had known him when he was a scrawny kid riding a half-broken horse to school. He had been the one to alert Tyler to the possibility of a job. Tyler suspected that he might have applied a little pressure on the Horseshoe's absentee owner on his behalf, and he was grateful.

A private man himself, Ben asked no questions. Better yet, he judged a man on things he himself had observed, not on the things he'd heard.

"Busy night?" Ben asked as he wrapped his leathery hand around the sweating glass. Tyler leaned against the bar and watched the crowd.

"It's better that way. Makes the time go faster."

"Just wait, son," Ben drawled as he reached into his shirt pocket for a cigarette. "When you get to be my age, you won't want time to go so damn fast." He struck a match and took a deep drag on the cigarette, puffing it to life.

Tyler shot another look at the clock over the bar. Nine hours until closing. Nine hours until he could be alone again.

Even though it had been eight months since he'd been let out of the cage that had been his home for thirty-seven months, he still craved solitude. Crowds, especially noisy ones like this bunch, made him edgy. Habit helped him shut out the constant racket, but casual conversation still came hard for him.

"You have any storm damage?" he asked Ben as he concentrated on wiping the condensation from the bar.

"Lost me two promising heifers," the stringy rancher muttered before lifting the glass to his mouth again.

"You insured?"

"Nah. Them companies got so many damn rules and regulations a man could strangle on 'em. I told 'em to go to hell last time they gave me trouble. Know what I mean?"

"Yeah, I know."

Tyler thought about the long list of rules and regulations that governed nearly every minute of his life, even now. Every week for the next sixteen months he had to call his parole officer and answer his inane questions.

Who had he seen that week? Had he gotten laid? Was he staying away from schools and playgrounds and every other damn place where children congregated?

Every fourth week he had to drive into Sacramento to see the patronizing bastard in person. He'd had to get permission to take this job, to renew his driver's license, to move in over the bar. Hell, sometimes he wondered if he should call his PO before he took a leak.

"Another shooter?" he asked Joselito Garcia as he emptied the brimming ashtray in front of Ben's foreman. The squat Chicano shrugged.

"Why not? Ain't got nothing better to do 'cept try to get Angie here to go out with me." He wiggled his black eyebrows at the approaching waitress. As she reached the bar, Angie shot him a disgusted look.

"You wish, cowboy."

Joselito flashed a white smile that showed off his new gold tooth. *"Sí, es verdad, señorita bonita."*

Angie pushed back her limp bangs and set her tray on the bar. "Lordy, my feet hurt."

Tyler handed her the glass of wine he kept for her under the bar. "How many have you taken Big Mike?" he asked as she plopped her tray of empties onto the bar and reached for the wine. She drank heartily until the glass was empty, then set it next to the others.

"Four, five, something like that."

"What's he drinking tonight?"

"Whiskey, but he's holdin' it pretty good so far."

Tyler disposed of the empty beer bottles and put the dirty glasses into the bin under the sink. "Let me know if he orders another."

"Will do." She yawned and flexed her sagging shoulders. "Damn, Gladys. I'm whipped, and the shift ain't half over."

"Take a break. I'll work the tables."

"Maybe I will, after I serve the uptown lady in booth six. Red wine."

"Uptown ladies don't drink the kind of wine we serve." He opened the cooler and pulled out a jug of cheap California burgundy, then stretched overhead for a glass.

Angie leaned forward. "No kiddin', Ty. We got us a classy one for once. I saw her soon as she come in. And I got a bulletin for you. She can't keep her eyes off you."

"Yeah, right." Tyler glanced toward the booth by the door. The blow came hard and fast, like a homemade shank in the gut.

"Know her?" Angie asked.

Tyler jerked his gaze to hers, surprising a look of speculation in her weary eyes. "Yeah, I know her."

Surprise flickered across Angie's face. "What's this, Ty? A secret love?"

He placed the glass of wine in the precise center of Angie's tray, then slowly raised his head to look at her. Her gaze was bright with curiosity, her red lips slightly parted like those of a child eager for candy.

"Serve the wine, Angie."

His voice was quiet, barely above a whisper. But the sudden white-lipped fear that crossed Angie's face was familiar. He had seen it often, on the faces of prison-wise cons who had mistaken his self-imposed silence for weakness. They had backed off then, just as she backed off now.

"Sure, Ty. Whatever you say," she murmured uneasily as she hefted the tray.

Shame brought a slump to Tyler's shoulders. He passed a hand down his cheek, tracing the faint scar edging his jaw. "Sorry," he said in the gentlest tone he could manage. "Just don't ask me any more questions."

Angie nodded and scurried away. Tyler's gaze followed her toward the booth where Cait was sitting. She was half-hidden in shadow, but the clean fragility of her profile and the sweep of her rich, dark hair was unmistakable. She was wearing it up, the way she did when she was feeling vulnerable and didn't want the world to know.

Vulnerable.

Yeah, sure, he thought in disgust. The woman who had turned on him like a fierce vixen defending her kit.

Tyler felt the tremors start deep in his gut where no one could see. He turned his back on the others and clenched his fists against his belly.

For four years he had lived with her contempt festering in his soul. For four years he had burned inside whenever he'd thought of her.

There had been times when he wondered why he hadn't given in to his needs ten years ago and buried himself so deeply inside her that she would never forget him.

There had been other times when he'd wanted to put his hands around her slender neck and press his thumbs into the carotid arteries until that honeyed skin turned blue and her accusing eyes were closed forever.

A monster. Caitlin believed him to be a monster. Knowing that, accepting that, had nearly broken him.

Sweat broke out on Tyler's brow. Sickness churned in his stomach. The hatred he'd had for Crystal had been pure and clean, the kind a man reserves for evil. But it wasn't hatred he felt for Cait.

"Uh-oh, looks like Big Mike's got delusions of grandeur," Ben muttered into his beer.

"The *señorita* don't look none too happy, that's for sure," Joselito wisecracked to the mirror.

Tyler turned in time to see Big Mike stop in front of Cait's booth. Instinctively he had one hand on the bar and his body braced to vault over, when he stopped himself. Cait was a big girl. Whatever happened, she'd brought it on herself.

Across the room, Cait saw Tyler turn his back on her. From the expression that crossed his face, she knew that he had recognized her. She knew, too, that he didn't intend to be the first to renew old acquaintances.

As the bleary-eyed biker leaned closer, she resisted the urge to look toward the bar again.

"Name's Mike Bronsky, pretty lady. My friends call me Big Mike." He favored her with a boozy grin, showing teeth in desperate need of cleaning.

"Mr. Bronsky." Cait tried to be polite, but her facial muscles seemed frozen.

"I just been sittin' over there tellin' my buddies that a classy broad like you shouldn't be all by her lonesome." His voice had a definite slur. The man was drunk, or close to it.

"I'm fine, really."

Bracing massive fists on the table, he leaned forward a few more inches, bathing her face with the sour stench of whiskey. "You waitin' for someone? Some guy, mebbe?"

"Yes, I am."

Mike grunted. "Looks like he done stood you up."

"I don't mind waiting. Really."

Mike frowned. Just then a new song blared from the jukebox, causing his expression to turn cunning. "While you're waitin', honey, let's you and me show them bozos how it's done." He grabbed her arm with a sweaty hand and pulled her to her feet.

Yelping in surprise, she jerked away. "No thank you." Her professional calm was unraveling at the edges. But a man like Mike fed on fear. Remaining calm was her only hope.

The drunken glint in his eyes hardened into anger. Before she could anticipate his actions, he hooked an arm around her waist and dragged her from the booth. Reacting on instinct, Cait stomped on his instep with her heel.

"You bitch!" he bellowed.

Cait saw his hand rise. She ducked, but he was too fast for her. The back of his hand struck her left cheek, sending her sprawling to the dirty linoleum.

Pain exploded in her cheek as tears sprang to her eyes. Adrenaline flooded her veins, and she began to shake. The metallic taste of blood nearly gagged her.

"You asked for this, bitch. Now you're gonna get it."

Clearly enraged, Big Mike stood over her. Voices erupted. Chairs scraped as the biker's buddies jumped up. She was alone in a forest of legs.

Almost strangling on fear, she hastily looked around for a weapon. There was nothing on the floor but cigarette butts and spilled beer. Desperate, she grabbed for her shoe and hefted it heel out, like a tomahawk.

"Mike, wait a minute!" Her voice was husky with urgency. "You don't want this."

"Better watch it, Mike," a drunken voice called out. "Bitch's about to make you into a soprano."

"Like hell," Big Mike bellowed, charging toward her. Before he had taken two steps, however, he was caught from behind and swung around.

"What the f—"

"Time to call it a night, Mike. Right now." Nothing showed on Tyler's face. Nothing had to. The too-quiet, too-silky timbre of his voice said it all.

Mike took a step backward, then caught himself. His buddies were watching. He'd heard that this guy McClane ran a clean, no-nonsense place by using muscle when he had to, but a man had his pride.

"Butt out, cowboy," Mike sneered with as much bravado as he could muster. "I'm about to teach this bitch a lesson."

Tyler didn't move. Nor did his gaze shift to Cait, but she felt certain he was intensely aware of her. "Seems to me she's the one doing the teaching," he said with a hint of amusement underscoring the stillness of his tone.

Nervous laughter rippled through the onlookers. "'Bout time you learned manners, Mike," a woman's voice shrilled.

"Damn right," added another.

The derision only served to fuel Mike's rage. His mouth drew down, and his chest heaved. "Outta my way, cowboy," he said, surging forward.

Before Cait had a chance to draw a breath, Tyler had the biker's massive arm twisted behind him and was marching him toward the door.

Big Mike struggled against the powerful hands controlling him, but Tyler had wrestled steers as a boy and knew how to exert the right amount of leverage. Seconds later Mike was sprawled in the dust outside and Tyler was facing the room again, one man against a dozen or more.

Out of the corner of her eye, Cait saw the waitress edge toward the pay phone by the rest rooms, then stop, as though she'd suddenly seen something in Tyler's face that had startled her.

Cait saw it, too. It was a cold, lethal rage, tightly controlled, utterly potent. In the past she had seen Tyler angry many times and never once had she been frightened. She was frightened now.

"Fun's over for tonight, ladies and gentlemen," he told the excited crowd.

"Like hell," someone muttered. "We ain't done drinkin'."

Tyler's gaze searched the room until he found the man who had spoken. He was almost as large as Mike and equally belligerent.

"I say you are, friend." The threat wasn't an idle one. Cait knew it. The others did, too.

Slowly the mood shifted. Within seconds, it seemed, the bikers and their ladies had thrown wads of bills onto the tables and left. The men at the bar returned to their drinks. The plaintive song on the jukebox ended and another began.

Cait let her shoulders slump and her face relax. Tyler remained where he was, watching her but saying nothing. It seemed an eternity before Angie hurried forward, concern written in the world-weary lines of her face.

"Can I get you something, hon?" she asked when she reached Cait's side.

"Anything but a mirror," Cait muttered, and then realized that her voice sounded very strange, as though it had been forced through the wrong end of a funnel.

"Ice and a clean towel." Tyler jerked his head toward the bar. Angie nodded and hastened to do as he ordered.

"You run a taut ship here, Tyler," Cait muttered.

He watched her without expression, the same way he watched everyone now. But inside his belly was knotted, and his jaw was tight.

"Good thing for you I do."

"True enough." She wiped her hand on her skirt before gingerly touching her fingers to her cheek.

"Ouch," she muttered, more to herself than Tyler. "This is certainly a first for me. Knocked flat because I didn't want to dance."

"Yeah, well, this isn't the Mark Hopkins," Tyler drawled. "A *lady* takes her chances when she walks in here."

"Thanks for the advice. I'll remember that the next time."

He lifted one eyebrow, and his face changed. From dangerous to sardonic. "Planning to become a regular here, are you, Dr. Fielding?"

Cait decided to ignore the sarcasm. Instead she took her time replacing her shoe and straightening her jacket. Spilled beer had soaked into her skirt. Her hands felt grimy where they had smacked the floor.

"Thanks for your help," she told him with a slight sharpness. "I have a feeling Big Mike and I weren't exactly evenly matched."

"Save your thanks, Cait. I didn't do it for you. I did it for me. The last thing I need is a bunch of cops hassling me."

"You? It was that cretin biker who should be arrested!"

Tyler rested his hands on his hips. He had always been lean, but his muscular body now seemed honed to new hardness.

"It's a funny thing about being on parole. All of a sudden you're guilty until proven innocent. But then, you know all about that, don't you?"

Cait flushed. "Please, Tyler. Let's . . . let's not dig up old pain."

"Just two old friends getting reacquainted? Is that the way this is supposed to go?"

Far too conscious of Tyler's steely eyes following her every move, Cait braced one hand on the seat of a nearby chair and prepared to lever herself to her feet. But her legs didn't seem connected to her body, and her head was suddenly swimming.

"I . . . there seems to be a slight problem." She tried to clear the thickness from her throat. As though from a distance, she saw Tyler take a step toward her, then stop.

"What hurts?" he asked.

"My pride, mostly."

"Anything else?"

She thought she detected a faint softening in those cold eyes, as though he might be smiling inside. "My head."

"Any nausea?"

"No."

"Dizziness?"

Cait shook her head. "Well, not much, anyway."

With an inner sigh, Tyler knelt down and pressed two fingers to her neck. In spite of the blood seeping into the capillaries to form bruises, her skin had the texture of the finest silk.

Beneath the softness that teased his fingertips, her pulse was fast but strong. Her color was good, warming her cheeks like a few hours in the sun. It hit him then that he hadn't felt a woman's distinctive warmth for a long time. Nor had he been distracted by the subtle scent that was rapidly disorienting him now.

His immediate reaction was instant and predictably physical. That he could handle. It was the subtle feeling of loss that caught him unaware. Tensing, he withdrew his hand and stood.

"You'll live."

Cait had expected the lack of interest in his tone. She hadn't expected the sadness it aroused in her.

"Is that your professional opinion?" she asked as she got to her feet.

"Bartenders don't have opinions."

Without seeming to, he looked for signs of weakness or fainting. He saw only a faint trembling of her hand as she pushed back the hair escaping from the pins. It seemed darker than he remembered. More black than brown. But then, a lot of things seemed different to him these days.

"Okay, Cait," he said with a trace of impatience now. "What's important enough to get you into a place like this?"

The swift slice of command in his tone rankled, but Cait kept her features serene. "I need to talk with you about something personal."

The lady had guts, coming here, he would give her that. There was a time, after the shock of the trial and the sentence had worn off, when he wouldn't have trusted himself alone with her.

"So talk."

Cait glanced around. The haze was still thick, and the music still blared. Half the tables were empty now, but those who remained were watching the byplay between the two of them with open interest.

"Is there someplace where we can talk privately?" she asked as her gaze came back to his.

"You want privacy, write me a letter. Right now I've got work to do."

Cait's patience was wearing thin. No one treated her rudely without her permission. Permission she had just withdrawn.

"Look, Tyler," she said in a slightly more chilly tone, "I know this is uncomfortable for you, but—"

"Uncomfortable?" His hard mouth slanted into a sneer. "Lady, you don't know the first thing about uncomfortable." He turned and walked toward the bar.

"It's about Kelsey," she shouted over the music.

He spun around. Three long strides brought him back to her. His hand grasped her arm. He was stronger, stronger even than she had imagined.

"Is she hurt? Sick? Tell me."

"She's not hurt and she's not sick," she said with feigned calm. "Now please let go of me before my arm is completely black-and-blue."

Tyler hadn't realized that his hand was wrapped around her upper arm. He jerked it free as red spread over his cheekbones. "Damn it, Cait—"

Angie returned then. In her hand she carried a white towel wrapped around a number of ice cubes. "Here, hon," she said, thrusting the towel toward Cait. "This should help some with that swelling."

"Thanks, Angie. I appreciate it." Cait pressed the makeshift ice pack against her cheek. Her skin felt hot and swollen, and the cut inside her mouth was still bleeding.

Angie hovered. "You're gonna have some kind of shiner by tomorrow."

"I can hear the questions from my patients already," Cait muttered.

"Tell 'em you were hit by a door."

"More like a truck."

Angie laughed. "Anything else I can get you, hon? More wine? A stiff Scotch?"

"Wine, please. I didn't quite—"

"That's the last thing you need," Tyler interrupted with a scowl. Before Cait could protest, he asked Angie to cover for him, adding that he would be in the office if she needed him.

"Office?" Cait lowered the ice pack. Suddenly the idea of being alone with Tyler wasn't as necessary as she'd thought.

"You said you wanted privacy, well, that's as private as it gets around here. Unless, of course, you want to come upstairs to my place."

"The office is fine, thanks."

Before Angie hurried away, she shot Cait a sympathetic look. It didn't help.

"It's at the end of the hall," Tyler said, nodding to a badly lit corridor by the phone.

She felt the curious looks of the men at the bar follow her as she walked a few paces ahead of him. The door to the office was closed. Trying the knob, she discovered that it was locked. She stepped back, only to stumble against Tyler's hard torso. Surprise that turned to heat spread through her.

"Excuse me," he said as he brushed past her to open the door. She noticed his after-shave then. It was a no-nonsense citrus that suited the man he'd become.

The door swung inward. Pocketing his key, Tyler preceded her into the small room. She left the door open, and he made no move to close it. Instead he moved away from her and waited while she took a quick look around.

The place was small and cluttered, but scrupulously clean. It contained a desk, one chair and a sagging couch in a drab shade of brown. On her left a lone window looked out on the alley. To her right stood an ancient filing cabinet in desperate need of paint. There were no pictures on the walls, no diplomas, no personal touches of any kind.

Tyler watched and waited with the utter stillness that was such a part of him now. It didn't take a medical degree to realize that the lady was uncomfortable and trying not to show it. Good, he thought. Let her sweat the way he'd sweated once.

He waited for her gaze to return to his. When it did, he saw apprehension gleaming between her luxurious lashes, and something more, something that made his jaw bunch. Pity.

"Okay, you've got your privacy." Frustration put a razor edge on his words that hadn't been there before. "Now what's this all about?"

Her chin stayed up, and Tyler watched temper replace the pity he hated. "Mind if I sit down first?" Without waiting for an answer, she chose the couch and settled onto the lumpy cushion.

Tyler leaned against the edge of the desk and crossed his arms over his chest. She decided to take the offensive. First she placed the now-soggy ice pack in the clean ashtray on his desk. Next she drew her feet together and sat straighter. Thus armored, she met his unfriendly gaze head-on. "I meant what I said. I'm here because of Kelsey. She was having problems at school and—"

"Okay if I come in?" Angie asked from the doorway. She was watching Tyler, who nodded. The mournful twang of a country song followed her into the room, grating on Cait's already taut nerves.

"I figured you wouldn't want this layin' out there in the booth." Cait noticed her forgotten purse then, slung over Angie's shoulder, and managed to thank her without wincing.

"If you'll hand me my wallet, I'll pay what I owe."

"On the house." Angie shot a quick look in Tyler's direction. "Right, Ty?"

He nodded curtly.

Angie dropped Cait's bag onto the cushion next to her before leaving. As she closed the door behind her, the latch clicked, metal on metal.

Because Cait was looking at Tyler, she caught the sudden bracing of his big shoulders. Habit, she thought. The leftover reflex of a man accustomed to locks he couldn't open.

"Now what's wrong?"

Cait heard the burr of irritation in his voice and realized that she was staring. "Nothing."

His mouth curled at one tight corner. "You never could lie worth a damn, Cait."

"I'm not lying."

"Aren't you?" His eyes were dark and shadowed, like the memories they carried of each other. And his mouth had a hardness that made her feel strangely sad.

Her confidence faltered. Where should she begin? How could she possibly find the right words? she wondered, then sighed inwardly. As if there were right words to explain the terrible regret she felt.

"Okay, so I'm not what you'd call at my best at the moment, but this isn't easy, you know. Seeing you again after...after so much has happened."

"You thought it would be?" His tone registered sardonic disbelief.

Cait shook her head. Had she ever been in control with Tyler? she wondered. Even now, when she'd counted on the advantage of surprise, he had somehow taken charge. Perhaps that was best, she told herself.

"No," she said truthfully. "I knew it would be a nightmare."

Surprise, quickly erased, flickered in his eyes. "You were telling me about my daughter."

Cait drew a long breath before beginning. "A few months ago, a few weeks after school started, Kelsey began to have problems. Poor appetite, bad grades, mood swings. I put them down to...to delayed grief over her mother's death." She paused to clear her throat. Her cheek was beginning to ache badly now.

"Go on."

"About a week ago she woke up screaming. She'd had a nightmare. Mostly about you and the trial."

His face froze, etching the lines of suffering even deeper into his lean cheeks. "Don't start that again, Cait," he ordered in the same dangerously calm tone that should have warned Mike and didn't.

"Just listen, Tyler. That's all I ask." Suddenly nervous, she wet her lips with a swift motion of her tongue.

It was an involuntary thing, he knew, that small quick sliding of her tongue over her slightly swollen lower lip. The stirring of his body in reaction was equally involuntary. Annoyed, he pushed himself from the desk and walked around to sit in the chair, which creaked under his weight.

"I'm listening," he prompted coldly.

Cait's chin inched higher. "She's had nightmares every night since. I've asked a colleague of mine, Dr. Hazel O'Connor, to put her in intensive therapy."

At the word "therapy" something sparked in his eyes. "For delayed grief?"

"Yes and no."

"What is this, Cait? Twenty questions?" He turned his wrist, revealing a dime-store watch. "Maybe you're not in a hurry, but I've got eight minutes left of my break. It's up to you how you want to use them."

Cait wished now that she had taken Angie up on her offer of a good stiff drink. "It's difficult to know where to begin—"

"As I recall, you usually say exactly what you mean." The utter truth in his words seared her.

"True, but in this case—"

"Eight minutes, Cait. After that, I go back to work. You can do whatever you please."

Anger replaced her indecision. Angling her chin, she caught his gaze and held it. He wanted words. She would give him words.

"I came here today to tell you that Kelsey has admitted that she lied."

Under the deep tan, his face turned parchment white. "Lied?"

"Yes, about the things she accused you of doing to her. I believe her. So does Hazel. All the signs point to a child in severe emotional shock."

He had been numb for so long that it took him a moment to feel the sharp, slicing thrust in his gut. "That's what you said the last time."

"Are you telling me I shouldn't believe her now?"

"You shouldn't have believed her four years ago!"

Life came back to his eyes. Along with it came an utterly cold, utterly bitter anger. Like ice crystals forming over steel.

"Three years I was in that place, Cait." The lethal quiet of his voice was far more frightening than any shout. "Three stinking years. Locked away from everything I cared about."

"I'm so sorry." Her voice caught. "I'll do everything I can, anything you want me to do, to...to make things right."

"Can you give me back those years, Cait? Can you take away the stigma? The shame? Can you get my license to practice medicine restored?" He stood so suddenly that the chair went crashing backward into the wall. "No, you can't do any of those things, can you?"

Two angry strides took him to the window. His back was rigid, his shoulders stiff. He braced a muscle-knotted hand against the wall and dropped his head. He was breathing heavily, like a drowning man desperate for air.

Cait wiped her palms on her skirt. There was nothing she could do about the shakes inside. "Please, Tyler. Please don't blame Kelsey. She didn't understand what she was doing."

"She understood right and wrong." He lifted his head and stared through the dusty panes at the row of garbage cans.

"Not really, Tyler. She was confused and frightened."

He turned to look at her. Cait had to work to stifle a gasp. He looked like a man who had aged twenty years overnight.

"Why? I've never hurt her."

Cait thought she detected a faint softening in his hard mouth. It was enough to give her the courage to stand and go to him.

"Crys told her that you would take her far away and she would never see her mother again." Her voice was steady, but hushed. "At five, a girl's mother is the most important person in her life, no matter how much she loves her father. She's even blaming herself for Crys's death."

"Way I heard it, Crys managed that on her own."

Somehow she had to reach past that terrible anger to the man he had been. The man who still loved his daughter.

"Kelsey needs you, Tyler. She desperately needs to know that you love her. That you don't blame her for the...for what happened to you."

"Then who should I blame, Cait?" he asked in measured tones. "You?"

"Yes, if that will help you put all this behind you."

She had tried words. Now, because she was desperate, she tried touching him. It was the lightest of touches on his arm, to show that she understood the anguish he was feeling.

Beneath the warm skin, his muscles pulled taut until his arm was as unyielding as stone. He didn't move, but Cait felt him reject her touch. Quickly she withdrew her hand.

"Please, Tyler. Will you help?"

"I'll think about it."

His answer was so counter to her expectations that at first she was certain she had misunderstood. "Think about it?" she questioned softly.

"That's what I said. I'll think about it."

Cait's face heated. "You'll *think* about helping your own daughter? What kind of man are you, anyway?"

The feeling that swept over him was different from the rage that always simmered inside him these days. He had learned to control rage.

This feeling, whatever it was, threatened the iron control he'd imposed on himself. The control that had kept him sane when he'd been shackled like a vicious animal. The control that had kept him from shriveling up inside when he'd been stripped and searched and shut into a space no bigger than a closet with two other guys.

"Treat a man like an animal long enough and he becomes one," he said impassively. "He stops caring about anything but himself."

"Not all men."

His mouth twisted. "All men."

"I don't believe that," she whispered. "Not of you. Not . . . of the man I knew."

Something shifted in his eyes, but his voice didn't change. "Give a man enough time to think and he learns things about himself that he hates. Put a man in hell and he does things to survive that no man should have to do. Things that make him sick inside. The worst part comes when you can't even feel sick anymore."

"Survival is a strong instinct. You shouldn't be ashamed of giving in to it."

"Who said I'm ashamed?"

"Aren't you?"

"What I *am* is angry the way a man has a right to be when he finds out he's been shafted by his own wife and daughter."

"Anger is healthy. Bitterness isn't."

"Is that your professional opinion, Dr. Fielding?"

"Professional *and* personal."

"There's that word again. Personal. Notice how you keep coming back to it?" His hand came out to smooth the collar of her blouse, then lingered. He had surgeon's hands. Supple, deft and incredibly strong.

"You've become a beautiful woman, Cait." His gaze flickered toward her mouth. Something in his gaze spoke of a terrible self-denial.

For years she hadn't allowed herself to think of Tyler as a sexual being—as a man with a man's needs. Not since he had married her sister. She found she was thinking of him that way now.

"This isn't about me, Tyler. It's about Kelsey. And you."

One side of his mouth slanted upward, saluting her attempt at control. "A man in prison has a lot of time to think. I thought about you often. Too often."

His thumb moved slowly, hypnotically, over the small bones protecting the vulnerable hollow of her throat. She felt heat rising along the curve of her neck.

"Every night, when I tried to sleep, I saw the contempt in your eyes. Every morning I woke up with a knot in my belly. Every day I had to find a reason to stay alive." His fingers tightened gently until she couldn't move. "Do you know what prison is like for a guy carrying a sentence like mine? It's like being thrown into a filthy black pit with no air and no light and no chance of escape."

Cait's eyes went wide with the pain that shafted through her. No man could hurt that much. It wasn't possible.

"Try to understand, Tyler," she pleaded softly. "I had to think of Kelsey. I couldn't take a chance that she was wrong. I'm sorry if you were hurt, but a man who truly loved his daughter would be grateful that I was trying to protect her, not feeling sorry for himself the way you are right now."

The color slowly drained from Tyler's face, only to return an instant later in a wash of dull red. "Get out, Cait. Before I do something that really is criminal."

"You won't hurt me. I know you."

Something flashed in his eyes. "No, Cait, you don't know me. Not the man I am now. Not the man you and your sister made me. I hope to God you never do."

Before she could react, Tyler dropped his hand and brushed past her. By the time she gathered her composure and turned, he was gone.

Chapter 3

It was close to ten when Cait pulled into Hazel's driveway and hurried to the front door. Hazel answered on the third ring. She was wearing a paint-spattered sweatshirt over an old pair of jeans and a painter's hat.

"How did it go?" she asked a split second before she began to frown. "Never mind. I can see."

She stepped back to let Cait enter. "Watch out for the ladder. I'm painting the entryway."

Cait glanced at her friend's shirt. "And yourself, I see."

Hazel laughed as she bolted the door. "Let's say that I don't let neatness slow me down."

She led the way into the kitchen, where she headed directly to the coffeemaker on the counter. She poured Cait a cup and silently handed it to her.

Cait smiled her thanks before taking a few sips. Because she hadn't eaten since noon, the caffeine hit her system undiluted, blasting some of the heaviness from her brain.

"Whoa, I needed that."

Hazel paused with the pot poised over her own cup. "That bad, huh?"

"Worse." Cait walked to the kitchen table, pulled out a chair and sat down. Hazel finished pouring her coffee, replaced the pot on the warmer and joined Cait at the table.

"You saw him?"

"I saw him."

"And?"

Cait wrapped her hands around her mug. "And I don't know."

Hazel turned sideways, but her gaze remained on Cait's face. "Did he agree to write the letter?"

"No."

"He refused?" Hazel's voice held a hint of disbelief.

Cait shook her head. "Actually, I never got around to explaining our strategy."

"Perhaps you'd better start from the beginning," Hazel suggested in a dry tone.

One by one, in the logical, emotional way of a trained therapist, Cait recounted the details of her visit. It took fifteen minutes. When she was finished, she was suddenly exhausted.

Hazel shifted in her chair until her feet were tucked under her and her elbows were resting on the table. Her expression was somber. "Tyler McClane sounds like a man in terrible pain."

Cait nodded. "It's like he's a different person. A stranger I'm half-afraid to get to know. There's an emptiness behind his eyes that scares me."

"I know what you mean. I've seen it, too, when I was doing my internship in a VA Hospital in Kentucky. In guys who had been POWs in Vietnam, mostly. Although the worst case I ever saw was a medic, a navy corpsman who was working with me on one of the wards after he'd returned from the war zone.

"Ryan was a cold bastard. Sarcastic with the patients. Unfeeling to the point of cruelty. I never once saw him smile. The guys on the ward called him a walking iceberg."

Cait had known Hazel for seven years. She'd seen her in all sorts of moods. She'd seen her on good days and on bad.

But she had never heard such depth of feeling in her voice before.

"What happened?"

Hazel took a quick swallow, then slowly lowered her mug to the table. A ghost of a smile crossed her lips. "You know me and my big mouth. One day I laid into him. Told him that he was a poor excuse for a medic and a man."

She stopped and drew a ragged breath. "That night he swiped a scalpel from the OR and sliced his own throat. It was touch and go, but we finally pulled him through."

"Oh, my God!"

"Turns out he was just the opposite of all the things I accused him of being. He cared *too* much. He took every casualty personally. He felt responsible for the guys he treated in the field who didn't make it. Each time he lost a patient, he stuffed his feelings a little deeper so he wouldn't hurt so much. Finally he just . . . lost himself."

"Did you help him?"

Hazel shook her head. "He never forgave me for the things I said. He refused to let me near him. I heard later that he left the navy and just . . . disappeared." Her chest rose and fell in a heavy sigh. "I've said a few prayers for him over the years. I hope they've done some good."

Silence settled as both women withdrew into their own thoughts. The clock on the wall ticked off the minutes until five had passed.

Cait gulped a mouthful of now-tepid coffee. It left a bitter aftertaste.

"Oh, Hazel, if you'd seen Tyler's face when I told him that Kelsey had admitted lying. For an instant, no longer than . . . than the blink of an eye, he looked as though I had just given him the most precious gift in the world. I would swear I saw a wild kind of joy in his eyes. And then it was gone."

Hazel walked to the counter, returning an instant later with the coffeepot. She refilled Cait's cup and then her own before placing the now-empty pot on one of the straw place mats.

"Give him time, Cait. You laid a heavy load on him today. And right out of left field, too. If he's the man you think he is, he'll work it out."

Cait bit her lip. What kind of a man was he, really? For years she had tried to erase Tyler McClane from her mind. He was dead to her and Kelsey, she'd told herself.

In a way, he was, she realized now. The man she had known, the man she had loved, was gone, replaced by a man with flint in his eyes and a terrible bitterness in his heart.

Because she couldn't bear that thought, she changed the subject. "What about Jackson Lamont? Did you ever talk to him?"

Hazel grimaced. "No, and I think he's stonewalling."

"Keep trying. I'll try, too, first thing Monday morning."

Hazel glanced over her shoulder. "How about we mix us up a batch of fudge and eat it all? Chocolate's better than booze any day for chasing the blues."

Cait thought about the cheap wine Angie had served her. It had been harsh and cutting. Like Tyler's memories.

Did he have someone to listen to him the way Hazel listened to her? A friend? Angie?

The cup she was holding clattered to the saucer. Hazel's gaze shot to her face and held there.

"What's wrong?"

"I've got to get home," she muttered as she got to her feet. "About that fudge, I'll take a rain check."

"Too tired?"

"Exhausted. And I want to check on Kels, make sure she's all right. I don't like to be gone too long."

Hazel got to her feet. "Cait, don't beat up on yourself. Okay?"

Cait hugged her friend. "I promise."

They walked together to the entryway. Cait opened the door, then turned to thank Hazel again. "I owe you a big one."

"Hey, what're friends for?" Hazel said in a light tone, but her eyes remained somber.

"I'll call you tomorrow."

Hazel's smile dimmed. "You still care about him, don't you?" she said softly.

Cait stared into the darkness. Clouds covered the stars, and wind rustled the bare branches. It was a lonely sound. A sad sound.

Her thoughts turned back to the night Tyler had admitted fathering her sister's baby. She had come close to walking into the sea that night.

"No," she whispered into the cold blackness. "I can't afford to care about him ever again." She walked alone into the night.

It was a few hours past closing time at the Lucky Horseshoe. The streets were empty. Shops were locked up tight. The tourists had long since left. The locals slept behind locked doors. Even the town's stray dogs had ceased their nocturnal prowling.

Tyler strode alone through the streets. The air was cold. The wind was from the north and carried a threat of snow. It stung his unshaved face and tossed his hair over his forehead.

He turned his face into the wind. The smells of winter were strong now. Wood smoke from dying fireplace fires. Pungent autumn leaves that had gone unraked. The first tart hint of snow.

From someplace behind him, Tyler heard an owl screech. It was a familiar sound to someone raised on a ranch. And a lonely one.

How many others in town were awake to hear it? he wondered. A sleepy mama nursing her newborn? A daddy calming his daughter's nightmare? Lovers curled together under warm covers?

Tyler quickened his pace. The restlessness was on him again. Walking helped. But no matter how hot his muscles burned or how exhausted he became, he couldn't drive Cait from his mind. Nothing had ever been able to do that.

Ten years ago he had wanted her with a young man's quick, selfish impatience. But even then Cait was a woman who deserved commitment from a man, not a hurried coupling on an empty bed in a sterile hospital room.

Someday, he had promised himself. When he had more to offer her than a shabby studio apartment and a pile of college loans. Someday when his future was assured. And then along had come Crystal.

She had been like a bright, vivacious comet blazing across the sky, eclipsing Cait's steady light. He knew now that she had played him like a pro. Asking his advice. Telling him her troubles. Offering to rub his tired shoulders when he stumbled home drained and exhausted after a long, difficult shift in the OR.

He had wanted her the way a man wants any beautiful sexy woman; he'd also known that an affair with her would kill any chance he had with Cait. His refusal had only made Crystal increase her attempts to seduce him. It had been a game to her, one she'd been determined to win.

One cold, rainy morning he had come home after thirty hours of duty to find her waiting for him. This time, unlike the others, she'd had a welcoming kiss on her lips and nothing beneath her trench coat but warm, bare skin.

Perhaps, if he hadn't been so exhausted . . .

Perhaps, if he'd had time to think about the consequences of taking what she was so enticingly offering . . .

Tyler uttered a silent, vicious curse. No use looking for excuses now. He had done what he'd done. He'd also regretted it as soon as he emerged from his foggy state the next morning. That afternoon, he'd told Crystal not to come around again.

The names she'd called him had been crude and accurate. He'd accepted her scorn because he'd deserved it. He'd also promised, although reluctantly and only after much tearful pleading from Crystal, not to say anything to Cait.

That had been the end of his infatuation with Crystal. Or so he'd thought. Until two months later, when she had presented him with the consequences: a baby on the way and a demand that he marry her—or there would be no baby.

Self-centered fool that he'd been then, he'd made a stupid mistake. But, God help him, he had paid a price that no man should have to pay.

He aimed a savage kick at a clump of dirt on the sidewalk. The noise ran like a hollow echo down the deserted street. He followed the lonely sound into the silent hills.

It was dawn before he returned.

Two days later Tyler drove to Sacramento to keep his regularly scheduled appointment with his parole officer, a middle-aged, overweight, balding bureaucrat named Harvey Shuffler. From the first interview, Shuffler had made known his intention to make the next two years a living hell. If the past eight months were an example, the man would succeed beyond his wildest hopes. Tyler was still seething from the endless questions and insults when he arrived at Jess Dante's office in Old Sacramento.

The two had met in grammar school when they'd been rivals for a rosy-cheeked little charmer named Melissa Jane Roth. They'd ended up in a wild free-for-all that, to this day, each insisted he had won.

The principal had marched them to his office, where they'd sat for an hour, sporting matching black eyes and sheepish grins. They'd left the office with aching bottoms and vows of eternal friendship, a friendship that lasted all through junior high and high school.

Both had left the mountains after they'd graduated—Tyler to work his way through Stanford, Dante to begin a meteoric rise as a Formula One race driver.

Eight years ago he was well on his way to number one in the world when a fiery accident during the Indianapolis 500 had cost him his right arm.

He'd returned to California and law school. In the close-knit society of the legal profession, he was known as a bulldog, a hard-as-nails tough guy who never gave up if he believed in his client's innocence. He was also known to turn down lucrative fees if there was any suggestion that a prospective client was lying to him.

Prosecutors and judges respected him. Very few liked him. Even fewer knew the man behind the aggressive words and tough bargaining. Tyler knew.

Dante had been one of the few people he'd known who had stood by him. During the trial, Dante had made the two-hour drive from Sacramento to San Francisco twice daily. He had put in long, arduous hours on a case that his colleagues warned him might very well damage his own promising career.

After Tyler's conviction, Dante had gone to Vacaville once a month to visit, the only visitor Tyler ever had. Nothing relating to Tyler's conviction was ever said between the two men. Nothing had to be said. They were friends. They usually had dinner when Tyler was in town. With Shuffler's permission, of course.

Dante's office was located in a renovated hotel that had once housed one of the most fashionable brothels of the gold rush days.

The inside walls had been stripped of the garish wallpaper to reveal handmade bricks. The floor, bare now of the thick plush carpeting, was pitted and scored with the marks of countless high-heeled slippers. The gaudy Victorian furniture had been replaced by modern chrome and leather.

Tyler had seen it for the first time on the day he'd been released from prison. Dante had been waiting for him outside the walls. They'd driven the distance to Sacramento in silence. Safe behind the old brick walls, Dante had gotten him quietly and thoroughly drunk, a violation of his parole that neither had ever mentioned again.

Dante was sitting at his desk, talking on the phone when Tyler entered. Like Tyler, Dante was taller than average. Also like Tyler, he carried most of his bulk in his powerful shoulders and torso. He was wearing his usual office attire—rumpled corduroy trousers, plaid shirt and a tie that belonged in a psychedelic nightmare.

As Tyler approached the desk, Dante grinned and nodded toward a chair. Instead, Tyler shed his jacket and walked to the window. Hands in his back pockets, he looked down at the angry snarl of rush-hour traffic.

It was little more than a month to Christmas. Peace on earth, goodwill toward men, he thought with a hard slant to his mouth. Last year and for two years before that, he had spent the holiday with four thousand other caged men. This year he would spend it alone. He wasn't sure which was worse.

Eyes narrowed, his gaze followed the streetlights toward the suburb of Fair Oaks, where Cait lived. He had her address and phone number memorized, but he had never been to her house. It wasn't permitted under the terms of his parole.

Just as well, he thought. Being around Cait made him edgy in a way that no other woman ever had. Hell, it made him edgy even thinking about being with her.

He shifted, trying to ease the tension that had been with him since he had seen her sitting across the bar in that dark booth.

He hadn't been ready to handle the feelings she generated in him. Now he knew that he never would be. Just as he knew it didn't matter much. The lady and the ex-con, he thought. A hell of an impossible combination.

Tired of the lights and garish decorations, he yanked on the cord that adjusted the blinds, closing them tight. Behind him he heard Dante conclude his conversation and hang up. Tyler turned to face his friend.

Dante cocked a black eyebrow over an impressive Roman nose and regarded him with the same laser-sharp intensity that had quelled many an unfriendly witness. Tyler was used to that look.

"Damn, Ty!" the attorney exclaimed in a deep-throated baritone. "You look like you're ready to take someone apart. Shuffler give you a hard time?"

"No more than usual."

Tyler made his way to one of the chairs opposite the desk and sat down. He stretched out his legs until the soles of his boots were braced against the desk.

"What's with the guy, anyway? You do something to tick him off?"

"Yeah. I haven't given him any reason to send me back to prison to finish my sentence."

Dante opened the bottom drawer of his big desk and pulled out a nearly empty quart bottle of Scotch. Tyler noted the distinctive label. It was the same expensive brand he once favored. In those days it had been important to have the best. Dante deftly unscrewed the cap with one hand and poured a triple into his coffee mug. This time he didn't ask Tyler if he wanted a drink.

"Weatherman promises a white Christmas in the Sierra," Dante commented after taking a long, thirsty drink. "You got any snow yet?"

"Not yet. Nights are cold as hell, though."

Dante eyed Tyler over the rim of his glass. "You up for Mexican tonight?"

Tyler grunted something noncommittal. Dante snorted.

"Don't overwhelm me with excitement, old buddy." The big attorney leaned back and propped his feet on the desk. Over the toes of his scuffed boots, he studied Tyler without seeming to.

Dante took another swallow of Scotch, then asked bluntly, "Tell me something, Ty. How long has it been since you've had a woman?"

Tyler scowled. "That's a hell of a question."

Dante continued to regard him impassively. "Take it from me, buddy. A man is vulnerable when he's horny."

"Not this man."

Dante took another drink. "So how long has it been?"

Tyler looked at his hands. Washing bar glasses had made them almost as rough as roping and mending fences. He thought of Cait's soft skin. Had he hurt her when he'd touched her in his office? It made him sick inside to realize that he probably had. Slowly he clenched his hand.

"I'm not interested in getting laid, if that's what you're asking."

"Well, something's sure as hell changed. Last week I thought you were finally coming to terms with the way things have to be right now."

"What things?"

"Parole. Losing your license to practice medicine. Giving up Kelsey."

Tyler shot his best friend a warning look. "I didn't give her up, damn it! The court took her."

"You signed the paper allowing her aunt to adopt her after Crystal was killed. Against my advice, if you'll remember."

"It was either that or let Kelsey grow up without really belonging to anyone." He rose abruptly and began to pace. The spacious office suddenly seemed confining and airless.

Watching, Dante knocked back half his drink, then set the glass on his thigh and ran his fingers up and down the slick surface. He knew better than to push Ty too far. Under all that surface sophistication, the man had a volatile temper.

"You still chewing on the things Caitlin Fielding laid on you Saturday?"

"No." Tyler returned to his seat and worked on disciplining his anger.

"You talk to her since then?"

"No." Tyler thought about the bruises that had marred her perfect skin. Had they healed? he wondered.

"I haven't seen her since the trial. How does she look?" Tyler shot him a wary look. "Fine."

"Pretty lady, as I remember. Elegant, but damn sexy."

"Is she?"

"Hmm. Not that her type appeals to me, you understand. There's too much going on behind those big brown eyes that I don't understand. Still and all, you have to admit that she has one great body under those tailored suits she wears. And those legs..." Dante shook his head. "Be tough for a man to resist."

Tyler narrowed his gaze. "Get to the point, Jess. If you have one."

"I've talked with that bastard Lamont. About the possibility of a new trial."

Tyler froze. "What did he say?"

"Let's say he wasn't overjoyed to hear that the star witness against you is now claiming she lied."

"I don't give a damn how he feels. Did he agree to re-open the case?"

Dante shook his head. "It's going to take a hell of a lot more than a phone call from me to force his hand. Convicting you made his rep. Rumor has it he intends to ride it into the attorney general's office one of these years. The last thing he'll want to do is admit he convicted an innocent man."

"Well, he did, damn it."

"True, but let's not get ahead of ourselves here. I did get him to agree to talk with—" he glanced down at the notes in front of him "—with Dr. O'Connor as well as Dr. Fielding."

"When?"

"Within the week. But don't hold your breath. In the meantime, be nice to Caitlin Fielding if she comes to see you again, but for God's sake, stay away from her otherwise."

"What's she got to do with it?"

Dante drained his glass and poured himself another triple. He knocked back half before answering. "You need her on your side, that's what. At the moment she's your only link to Kelsey. With your wife—"

"*Ex*-wife."

"*Ex*-wife dead and therefore unavailable for cross-examination, Kelsey is your only hope. No doubt she's very attached to her aunt now. Which means Caitlin Fielding has a lot of say over what the kid does and doesn't do. Plus, we need her to testify to the kid's statements that she lied. Being a shrink, she'll have a great deal of credibility, not to mention the effect those big brown eyes will have on the jury, especially the males."

"Go on," Tyler ordered in a cold voice.

"To tell you the truth, she's the last person I want on the stand, especially after she let you twist in the wind four years ago. But…we need her. So that means we have to cover our butts. No personal contact with her. No phone calls, no visits, nothing that Lamont could remotely challenge as coercion."

Tyler felt a flare of anger. "What about Kelsey? Cait says she needs my help."

"Maybe. Maybe not."

"That's damn cold-blooded, Dante."

"So is a false charge of child molestation. I've said all along that Crystal was running a bluff on you. If it hadn't been for Caitlin Fielding, I think your ex wouldn't have had the guts to go through with it. But once Fielding bought in, everything went to hell. Or don't you remember what she was like?"

Tyler looked down at his right hand. Once he had used it to heal. Now he poured drinks and mopped up spills.

"I haven't forgotten," he said as his hand slowly made a fist.

Dante finished his drink and stood. "Stay away from her, Ty. The lady is not your friend, no matter what she says."

Chapter 4

It was close to five, and Cait's last patient had already left. Already she had kicked off her shoes and shed her suit jacket. Now she undid the top button of her silky blouse and tried to ignore the mess four-year-old Jason had made during play therapy.

"This is ridiculous," she muttered into the phone clamped between her shoulder and her ear. Jackson Lamont's secretary had her on hold again—for the third time in five days.

Annoyed and impatient, she let her shoulders slump against the chair and rubbed her tired eyes. She was running out of voice. And steam.

That had been happening a lot lately. Her temper was shorter than usual, as well. Yesterday she had yelled at a woman in trendy exercise clothing who had beaten her to the last parking place at the supermarket. This afternoon she had nearly taken the head off a phone solicitor wanting to sell her a time-share in a condo.

Hey, everybody, she thought. Step right up! Watch the serene, always-in-control shrink turn into a neurotic shrew, just because she can't get one particular man out of her mind.

She closed her eyes and tried to shut out the elevator music playing in her ear. It had been three days since she had seen Tyler. And three nights. Restless, nearly sleepless nights.

"I'm sorry, Dr. Fielding," a disembodied, slightly nasal female voice said in her ear. "Mr. Lamont is tied up in a meeting at the moment, but I'd be happy to take a message."

"Ms. Putnam," Cait replied in a tight voice, "I have already left enough messages to fill the San Francisco phone book—as you well know."

"I can assure you that Mr. Lamont does have all your messages, Dr. Fielding. But he's been very busy this week."

"Did you explain that this is about new evidence in the case he once prosecuted against Dr. Tyler McClane?"

"Your message was most explicit, Dr. Fielding." The woman hung up without saying goodbye.

Cait gritted her teeth as she replaced the receiver. Disgust crossed her face as she snatched up a page of notes and crumpled it into an angry wad.

"Arrogant ass," she muttered as she tossed the ball toward the wastebasket by her desk. It hit the rim instead and bounced onto the thick, rose-colored carpet.

"You missed."

"Tyler!"

He was dressed much as she'd seen him in Sutter Creek, in jeans and boots. This time, however, he had added a fleece-lined denim jacket over a red flannel shirt and a buff-colored Stetson. The combination suited him, perhaps better than the conservative suit she remembered.

"Hello, Cait. Do you have a minute?"

"I . . . sure. Come in." Her voice was strangely scratchy. "My last patient left twenty minutes ago. I'm just sitting here decompressing before I have to face the holiday traffic."

As he entered, he swept off the Stetson with one hand and finger-combed his hair with the other. It was long enough to cover his ears and curl over the collar of his shirt. In the artificial light it seemed more gun-metal gray than silver.

"Rough day?" He was still remote, but the fury was gone from his eyes.

"Patients I can handle. It's the idiots with a little taste of power I can't abide."

"Any particular idiot?" he asked. "Or idiots in general?"

"Jack Lamont."

"Oh, yeah? I didn't realize the two of you were such close friends."

Cait ignored the sarcasm. Arguing with Tyler wouldn't benefit either of them. "About as close as the two of you, I suspect."

"I doubt it."

Cait grinned, and for an instant she thought he might grin back. He didn't. Instead, he dropped his hat onto one of the two chairs opposite the desk and sank into the other. A hint of the up-country mountains came with him, as though he'd carried the wind in with him on his clothes and in his hair.

"Nice office. Cheerful."

His swift, assessing gaze noted every corner before coming back to her face. Even though he was sitting very still, there was a restless, exclusively masculine energy about him. It was there in the subtle narrowing of his eyes and in the confident stretch of his long, muscular legs.

"My patients seem to like it."

"Especially that pillow, I imagine." Cait glanced toward the red vinyl "pounding pillow" in one corner. Five or six plastic bats in various sizes were conveniently close at hand.

"Actually, that's really there for me. If you'd come in a few minutes later, you would have found me walloping the heck out of it."

"Sounds interesting."

"Would you like to try it?"

One corner of his mouth yielded to an involuntary half smile. "I just might—one of these days."

"Anytime."

His eyes were the color of storm clouds as he watched her. For a second Cait felt pulled into those eyes. There was so much she wanted to say.

"Looks like you're healing."

"Healing?"

"The black eye."

"Oh, that." Cait lifted her hand and touched the fading bruise under her eye. "It doesn't even hurt anymore."

"Good."

Tyler ran his hand over the arm of the chair. It annoyed him to realize that his palms were sweating and his respiration was faster than usual. It annoyed him even more to realize that his body was reacting involuntarily to Cait as though they'd just met. Dante was right. The lady could fire a man's blood with just a glance from those soft eyes.

Suddenly tense, he leaned forward to shrug out of his jacket. "I'm here because of my daughter," he said as he folded his jacket over the arm of the chair. "It took me a few days to get permission from my parole officer to be in the same city with her."

Cait felt a small shiver of relief. So she hadn't read him wrong. Under the hard-edged reserve, Tyler still cared about his little girl.

"Hazel has begun therapy. We've decided on twice a week for the time being. Anything more than that might push Kelsey into a worse collapse."

His eyes went blank with shock. "Collapse?"

"I thought you understood. She's very close to a complete breakdown. Unrelieved guilt can do terrible things. In this case, it's exacerbated by the fact that she's convinced you hate her."

"She's wrong. I love her. I always have."

"Would you be willing to tell her that?"

His eyebrows lifted. Whether in surprise or refusal she wasn't certain. "You were in court. You heard the sentence. I'm not allowed to have any contact whatsoever with her."

"If I could clear it with the judge and your parole officer so that you could write her a letter, would you?"

"*Can* you clear it?"

"I can't promise, but, yes, I think I can."

He noticed that there were faint shadows under her eyes and wondered if she'd been having trouble sleeping, too. He told himself he couldn't afford to care one way or the other. His concern was for Kelsey. Only Kelsey.

"What do you want me to say in this letter?"

Cait allowed herself a pleased smile. "She needs to know that you don't blame her for lying. Hazel will read it to her in a controlled atmosphere, and then they'll talk about it. Hopefully, it will serve as a catharsis."

"If it doesn't?"

"Then we'll try something else."

A catharsis. Controlled atmosphere. Tyler glanced at the diplomas arrayed on the wall behind her. His own were packed away in a box in his closet. One of these days he would get around to throwing them out.

"I'll do my best," he said, as much to himself as to Cait.

"That's all anyone can do." She picked up a pen, then realized that she had no use for it and carefully replaced it on the polished desktop.

Tyler saw the nervous gesture and remembered a younger, less confident Cait. A woman of emotion with a lusty passion for life. A prettier-than-she-knew woman who had laughed as often as she'd cried.

He could still see her bustling down the corridor of the pediatric wing, her hair mussed from the absentminded twirling of her fingers as she agonized over a particularly heartbreaking case. She had worried about everything in those days. Her patients. Her friends. Even an insecure resident from the sticks.

He'd worried about his patients and his future. Nothing else had mattered to the man he'd been then. He rose so abruptly that Cait blinked in almost comical surprise. He'd been indoors long enough. He needed space. Air.

"Talk to the judge," he ordered. "Call me when you have his answer."

He reached for his jacket and shrugged into it. Cait had a sudden image of hard-packed muscles moving against flannel. As his gaze came to her again, she was suddenly intensely conscious of her mussed hair and wilted makeup.

It struck her that no one had ever made her more aware of her own femininity than Tyler. Perhaps because he was so intensely masculine.

"Uh, I need your home number," she reminded him as she pushed back her chair and stood.

"You can reach me at the Horseshoe. I have an extension upstairs." He took one of her cards from the small wooden holder and wrote his number on the back. He left both pen and card on the desk.

"Anything else you need?"

Yes, she thought. I need a glimpse of the man I used to idolize. "No, nothing. I'll call when I have news."

She walked around the desk and extended her hand. Tyler hesitated, then touched his hand to hers. The contact was impersonal and withdrawn quickly.

"Thank you for coming." She waited for the knot in her stomach to ease. Instead, it twisted tighter.

"You knew I would."

"No, I didn't," she said gently. "I only hoped."

Barefoot, she was nearly a head shorter than Tyler. In order to keep her gaze on his, she was forced to tilt her head, exposing her throat to his view.

The skin was paler there, especially in the fragile hollow where her pulse was beating abnormally fast. He felt his awareness quicken, followed almost immediately by a hot, swift shaft of desire. Easy to label, he thought. Not as easy to ignore.

"Goodbye, Cait."

He caught up his hat and tugged it over his forehead. He nodded once and turned to leave.

"Wait!"

"Something else?" he asked, half-turning her way.

"I, um, just wondered ..."

"Wondered what?"

Cait glanced toward the framed photograph of Kelsey on her desk. "I have something for you," she said as she reached for the photo. She freed the brass catches holding the picture in the frame and removed the photograph.

"This was taken about two months ago," she said as she held it out to him. His gaze held hers for an instant before dropping to the face in the picture.

"Thanks," he murmured as he took it from her. Cait saw that he swallowed hard and his hand shook.

"She still looks like you."

"No doubt she hates that." His voice was soft and surprisingly without bitterness. Cait wondered if he realized how he changed when he spoke of his daughter.

"I'm not sure she knows how alike you two really are. She was so young when you went to prison."

Tyler stared at the small face of his child. The judge had refused him permission to keep her photo in his cell, so he had tried to keep the memories alive in his mind. Like a miser, he had hoarded every small remembrance—the quick burst of her smile, the music of her laughter, the sound of her voice calling for her daddy. But his memories were fading.

"Does she still hate tomatoes?" he found himself asking.

"Like the plague."

Her gaze meshed with his. It was a mistake. Something softened inside her, urging her to remember other times alone with him.

"Does she ever ask about me?"

She shook her head. She couldn't bring herself to say the words. The softness disappeared from his face.

"Just as well."

He tucked the photo into his shirt pocket, nodded and headed for the door. Watching, Cait knew the exact instant when he caught sight of the poster. He stopped to read the hand-stenciled letters.

"Sunset View School. Is that Kelsey's?"

"Yes. It's her first Christmas play."

"Says December nineteenth. Two weeks from now."

"That's the night before Christmas vacation. She's playing one of Santa's elves. She has one line, which she practices for hours in front of the mirror."

"Are you going?" he asked without turning.

"Yes, of course." He heard confusion in Cait's tone. But then, he should have known that she wouldn't miss such an important event in his daughter's life.

His daughter. How long would it be before he stopped thinking of Kelsey that way? Months? Years? A lifetime?

His hands balled into fists. Never, he thought. Kelsey was part of him. She carried his blood. No matter what the judge said, she would always be his child.

His face set in grim lines, he turned to face Cait again. "Seven o'clock on the nineteenth. I'll see you there."

"No! You can't do that."

He raised one eyebrow. "Why not?"

"She might see you." Cait forced authority into her voice. "It could be very traumatic. Set her back weeks, perhaps months."

"I'll come late. Stay in the back. I'll make sure she doesn't see me."

"But someone else might see you. Someone who could recognize you."

"In Sacramento? Who would recognize me?"

Cait's courage wavered, but she made herself plunge ahead. "Kelsey's teacher Mrs. Eddington, for one."

"Kelsey's teacher? How could she possibly recognize me?"

Cait's gaze slipped from his. "When I enrolled Kelsey in Sunset View, I showed Mrs. Eddington your picture and told her to call the police if... if you showed up asking to see Kelsey."

Tyler felt a tightness gripping his chest. He had trouble breathing. Inside, where it had been deeply sheltered and fiercely protected, something very fragile withered and died.

"I knew that you hated me, Cait. I just didn't know how much until this minute."

He slammed out of her office and took the stairs two at a time. At the bottom he shoved open the exit door with the flat of his hand and kept going.

Dark had settled while he'd been in Cait's office. The fog was rising. The air was dank. Tyler quickened his pace. He craved a drink, but he didn't dare.

Three cars remained in the small lot: a van parked in the far corner, a red convertible in a reserved space near the door and his truck, parked under the security lamp.

He was about to unlock the door when he froze. It wasn't much of a sound, the faint rustle of fabric, perhaps, but the back of his neck tightened.

They came from the other side of the truck, three big men dressed in dark clothing. Acting on instinct, Tyler turned so that the truck was at his back.

"Hey, buddy, got a match?" one of the men asked. The slur in the rough voice and the stench of rotgut whiskey told Tyler that he was drunk.

"Don't smoke."

They were all around him now, hulking shadows without faces. "How 'bout a little drink, then?" another voice wheedled. "You got yourself a bottle in that there truck?"

"Don't drink, either."

Tyler gauged the distance between himself and the others. Two of them looked slow. The third, the heaviest, had the moves of a boxer. If he had to, he would take that one out first.

"Don't drink, don't smoke," barked out a new voice. "Looks like we met us a Boy Scout, boys."

Tyler knew that voice. But from where? An ex-con from Vacaville? Someone nursing a grudge? It was possible, he knew. He'd made more enemies than friends in prison.

"That right, cowboy? You as straight as you advertise?"

"Nah, he's got him plenty of bad habits," interjected the familiar voice. "Ain't you heard? Our boy here's done hard time."

Tyler saw the knife then, a big one with serrated edges. "You got a problem, friend?" he asked with just enough ice in his voice to let them know it would cost them to jump him.

"'Pears like you're the one with the problem." The man speaking walked into the light, deliberately giving Tyler a good look at his face. It was Big Mike.

"Surprised, cowboy?" The biker's grin was a malevolent slash in the cold fog.

"Hello, Mike." He flavored his words with contempt. "I thought I smelled something rotten."

Mike's grin vanished. "Big talk for a guy who's about to eat this here blade." The others laughed at that and edged closer.

"Three against one and a knife?" Tyler taunted. "Didn't know I scared you that bad."

"Screw scared, McClane. You'll be begging me to kill you after I'm done with you."

"Not on your best day, slick."

"Bastard," Mike hissed. "I been following you for days, waiting for just the right time. Looks like this is it, don't it?"

A familiar calm came over Tyler. He figured he had no more than minutes before Cait walked out of the door behind him. Whatever he did, he had to do it now.

Mike had him on reach, but he was quicker. Folding into a wrestler's crouch, he beckoned derisively.

"C'mon, slick. Let's see what you've got."

With a guttural cry, the biker lunged out with the knife. At the same time, one of the others hurled a punch at Tyler's jaw.

It was an old prison trick, take a man from all sides, one that Tyler had anticipated. He ducked, and the man's fist smashed into the window behind him. It exploded inward, showering the inside of the truck with safety glass. At the same time Tyler sent his knee crashing into the man's groin and shoved him toward Mike. The two collided in a tangle of arms and legs.

Meanwhile, the third assailant aimed a haymaker at Tyler's gut. Tyler moved, but not fast enough, and the blow smashed into his ribs, doubling him in two and knocking off his hat. Pain seared through him, paralyzing him for an instant.

By this time Mike had freed himself and come at Tyler from the left. The knife flashed. Tyler leaped backward, but the truck impeded his escape. His jacket and shirt slowed the blade, but the edge still managed to slice deeply into his shoulder. Pain seared his flesh like a hot lash.

As he dodged away from the blade, he saw Cait come through the door and into the circle of light from the security lamp. She was so close he saw the shock come into her eyes.

Cait stopped in midstride. Oh my God, she thought on a swift indrawn breath. The biker from the bar! And he was trying to kill Tyler.

"Stop it, you bastards!" she shouted. "Right now!"

Heads turned in her direction. Someone spat out an obscenity. Tyler shot her a quick glance. At the same time he hit the smaller one low and hard, a quick one-two that doubled the man into a helpless ball. He heard Cait shouting something about the police.

"No police!" he rasped as loudly as the pain permitted. "Just get out of here."

"Are you crazy? You need help!"

Cait jerked open the door and ran inside. Instead of waiting for the elevator, she ran full tilt toward the stairs. Halfway there, she slipped on the marble floor and nearly went down.

Muttering a curse, she paused to kick off her suede pumps before sprinting for the steps. She took them so fast her breath was coming in harsh gasps by the time she reached her office.

She wasted precious seconds unlocking the door, and then she was racing across the waiting room into her office. Fighting for breath, she snatched up the receiver and punched 911.

No police! Tyler had sounded so insistent. But why?

She smashed down the button and bit her lip. Think, Cait. Why...? The answer came quickly. What had he said to her, a man on parole didn't need the police hassling him?

But that was a minor scuffle. This was serious. Tyler could die. If she made the wrong choice...

The wrong choice. Once Tyler had asked her to trust him. She had refused. This time she would do as he asked. Quickly, before she could think better of it, she flipped her Rolodex to the *D*s.

"Dante, Dante," she muttered. "Here it is...home... office." She glanced at the digital clock on her desk. Six forty-five. She would try the attorney at home.

"Please be home, please be home," she repeated as she punched out the number. There was an agonizing pause; then the phone began to ring.

It had been pure reflex that sent Tyler's head turning her way as she disappeared inside. In that split second his mind was on Cait, not the man with the knife.

Mike lunged. Tyler moved, but not fast enough. The blade gouged his side. Stumbling backward, he fought to clear his head. Already blood was saturating his shirt.

Mike moved toward him, arms outstretched, knife poised. The others yelled obscene encouragement. Oozing confidence, the biker put his head down and charged.

It was the mistake Tyler had been waiting for. He sidestepped clumsily but managed to plow a fist into Mike's throat. The knife flew sideways as Mike's hands came up to clutch his gullet. Tyler managed to scoop it up before the nearest man could get to it.

"Don't try it," he warned. One of Mike's friends turned and ran toward the van. The other one froze.

Mike coughed violently before bringing up a mouthful of blood. He spat viciously. Blood spattered his boots along with the pavement.

"You win this time, McClane. But I know where to find that whore of yours now. You can't watch her all the time."

"I won't have to." Tyler's words were dangerously hushed, like stones falling one by one into a quiet pond.

"Oh no? Why not?" Mike sneered.

Tyler's slow smile had chilled edges. "Because you're too much of a coward to want to die."

Mike gaped at him. "I heard you put the first guy who made a move on you in the prison hospital for a month, but that don't make you tougher'n me. I was *king* when I done *my* time."

Tyler held up the knife and tested the edge with his thumb. A thin line of blood appeared. The light was full on his face, and he let Mike see the man he'd had to be in prison, the man he'd never wanted to be again.

"I was a surgeon once. A good one. I can carve up a man in seconds without raising a sweat. On the other hand, I can take a long, long time before I let him die."

Mike's mouth twisted and he spat. "Go screw yourself, McClane. I ain't impressed."

"If you show up here again, if you even set eyes on the lady again, I'll kill you."

"C'mon, Mike," one of the other men rasped. "This ain't goin' down the way you promised."

"Screw you," Mike muttered before lurching to his left, away from the knife, away from the man with a steady hand and steel in his eyes. The others followed.

Tyler managed to hold on until the van peeled out of the parking lot. And then he crumpled unconscious to the tarmac.

Chapter 5

"Jess Dante."

"Dante, this is Caitlin Fielding. Don't talk, just listen. Tyler came to see me at my office tonight. After he left, some men attacked him in the parking lot. They're still here. He needs help."

"Where's your office?"

Cait told him. "Tyler said not to call the police, but—"

"He's right. No police. Stay where you are. Lock your door and don't open it for anyone but me or Tyler. I'll be there in ten minutes." He hung up.

Cait let the receiver fall from her hand. It hit the desk with a sharp crack, but she was already running. Seconds later she reached the door to the parking lot. As she pushed it open, she saw him. He was lying near the fender of his truck. There was no sign of Mike or the others.

It seemed like hours instead of seconds before she reached his side and sank to her knees. He was lying on his side on the dirty pavement. Mike's knife was in his right hand. His knuckles were swollen and bruised.

"Tyler." She thought she was shouting, but her voice came out in a shaky whisper. She touched his shoulder, and her fingers encountered something wet and sticky. Blood.

Choking back a cry, she leaned closer until she could see his face. His eyes were closed, but he was breathing. With shaking fingers she checked the pulse in his neck. Rapid but strong, thank God. And his skin, though waxen, was warm.

"Tyler, it's Cait," she cried. "Can you hear me?"

He felt himself drifting. Grit dug into his hip where it rested against something hard. The air was clammy and smelled of old oil and dirt. His body was numb with cold, except for a hot spike stabbing his side. He tried to turn away from the pain. It followed him.

"Tyler, listen to me." Cait's voice caught, and she paused to repair her faltering composure. "Dante is coming. Everything's going to be all right."

His eyes opened, then narrowed immediately as he winced. Slowly he rolled to his back. Even that simple movement sent agony spiraling into his side.

"Shouldn't be here," he muttered. "Dangerous. Might come back." His voice was slurred but strong. His eyes were glazed. Shock, she thought. And pain.

"Don't try to talk, please. Just lie quietly."

Tyler felt the softness of wool beneath his cheek. Cait's body, warm and supple, was curled around him. Gentle, soft hands stroked the damp hair away from his face.

The clean flowery scent of her skin enveloped him. It was so foreign to the life that he had led for so long that it stunned him. A rough yearning uncoiled from the dark, cold emptiness inside him.

"Cait," he muttered. His hand was heavy. Clumsy. Somehow he managed to lift it high enough to touch her cheek.

"I don't want you to be hurt anymore," she whispered with a sob in her voice. Her fingers closed around his hand.

"Used to it." His eyelids closed drunkenly. In the harsh light, his thick lashes made dark crescents on his too-pale skin. He muttered something she didn't catch, and his hand fell away.

Cait bit her lip. She cradled him against her and tried not to think of the pain that had put deep lines in his face and silver in his hair.

His body was a dead weight against her thighs. It had a hardness to it and a heat that penetrated her clothes to touch the skin beneath. She smelled blood and sweat and dirt, harsh masculine scents. His jacket was torn. His shirt hung open where the buttons had torn loose. He—

It was then that she saw the large splotch of fresh blood, low on his belly where his jeans rode. The waistband was frayed and sodden where Mike's knife had sliced.

The panic that had begun to subside flared anew. She bit her lip and shot a frantic glance toward the lighted window on the third floor. At that moment she heard the throaty rumble of a high-powered motor.

The car came from the west, moving fast. She knew that it was Dante's the moment she saw it. It was a low-slung, vintage Mercedes, exactly the kind of a car she would expect a former race driver to own.

The light at the intersection was red, but Dante slowed only long enough to make sure there was no cross traffic. Seconds later the Mercedes screeched to a stop only yards from her. Dante was out of the car and moving toward her before she could call his name.

"How is he?" he threw at her as he bent over them.

"Bleeding badly. Methodist Hospital isn't far. We can have him there in minutes."

"No hospital." The voice was Tyler's. Cait felt him stir against her.

"This is serious, Tyler," she said as she gently but firmly tightened her grip on his uninjured shoulder. "You need a doctor."

"I *am* a doctor," he muttered. "Or I used to be. Forget sometimes."

Cait and Dante exchanged looks. "We can't take him to my house," she whispered. "Kelsey's there. And Sutter Creek is too far."

The big attorney hesitated before replying curtly, "My place."

Dante cast a quick glance up and down the street, then bent closer. "C'mon, buddy, let's get you out of this parking lot before a beat cop comes nosing around."

Dante slipped his arm behind Tyler's back and helped him to his feet. Tyler's face turned white, and he bit off a groan.

"Bastards jumped me," he muttered as he draped an arm over Dante's wide shoulders.

"So I hear. You must be losing your edge."

"Had...something on my mind. Got careless."

With Dante's help, he managed a few steps, then a few more. Big as he was, Dante, too, was staggering under Tyler's weight.

"You're both going to need a doctor," Cait muttered. Before either man could protest, she took Tyler's other arm and draped it over her shoulders. He staggered, throwing the hard weight of his hip against hers. She reeled but managed to remain upright.

The three of them headed for the Mercedes. It was slow going. Tyler was breathing heavily. His teeth were clenched and large drops of moisture beaded his brow.

By the time they reached the passenger side, Tyler's arm was a crushing weight on her shoulders. His head sagged and his eyes were closed.

Dante took a tighter grip on Tyler's almost-limp body. "I've got him," he grated to Cait. "Get the door."

Cait leaned forward and opened the car door. Between the two of them they managed to get Tyler into the bucket seat. He slumped against the leather upholstery and closed his eyes.

The old Mercedes was equipped with a lap belt only. Cait's fingers shook as she slipped the metal end into the buckle and pulled the strap tight.

"It'll be okay," she murmured, but her voice shook. "Dante will take care of you."

There was more blood now. On her skirt, on her breast, on the hand she'd used to smooth the thick hair off his wet forehead. He groaned and turned his head away from her.

"Hang on, buddy," Dante murmured as he muscled past Cait to make sure the seat belt was fastened. When he was finished, he gently closed the door and turned to face her.

Cait clutched his arm. "He's lost a lot of blood. There may be shock, infection, anything. He needs professional care."

Dante's Latin features took on a fierce scowl. "He'll get it."

"How?"

"My neighbor is a vet. She's sewn me up a time or two."

Cait's eyes rounded. "A vet!" she snapped. "You're out of your mind. He needs a doctor, and I intend to call one."

She took two quick steps toward the door before Dante's big hand came down on her shoulder, stopping her. He swung her around until they were only inches apart.

He towered over her, his face close to hers. "Let me spell it out for you, Dr. Fielding," he said in a low, rough voice. "Because of you and that vindictive sister of yours, Ty just might spend the rest of his life branded as a sex offender."

Cait flinched, but Dante wasn't in the mood to be gentle. He bored in. "At the moment, he's just trying to get through one of the most restrictive paroles I've ever known the board to order. So far he's managed to keep his PO off his back. But one slip, one mistake, one violation of the rules, and Ty's freedom, such as it is, is history." He inhaled swiftly, but he wasn't finished. "A street brawl, no matter how justified, is definitely not permitted."

Cait tried to blink away the tears, but there were too many. "But if I testified on his behalf, if I told the board that he was just trying to protect me—"

"Like you testified on his behalf at the trial, you mean?"

Cait winced. Visibly trying to control his temper, Dante let her go. "Ty is the best friend I ever had. He's also one of the kindest men I know, and the most honorable. I watched him dying by inches in that hellhole. He's not going back there, no matter what I have to do."

He turned away from her and hurried to the driver's side of the car. Seconds later the engine roared to life. An instant later they were gone, leaving behind a plume of exhaust and a woman with tears streaming down her face.

She was there, smiling down at him in that slightly crooked way he remembered. This time she was so close he could feel the sweetness of her breath bathing his face.

"Darling," she whispered. "I'm here."

Her eyes warmed until they were shot with seductive gold lights, and her tongue ran along the gentle curve of her lower lip, sending his pulse rocketing. He tried to smile, but he had forgotten how.

He struggled to get closer, but unseen hands anchored him to the cold, wet ground beneath him. Panic shot through him, rising in a wave to his throat. But he knew better than to cry out. A man who broke was a dead man.

Tyler awoke in a cold sweat. Panic sent him jackknifing into a sitting position. Pain like hot needles nearly cut him in two. Crying out, he doubled over and fought for breath.

When the pain eased enough to allow rational thought, he discovered that he was lying naked under wool blankets. A large gauze pad was neatly taped to his hip. Another covered one shoulder.

He remembered then. This was Dante's house. Probably Dante's bed, too, from the size of it. Seconds later the sound of his friend's voice told Tyler that he had guessed right.

"Morning, buddy. How 'bout a quick game of racquetball?"

Tyler turned his head too quickly, sending pain spiking through his shoulder. He bit off a groan.

"Can it, Dante," he grumbled. "I'm not in the mood."

Dante leaned his truncated shoulder against the doorjamb and grinned. It took much of the harshness from his face.

"Hell, Ty. You got to be rarin' to go. You slept almost sixteen hours after Clancy sewed you up."

Tyler ran his hand down his stubbled cheek. His eyes were gritty, and his mouth tasted like the bottom of a well. No doubt he smelled like a hibernating bear.

"Tell me the truth, Jess. The lady with the needle wasn't really a vet, was she?"

"Absolutely. She owed me a favor or two."

"She's damn good, whoever she is. I hardly felt a thing."

Dante stepped into the room and crossed to the bed. He was wearing jeans and a T-shirt bearing the logo of a famous oil company, one of his former sponsors when he'd been on the racing circuit. In his hand he held a steaming mug of coffee that drew Tyler's narrowed gaze.

"That for me?"

"Yeah. Thought you could use the caffeine."

Dante set the mug on the nightstand and helped Tyler pile the pillows against the headboard. Tyler grunted his thanks before easing himself into a semireclining position. The pain receded slowly, leaving him feeling sick to his stomach.

"What did you slip me last night, a Mickey?"

"Codeine. It was about eight years old, but what the hell? It worked."

Tyler stretched out one leg and tried to work some of the stiffness from his back. If pressed, he might be able to find a place on his body that wasn't sore. Or he might not.

"What time is it?" His watch was on the dresser across the room, along with his keys and the picture of Kelsey that Cait had given him.

"Almost eleven."

"Damn, I have to call Angie."

"I've already taken care of it. Told her you had a problem with the truck. She said she would cover for you."

Tyler nodded. "I hope that bastard Shuffler doesn't decide to make another one of his surprise visits."

"I hear ya."

Dante crossed to the window and threw open the curtains. Sunlight streamed through the window to splash on the bed. The sky was a bright, deep blue, startling Tyler with its intensity. During those first few weeks after he'd been released, he'd felt disoriented with all the colors and sounds of the outside world.

"How do you feel?" Dante asked as he turned away from the window.

"Like I lost."

"Way I heard it, it was three against one."

Tyler managed a grunt. "Two and a half anyway. One was dead drunk."

Tyler waited for the stabbing pain in his side to ease before reaching for the coffee. It was hot and bitter. He thought he'd never tasted anything better.

"By the way, you had a couple of calls." Dante pulled up an old-fashioned rocking chair and sat down. The aged wood groaned under his weight. "One last night after you were asleep. Another early this morning."

Tyler frowned. "Me? Who from?"

"Caitlin Fielding. Both times."

Tyler stared into the dregs in the cup. "She say what she wanted?"

"To know if you were okay. Seems she's concerned. Wants you to call her back. She left her home number and her office number. Made me repeat them, even."

Leaning back, he slipped his hand into his pocket and pulled out a slip of paper. He dropped it onto the nightstand. Tyler ignored it.

Dante settled back in his chair and shook his head. "You don't listen worth a damn."

"I listen."

"Oh yeah? So why didn't you stay away from Caitlin Fielding?"

"Because of Kelsey. And don't worry. I had Shuffler's permission to see Cait."

Dante's gaze went to the dresser. He'd found the photo of Tyler's daughter when he'd stripped off the bloody clothes. The little girl had changed a lot since the trial. He turned back to find Tyler watching him with those too-empty eyes.

"Ty, do you have any idea what could have happened if Kelsey happened to be in Fielding's office when you showed up?" Without waiting for an answer, Dante went on. "You'd be back in Vacaville serving the rest of your sentence, that's what."

"It didn't happen."

"But it could have. You were just damn lucky."

Tyler gulped the last bitter drops of coffee and turned to put the cup on the stand. A hot lash of pain stopped him. Dante leaned forward and took the cup from his hand.

"Thanks," Tyler muttered as he let himself sink back against the pillows. The cut in his shoulder was beginning to throb.

"Jess, I want you to do something for me."

Dante eyed him warily. "Why do I think I won't like this?"

"Arrange for me to see my daughter."

Dante scowled. "Damn it, Ty. Haven't you heard anything I've just said?"

"I heard."

Dante braced his arm on his knee and leaned forward, suddenly all business. "The court has taken her away from you permanently. My hands are tied."

Tyler scowled. "File a petition."

"Useless, unless you're acquitted in a new trial."

"Then get me a new trial, damn it."

"I'm trying, but you keep sabotaging me."

The two men glared at each other, power against power. Determination against determination. Dante was the first to look away.

"I thought you'd learned a few things in prison, like patience."

Tyler closed his eyes. Dante was the best friend he'd ever had. He was also a damn good lawyer. A man would have to be crazy not to listen to him.

"Kelsey's in a school play on the nineteenth," he said, opening his eyes.

A look of alert suspicion replaced the frustration in Dante's black eyes. "How do you know?"

"I saw a poster in Cait's office. I'm thinking about attending."

Dante shot a quick gaze toward the ceiling. "To see Kelsey?"

"Yes."

"You sure it's not to see Caitlin Fielding again?"

A scowl furrowed Tyler's brow. "I might have lost my license, but I haven't lost my mind."

"Every man loses his mind when he wants a woman. It's built into the damn hormones." Dante's powerful voice rang with all the conviction of a man used to commanding six figures just for walking into a courtroom.

"And don't try to bs me, old buddy. I saw the way the lady was holding on to you in that parking lot. Bloody and hurtin' like hell, you were lovin' it."

Tyler kept his temper pulled tight. "She's Kelsey's mother now. And that's all she is."

Just because she'd been worried about him, even cried for him, didn't mean that she was offering anything more than temporary compassion. A man would be a fool to think she was.

Dante stood. His gaze caught Tyler's and held. "Remember this, Ty. Get caught in the vicinity of your daughter without permission, and I guarantee the board will revoke your parole. In case you've forgotten, that means three more years of hard time. And maybe even an extra year or two tacked on for contempt of court. Think about that before you do something stupid."

Chapter 6

Seven-year-old Steven Goldberg slapped his Forty-Niners cap on his head and opened the door to the outer office where his mother was waiting.

"Bye, Dr. Fielding."

"Bye, Stevie. See you next week."

"Yep, I'll be here." He flashed her a cocky grin and closed the door. Smiling to herself, Cait jotted down a few notes before she tossed his folder on top of the day's stack. Stevie had been coming to her every Saturday morning for almost a year.

Before long, he would no longer need her. It would hurt, saying goodbye, just as it always hurt when one of her patients left her.

Her gaze went to the photograph that had replaced the one she'd given Tyler. Her daughter was the most precious thing in her life. If she ever lost her...

The phone rang. It was the answering service with her calls. One of them was from Hazel. She returned it first.

Ten minutes later, Cait pulled out the card with Tyler's number scrawled on the back and dialed. It rang twice.

"Horseshoe. McClane here."

Cait swallowed the sudden flutter of nerves in her throat. "This is Cait."

Silence burned through the line. Cait wondered if he was going to hang up. She wasn't sure she would blame him if he did.

"You sound as though you're recovering," she said quickly.

"I'm doing okay."

"I wanted to let you know that Teri Grimes at Children's Protective Services has gotten Hazel and me an appointment with an appellate judge next week. Looks like we might be able to convince him that Kelsey's recovery requires some limited contact with her father."

"When next week?"

"Wednesday at four."

"I'll call you at five."

Cait smiled. That was more like the Tyler she'd known. "Better make it six, at home. Let me give you the number."

"No need. You left it with Jess."

"Along with a request that you call me back. As I recall, you never did."

Silence fell. This time Cait resolved to wait it out. As she did, she wound the phone cord around her index finger. The silence was long enough to let her unwind it again. It was also long enough to make her feel like a fool for calling in the first place.

"You're right. I should have called." His voice was clipped. "My manners must be rustier than I thought."

"Mike was looking for me, wasn't he?"

"No. He was following me."

"It was because of me, though. Wasn't it? He was after you because you threw him out."

"Let it go, Cait."

"I've, uh, been thinking about the play tomorrow night. If you promise to stay in the back..."

"Don't worry, Cait. You won't have to post guards. I won't be there." He hung up without saying goodbye.

* * *

Kelsey's class was gathered with all the others in a class-room next to the cafeteria. Devoid of tables now, the lunchroom was doing double duty as an auditorium.

The classes were appearing in order. At the moment the third-graders were onstage. Kelsey's class was next.

Cait was helping the "elves" with their costumes. Some of the other mothers and a few fathers were performing similar tasks. Inseparable as always, Kelsey and her friend Sarah chattered back and forth like bright, very nervous magpies.

Cait settled the green felt cap over Kelsey's soft curls. A sudden panic widened Kelsey's eyes.

"What if I forgot what to say, like Sarah did in prac-tice?" she whispered in a tremulous voice.

"No big deal, sweetie. Just make something up."

Kelsey continued to fidget, but the panic had subsided. "You're sure you're going to be in the audience?"

"Absolutely. With my fingers crossed." Cait held up two crossed fingers to demonstrate. "Hazel will be there, too, remember? She's saving me a seat. We both love you very much, you know. And we're very proud of you."

Kelsey shifted from one foot to the other. "Sarah's grandma and grandpa came all the way from New York to watch us."

"I know."

"I don't have a grandma or a grandpa, do I?"

"No, not anymore." Cait brushed an imaginary speck of lint from Kelsey's shoulder. Her parents were both dead. So were Tyler's, or so he'd told her once a long time ago.

Kelsey's soft little mouth trembled. "Sarah says that I'm an orphan, 'cause you're really my aunt and not my mommy."

"Sarah's wrong. I'm your aunt *and* your mommy. That makes you one very special little girl, don't you think?"

Kelsey nodded, but her eyes didn't smile.

The school had been transformed into a winter wonder-land. Snowflakes hung from the ceiling. A heavily laden

Christmas tree stood in one corner. Red and green garlands were draped along every wall.

The play had drawn a capacity crowd. Standing on the periphery, Cait stood on tiptoe and searched for Hazel's bright curls.

In the dim light it took her a few seconds of scanning faces before she spied Hazel in the back row, near the end. The seat on the aisle was empty.

"How is she?" Hazel whispered as Cait slipped into the empty seat.

"Nervous."

"How are *you*?"

"Even more nervous!"

Hazel chuckled and handed Cait a program. "She'll be fine."

Cait held up her still-crossed fingers. "I hope so."

She settled into the hard seat and tried to swallow the nervous tickle in her throat. Onstage, a troupe of eight-year-olds dressed as reindeer giggled and mugged through a ragged two-step in time with "Rudolph, the Red-nosed Reindeer."

A quick glance at her watch told Cait that the evening was nearly half over. Soon the third graders would take their final bows, and then it would be time for Kelsey's class to take the stage.

"*...and that's how Rudolph became the ninth reindeer!*" the third-graders chorused in unison.

At that moment the curtain came down swiftly, nearly bonking the last reindeer on his antlers. Tentative clapping swelled into a storm of applause.

Just as the clapping began to abate, Mrs. Eddington, looking like Mrs. Santa herself in red velvet, walked to center stage and beamed at the faces turned her way.

"And now, moms and dads, brothers and sisters and friends, I am proud to present our fourth-grade students in a play of their own creation entitled *The Elf Who Hated Christmas.*"

The rotund teacher executed a small, formal bow and walked off the stage to another burst of applause. The audience murmured in anticipation. Hazel cleared her throat and straightened in her chair.

Cait felt a gust of wind shiver the back of her neck and swiveled around to see what was causing it. Someone had just come in through the door leading to the parking lot.

As soon as she saw the broad shoulders, she knew. It was Tyler. As she watched, he took a quick look around before edging closer to the wall where other latecomers were standing.

He could have been any of the fathers in his conservative blue blazer and tailored slacks. His hair, disheveled by the wind, looked as though it had been recently trimmed, and his jaw had the shiny hardness of a recent shave.

It was the bruised jaw that set him apart. That and the tension in his big shoulders. Cait was certain she hadn't made a sound, but suddenly Tyler's gaze was aimed directly at her.

"That's Kelsey's father, isn't it?" Hazel murmured, close to her ear.

"Yes," Cait whispered over a swell of music from the boom box near the stage. "How did you know?"

"For one thing, they look alike. For another, you're about to mangle that program."

Cait glanced down at the tube of paper now crushed between her fingers. "He said he wasn't coming," she whispered.

"Well, he's most definitely here now," Hazel whispered back.

Cait drew a shaky breath. To the accompaniment of trumpets the curtains rose on Santa's workshop. Santa and some of his elves were staring helplessly at an empty corner where the sleigh should have been but wasn't. After hours of helping Kelsey with her lines, Cait knew the play by heart. Kelsey would soon make her entrance.

Cait handed Hazel her program and stood. Moving quietly, she went to him.

"I didn't think you were coming," she whispered when she reached his side.

"Changed my mind."

The music changed, and Cait recognized Kelsey's entrance cue. Her heart raced, and her throat threatened to close as she touched Tyler's arm.

"There she is," she whispered softly. "In the front row, with the green hat and purple doublet." A smile hovered softly at the corners of her mouth. "She's afraid she'll forget her line. I told her to improvise."

He tried to smile at that. Failing, he shifted his gaze to the stage. Each breath he took seemed squeezed from him. He was afraid to move. Feelings he hadn't acknowledged in a long time whipped through him. Feelings he was helpless to withstand.

"Here it comes," Cait murmured. Her hand groped for his elbow, and she held on. "Keep your fingers crossed that she doesn't forget."

Tyler experienced a moment of panic. What would happen if she did? Her mother would have burst into tears. As for him, he just got calmer under stress—until the problem was solved. That was when his temper usually exploded.

He held his breath. Santa was speaking. And then it was Kelsey's turn.

"But Santa? How...uh..." Her high, clear voice stuttered into silence. Kelsey ducked her head, causing the bell on her cap to tinkle loudly. Tyler and Cait shared an agonized look.

Hang in there, baby, he thought. You can do it.

Onstage, Kelsey's face was getting pinker and pinker. The other elves exchanged anxious looks. Santa looked toward the wings. And then Kelsey straightened her little shoulders and said with great drama, *"But, Santa, how can we have Christmas without the sleigh?"*

Kelsey's fellow elves looked relieved. Eyes sparkling, she grinned toward the footlights as though to say "I did it." Santa picked up his cue, and the dialogue continued.

"Proud of herself, isn't she?" Tyler whispered in a gruff tone.

Cait managed a shaky nod as she whispered back, "She's got this...this tough little center that won't let her give up."

Because it seemed right, she raised her gaze to his and added softly, "Like her daddy."

Tyler found his throat blocked by a thickness that he couldn't swallow away. It had been a long time since anyone had looked at him with approval.

Suddenly he felt as though the walls were pushing against him. The dark was smothering. He needed air.

He turned, only to realize that Cait blocked his escape. He pulled his hands from his pockets. With his left, he captured hers. With the other he took an envelope from the inside pocket of his blazer and slapped it into her palm.

"What's this?" Her voice was barely audible over the sudden burst of applause swelling over them.

"The letter you wanted. Use it as you think best." He dropped her hand and turned away.

"Tyler, wait," she called after him. He didn't stop.

Cait shot a quick glance toward the stage, where Kelsey and the others were taking their bows. Kelsey's eyes were shining like Christmas stars. She was fine. Tyler wasn't. Cait turned to follow him into the cold night.

As soon as she left the building, she felt the cold wind buffeting her. The parking lot was full. Even with the bright lights overhead, it took several seconds before she saw him.

He had both hands on his truck's right front fender as though he were determined to rip it free from the chassis. His head was bent, and his broad back faced her.

She was less than a dozen yards from him when he spun around quickly, as though to fend off another attack. The cold glitter in his eyes stopped her in midstride. As soon as he recognized her, his body relaxed. His eyes, however, remained coldly guarded.

"You left before I could thank you," she said, indicating the letter still in her hand. His shoulders moved in the barest suggestion of a shrug.

"I hope it's what you wanted."

"Are you sure you should give this to me without permission? Because of your parole, I mean. What I mean is, didn't you take an awfully big risk?"

There was a pause before he said tersely, "Not much."

"But Dante said—"

"Forget Dante. He's gotten paternal in his old age."

Cait laughed at the thought of the virile, dynamic attorney getting old. "Whatever you do, Tyler, don't let him hear you saying that."

His face relaxed for an instant, as though he were smiling inside. "If you don't tell, I won't."

"It's a deal." She moved closer.

His face tightened again. "If I could do more, I would."

"I know. I just wish it were possible. For your sake as well as Kelsey's."

There was a measured silence during which his eyes searched her face intently. "You really mean that, don't you?" he said at last.

"I never say anything I don't mean. I thought you knew that."

"Did you mean it when you said you believed I was innocent?"

"Yes. I believe it. Unequivocally. I made a mistake four years ago. I realize that now."

His big shoulders flexed as though they had wearied of carrying a great weight. "I made mistakes, too. Too damn many," he said slowly, deliberately, as though measuring each word. "I wasn't home when I should have been. I saw my daughter when it was convenient for me. Sometimes I went days without seeing her. No wonder it was so easy for Crys to convince her I'd take her away. Furious as I was with Crys at the time, I just might have. I thought about it enough."

He passed his hand through his wind-whipped hair before raising his gaze to the sky. "God, I'd give anything for another chance."

"Don't, Tyler." Cait moved closer until only a few inches separated them. "That's all in the past."

"No. Some mistakes take a long time to erase." His voice broke, and his chest heaved as he struggled for control. "I would have killed anyone who did what they accused me of doing, Cait," he said in a harsh whisper. "I swear it."

The wind snatched at her hair, leaving tendrils clinging to her neck. He lifted a hand to brush them away. His fingers lingered, but there was no hint of seduction in his touch. Only an abiding need for human contact.

"It's cold. You'd better get back inside."

She covered his hand with hers and leaned into his touch. Surprise flickered in his eyes.

"Do you remember that night on the hospital roof when you found me crying because I'd lost a patient to suicide?"

"No." But she saw by the quick flash in his eyes that he did.

"First you dried my tears, and then you held me. You were so gentle. So tender."

"Don't." His voice was ragged, his fists clenched.

"I needed a friend that night, and you were there," she continued softly. "Tonight I think you need a friend."

Very gently she threaded her arms around his waist and rested her head on his shoulder.

As soon as she touched him, Tyler felt a surge of longing so great it stunned him. But it wasn't physical need that threatened to drive him to his knees. It was a deep hunger to belong. To matter to someone. To make a difference in someone's life.

He resisted for as long as he could, and then he was dragging her against him. His need to feel her warmth was savage. His arms strained to withstand the need to hold her even tighter.

Her scent swirled on the breeze. Her breath warmed his neck. Her soft breasts cushioned his chest. The quiet came gradually. Little by little he felt himself relaxing.

It was habit that had his hand beginning a slow movement against the small of her back. Even the lightest friction of skin on soft wool, however, was more than he could take. Stifling a groan, he closed his fingers into a hard fist.

Cait was returning a favor tonight. He had no right to want more. Slowly he lifted his head and released her.

"Consider us even," he said with a slow smile that felt stiff on his face.

Cait surfaced slowly. "I really am sorry, Tyler."

"So am I. More than you know."

The night grew very quiet. Overhead, stars gathered strength. The breeze blew fiercely, but Tyler's big body protected her from its bite. Nevertheless, she shivered.

"You should be inside. And I should be on my way." He touched the curve of her jaw.

"I'm glad you came." The warmth inside her was suddenly slipping away.

"Thanks for being my friend tonight," he said in a voice so low and deep that she felt as well as heard the vibration. "You were right. I needed one."

It was the gentlest of kisses, a warm sweet pressure of his mouth against hers before he took a determined step away. The warmth of his mouth lingered.

"Good night, Caitie."

She managed a smile. "Good night."

He watched her until she was safely inside, and then he let his shoulders slump. It was going to be a long, lonely drive home.

Chapter 7

The phone rang just as Cait and Kelsey were sitting down to dinner on Wednesday. It was six o'clock on the dot.

"I'll get it," Kelsey cried.

"That's okay. It's for me." Cait was already out of her chair and heading for the den. She closed the door carefully before reaching for the phone.

"Hello?" She found she was slightly breathless. From running, she told herself.

"Cait? It's Tyler. I assume you kept your appointment with the judge today." She heard music playing in the background. "Jingle Bells" with a western beat.

"We did indeed." She took a deep breath.

"Well?" His impatience fairly sizzled down the line. She imagined him scowling as he spoke, but his big hand would now be white around the phone. He guarded his heart well. Sometimes, however, the intensity of his feelings spilled over those walls he'd erected. Something warm uncurled inside her.

"We won," she said with a pleased grin. "Big time."

"We?"

"You and Kelsey, Hazel and me."

"Cait—"

She shifted the phone from one ear to the other and grinned at her reflection in the window. "Actually, Haze was the one who did most of the talking," she went on, as though she hadn't heard his frustrated growl. "I was mainly there for moral support. I wish you could have seen her, Tyler. She went in there like a little redheaded bulldog. Judge Alexander didn't have a chance, although he was thorough, I'll give him that. He asked just about every question I expected and a few more. Bless her heart, Haze had answers for them all. She could have been a politician, although for heaven's sake don't tell her I said so. She would kill me."

There was a pause. "Is there a bottom line to this?" He sounded annoyed, but there was a definite thread of indulgent humor mixed in with the masculine rumble.

"Sure. Bottom line, the judge agreed that Kelsey's emotional stability depends on believing that you don't hate her. So he's going to allow limited contact. By letter only, at the moment. But what the heck, it's a start. Right?"

In the sudden silence she imagined him sitting rigidly, staring straight ahead the way he'd done when the bailiff had read the verdict.

"What's the next step then?"

"Next we wait for the right moment, when Kelsey seems especially receptive, and then I'll read your letter to her."

"You? I thought you said Dr. O'Connor was going to read it."

"Hazel thinks it would be better if I did. Actually, she *ordered* me to read it. She can be very bossy sometimes, although to tell you the truth, I usually ignore her and do what I want anyway. Maybe that's why we're still friends."

"Why doesn't that surprise me?" Was that husky note in his voice the beginning of laughter?

"Beats me."

Even over the din of the early-evening crowd, Tyler caught the slight lilt of a smile in her voice. It wasn't a big deal. Except to a man who'd never forgotten how special one of her smiles could make him feel.

"So are you?" he asked as the silence lengthened.

"Am I what?"

When she was annoyed, he remembered, two tiny vees formed above the bridge of her nose. In his mind he saw them now. There were freckles on that little nose. Usually she'd covered them with makeup. He had always meant to tell her not to bother. Sooner or later they peeked through, tempting a man to count them with his tongue.

His mind took hold of that thought and refused to let go. Across the bar, Ben Hadley gave him a strange look.

Tyler turned his back and stared down at the scuffed toes of his boots. Ten years had passed, and she still had the power to beguile him.

"Are you going to read the damn letter?"

"Well, sure. I thought I just *said* that."

"No, you didn't."

There was a pause before she asked softly, "Tyler, are you gritting your teeth?"

Tyler relaxed his jaw. "No."

"Yes, you are! I can hear that sound you make when you're getting impatient."

Old memories tugged at him. Old longings stirred. His mood took on a stark edge of loneliness. "I'd better get back to work."

She burst out laughing. "You never could stand it when I was right, could you?"

He felt a loosening at the back of his neck. It took him a moment to realize he was relaxing. It wasn't an unpleasant sensation, simply unfamiliar, which was why he didn't trust it.

"That's because you thought you were always right," he said.

"So?"

"Sometimes you're wrong. And sometimes you're not the one who pays when you are."

There was a pause before she said slowly, "That's true. I guess I'd forgotten. But then, I don't have the same reason to remember, do I? As you say, you're the one who paid."

98   *Paroled!*

The lilt was gone from her voice. It occurred to him that perhaps that had been his intention.

"That was out of line. Forget I said anything."

"Why do people always say that?" she mused in a low tone tinged with an emotion he couldn't identify. "Once something's been said, it can never be called back, can it?"

She hung up without waiting for his reply.

Tyler stood with the phone in his hand. The dial tone buzzed angrily in his ear, but it was the long string of curses slicing through his head that he heard.

During Cait's childhood, the Christmas tree was never decorated until Christmas Eve. That was one of the things she had resolved to change when she had her own family. It was a full week until Christmas, but the den blazed with lights and smelled deliciously of pine needles.

The tree was a specially ordered noble fir tall enough to touch the ceiling. Cait was in charge of the lights and the tinsel, while Kelsey took care of the ornaments.

She'd been hoping that a tree-decorating party would put sparkle in Kelsey's eyes. Instead, it seemed to have made her more withdrawn.

"What do you think, sweetie?" Cait asked as she stepped back to inspect her handiwork. "More tinsel?"

Kelsey shrugged. "Mommy always had a silver tree, with lots of red balls."

Cait heard the forlorn note in the child's voice and knew that she was remembering last Christmas. The three of them had spent it together at Crystal's home in Hillsborough. A week later, on New Year's Eve, Crystal had been dead.

"Are you disappointed that our tree isn't like Mommy's?" Cait asked softly.

Kelsey stared fixedly at the carpet. "Not exactly," she mumbled. "It's just . . . different."

Her brow was still furrowed. Kelsey was a lot like her father. She couldn't be pushed into anything, not even conversation.

"I understand. Different can be scary sometimes." Cait dropped an arm over Kelsey's thin shoulders and led her to the chair by the fire.

"I need a hug," she said as she drew the little girl close to her. As Kelsey's arms immediately wound around her neck, Cait thought of Tyler. How terrible it must be for him to know that he could be sent to prison for hugging his own child.

"Mmm, that was just what I needed," she murmured as Kelsey released her. "Thank you."

Kelsey snuggled closer. "Welcome."

"The fire feels good, doesn't it?"

Kelsey didn't answer. Instead, her gaze trailed upward to the photograph of Crystal and Caitlin on the mantelpiece. It had been taken when Cait had graduated from college and Crystal was just beginning.

"Mama Cait, was my mommy pretty?"

Mixed emotions stabbed at Cait, just as they always did now when she thought of her sister. "Yes, darling. Very pretty."

Kelsey's eyes grew very solemn and dark. "Sarah says that her mommy is the prettiest mommy in California and her daddy is the handsomest."

"Does she?" Cait's voice was calm.

"Uh-huh. She asked me if my daddy was handsome."

Cait realized that her throat was suddenly tight. "And what did you say?"

"I didn't say anything."

"Why not, sweetie?"

"'Cause I don't remember what he looks like." As though she were ashamed, Kelsey dropped her gaze and hunched her shoulders. "Sometimes I think I remember, but I'm not sure."

Cait glanced toward her desk. "Would you like to see a picture of your daddy?"

Kelsey nodded again, but apprehension pinched her mouth and darkened her eyes.

"Let me up for a minute, so I can get to my desk."

The yellowed newspaper clipping was in the bottom drawer, under a stack of personal papers. Kelsey watched intently as Cait returned to her seat and unfolded the clipping.

The article was a laudatory one, praising Dr. Tyler McClane for reattaching an eleven-year-old Little League pitcher's right arm after it had been severed in an accident. The grainy photo accompanying the article showed a gangly half-grown kid in a hospital bed grinning at the camera while Tyler was standing next to him. He wasn't smiling. Nor did he look particularly pleased at having his picture taken.

Kelsey stared. "Did he really sew that boy's arm back on?"

"Yes, he really did. And one year later that boy was pitching for his team again."

"Honest?"

"Cross my heart."

Kelsey looked startled and just a little bit awed. Cait knew the feeling. She had felt the same way about Tyler once, especially when she'd been a green psychotherapy intern listening to the surgical residents sing his praises.

Kelsey traced the headlines with her fingertip. "Auntie Hazel says my daddy isn't in prison now."

"That's true. How do you feel about that?"

"Good, I guess. Sometimes I don't know how I feel about anything anymore."

"You know something, Kels? Sometimes I don't, either. It's a scary feeling for me."

Kelsey blinked solemnly, as though the idea of Mama Cait being scared of anything was a novel one.

"Me too," she admitted belatedly. "Sometimes I can't sleep 'cause I get so scared."

"Me too," Cait echoed with a soft smile.

She drew her daughter close and kissed her forehead. She wanted to promise that nothing would ever scare her again. But that was a promise no one could make.

"Mama Cait?" Kelsey asked when Cait released her.

"Yes, sweetie?"

"Do you think my daddy gets scared?"

Cait hadn't expected the question. Stalling, she glanced down at the man in the white coat. His tie was askew, and he needed a haircut, but his eyes burned with a fierce dedication that still touched her, even after so many years. "I think your daddy gets scared a lot."

Kelsey's smooth forehead suddenly took on frown lines. "What's he scared about?"

"I don't know for sure, but I imagine he's scared that people will think he's a bad person because he's been in prison. Sometimes I think that makes him very lonely inside."

"Mommy said I shouldn't ever tell anyone that Daddy was in prison. She said other kids wouldn't play with me. But they already knew, 'cause my daddy's name was in the papers. His pictures, too. Lots of 'em."

"Yes, I know."

The media had had a field day. Most of the papers had had him tried and convicted before he'd even come to trial. But then, so had she, hadn't she? Cait glanced toward the fire. Suddenly all the joy had gone out of her tree-decorating party.

Careful not to tear the clipping, she refolded it before slipping it into the pocket of her robe. Kelsey watched glumly. Cait noticed that her small mouth had taken on a definite droop.

"What's wrong, Kels?" she asked softly. "Are you sad because we've been talking about your daddy?" .

Kelsey nodded. "Will I ever see him again?" the little girl asked after a moment's thought.

"Would you like to?"

Kelsey gnawed on her lip. As she did, her expression grew even more apprehensive. "I think so," she said in a tentative little voice. "I mean, if he wants to see me. Mommy said he really didn't like being a daddy much. 'Specially since he only married Mommy 'cause she was going to have me."

The forlorn droop to Kelsey's mouth tore Cait apart inside. How could Crys have been so cruel to her own child?

she raged. No wonder Tyler had grown to hate her. Cait was very close to that herself now.

"Kels, there's something I need to tell you. Okay?"

Kelsey looked startled but curious. "Okay."

"It's about your daddy."

Kelsey blinked but didn't say anything.

Cait took a moment to order her thoughts before she continued. "Remember that Saturday when I drove to the mountains? When you were at Sarah's for the day?"

"You mean when you went to see an old friend?"

Cait nodded. "That old friend was your daddy."

"You saw Daddy?" She sounded frightened, and just a little awed.

"Yes. Mostly we talked about you."

"You did? What did you say?"

"I told him how big you were getting and how smart you were. And I told him about the bad dreams."

"What . . . what did he say?"

"Actually, he gave me a letter to read to you. Would you like to hear it?"

Kelsey's small white teeth worried her lower lip as she tried to make up her mind. Finally she peeked at Cait through her thick lashes and asked shyly, "Would you be mad at me if I said yes?"

"Of course not! That's why I have it here, so that I can read it to you."

Kelsey's gaze dropped, her lashes trembling. "Mommy would have been mad. She said I shouldn't talk about Daddy to anyone ever again."

"Well, *I* think it would be a good thing if you talked a lot about your daddy. To me, if you'd like, and to Auntie Hazel, too, when you go to see her in her office. Especially to Auntie Hazel."

"Really?" Kelsey's face mirrored confusion, but Cait thought she saw a small flicker of relief in the little girl's eyes.

"Really." Cait stood and held out her hand. "C'mon, let's go upstairs to my room, and I'll get that letter for you."

Kelsey slipped her hand into Cait's, and together they climbed the stairs and entered Cait's bedroom. While Cait switched on the lamp, Kelsey walked to the bed and sat down with her hands folded primly in her lap. It's okay to be scared, Cait wanted to say, but she didn't dare. Kelsey's emotions were still too finely balanced.

The envelope was safely tucked away in her underwear drawer. As she drew it out, she realized that she was nervous.

Her hand was surprisingly steady, however, as she removed the single sheet from the envelope and unfolded it. The words were printed in careful letters, bringing a lump to her throat. Like most doctors, Tyler's handwriting was little more than a scrawl. Obviously he'd taken great care to make sure Kelsey could decipher his words.

"Here, sweetie."

Kelsey pushed the letter back toward Cait. It crinkled loudly in the silent room. "You read it to me out loud, okay?"

"Okay," Cait said before clearing her throat and raising the paper. Her vision blurred for an instant before she gathered herself together and began to read.

"Dear Button,

Guess what? It's almost time for your birthday. A little less than three months, right? I bet you're looking forward to it.

Are you having a party with your friends? You always did love parties, especially the presents. And you always wanted chocolate cake with extra icing. Maybe if you whisper in Aunt Cait's ear, she'll bake you one just like the one she made for your first birthday."

Cait glanced up to see Kelsey smiling softly. Her eyes misted, making it difficult to read on.

"Button, it's hard for me to think of you as a big girl of nine. Not only because it's been a long time since I saw you last, but also because I keep remembering the first time I saw you.

It was the day you were born, and you were only a few minutes old. You were impossibly tiny and perfect and cute as a button. When the nurse put you in my arms for the first time, I knew that nothing in the world was more precious to me than you.

Button, that's still true. I love you more than I have words to tell you. I loved you when you were saying those things about me in the courtroom, even though I didn't understand why. And I loved you during all the months when they made me stay in a place where I really didn't want to be.

Your Aunt Cait has told me that you've been having bad dreams. They can be really awful sometimes, I know. She also said that you're feeling bad because you think I blame you because the judge sent me to that place, to prison. But I don't blame you for any of the things that happened.

Now that I've had a lot of time to think about it, I know I wasn't much of a daddy, and I'm very, very sorry about that. But please, baby, don't ever think that I will ever stop loving you, no matter what.

So now I want you to do what Aunt Cait tells you. I know that she loves you very much and is trying very hard to be a good mommy to you. Also, I want you to do what Dr. O'Connor tells you so that you won't have any more bad dreams. Okay?

Imagine me kissing you on your button nose and telling you that I love you.

                                                      Daddy."

Tyler had come to hate Sundays. In prison, it had been the day when families visited. On the outside, it was still a day reserved for families. He always worked Sundays.

It was a few minutes past ten. In two hours the Horseshoe would open and the regulars would stream in. The day was overcast. Worse, snow was predicted for the higher elevations, which meant the place would also be full of tourists.

As soon as he finished washing the glasses from the Saturday-night rush, he would need to haul up a few cases of beer from the basement.

He dried his hand on his thigh and reached for his coffee. It was his sixth cup of the morning. Or maybe seventh. He'd lost count. He just knew he needed the caffeine to clear his head. Sleep had eluded him for most of the night, and when he *had* slept, he'd dreamed of Cait again.

But this time the dream was different. This time he was holding her in his arms and kissing her. This time, when he awoke, he couldn't make himself stop thinking about those few moments in the school parking lot when she had walked into his arms and nestled there.

He was enough of a realist to know that it had meant nothing. Hell, she used to hug him all the time. She'd hugged everyone. There wasn't anything sexual in her hugs. Cait wasn't a tease like her sister. Sometimes he'd wished that she had been. It was easy to resist a tease.

He downed the rest of his coffee, then flexed his shoulders and reached for another dirty glass. It was foolish to remember the sleek softness of Cait's hair against his face, just as it was foolish to recall the feel of her soft body against his.

Sex had been the furthest thing from the lady's mind, he told himself as he concentrated on rubbing the soap from the slick glass with his fingers. Truth was, it hadn't really been in his mind, either. Not then.

Then he'd been thinking of Kelsey, and he'd been hurting. Cait had sensed that and offered comfort. On the long drive home it had occurred to him that she had been motivated by guilt. It also occurred to him that she might have been motivated by pity.

Guilt he could handle. The thought that she pitied him had his belly in knots and his frustration level soaring. He rinsed the glass and upended it in the drainer.

As he did, the door to the street screeched open. Daylight splashed into the gloom, and he saw a woman's slender silhouette.

"Sorry, we're closed until noon," he called over the sudden sound of street noise.

"I suspected that when I didn't see the hogs parked outside."

Mentally Tyler jerked himself erect, although he didn't move. "Cait?"

"Good morning. Terrific day, isn't it? The wind smells like Christmas."

She let the door close behind her and walked toward him. Unlike the last time she had dropped in on him, she was dressed for the mountains in jeans and a heavy sweater. More appropriate, perhaps, he thought as he dried his hands. But a hell of a lot more trying for a man who had been celibate for longer than he cared to remember.

Not that the jeans were tight. They weren't. Cait was far too elegant for that. But they were old and worn smooth across the seat. And her sweater was an unusual shade of gold that added sparkle to her eyes.

"I was in the area and thought I'd drop in," she said as she dropped her purse onto the bar and slipped onto a stool. "Aren't you pleased?"

She smiled, and Tyler realized that it was her smile that bothered him the most. It was just a bit crooked and softened her lips into a perfect shape for kissing.

"Law says I can't offer you anything alcoholic until noon."

"How about a few minutes of your time instead?"

He could almost feel her softness pressed against him. Almost. Had he ever wanted to hold a woman more than he wanted to hold her? he wondered, but he already knew the answer.

When he spoke, his voice was deliberately remote. "That I can handle."

Her sudden appearance had taken him by surprise. Because his guard was down, he'd revealed a glimpse of the man behind the stone wall. Now, however, all his defenses were in place, stronger than ever.

She wondered why she'd thought they wouldn't be. Someday she would learn that things were not always going to be the way she thought they should be. Or the way she wanted them to be.

Ignoring the coolness that had returned to his eyes, she allowed her gaze to trail slowly and thoroughly around the place where he spent most of his time.

She discovered hidden treasures. A marvelous brass wall fixture to one side of the mirror. A wealth of intricate carving on the floor-to-ceiling paneling behind the bar. Initials and dates carved into the thick walnut going back to 1878.

"This place looks different without people," she said when she realized that he was watching her. "More... welcoming, somehow."

Tyler gave the place he'd called home for eight months a quick once-over. It hadn't changed.

"Somehow that's not exactly the word I would use," he said wryly.

"No?" Lacy dark lashes narrowed slightly over brown eyes dancing with challenge. Maturity had honed the youthful lines of her face into an elegance that stunned him. Unlike Crystal, however, Cait seemed completely oblivious to her beauty. Perhaps that was why he didn't distrust it. Perhaps he was a fool not to.

"What word *would* you use?"

"Try seedy."

"No way. More like charming." Her tone was just the tiniest bit belligerent now, and her flashing eyes could entice an argument from a stone.

"A realist would see right away that it's dilapidated," he muttered with a telling look at the worn spots on the linoleum.

Cait's gaze lovingly traced the carved flowers twining down a graceful pillar framing the mirror.

"A romantic would know immediately that it's wonderfully historic," she maintained stubbornly.

The light of battle turned her eyes to shimmering amber. Her soft mouth took on a stubborn cast that dared a man to explore her lips with his tongue. Something stirred in him that he'd thought safely hidden.

"You win. If you want it to be historic, it's historic."

Triumph flickered over her face. "Don't forget charming."

Her hair was loose today, swinging freely against her neck whenever she moved her head. It had the luster of soft dark satin, making him wonder what it would look like spread out on his pillow.

"And charming," he conceded before focusing his attention on the glass in his hand.

"And welcoming."

His head came up at that. "Don't push it, Caitlin," he said with a half smile that might have seemed boyishly indulgent on a less masculine face.

"You're right," she said with a rueful grin. "I tend toward excess."

"Tend toward it?" he said with a sardonic slant to his hard mouth. "I'd say you were off the scale."

Just as he'd known they would, her eyes lit up a split second before she laughed. The pull came again, stronger this time. He reached for the last glass and plunged it into the soapy water as desire stirred low and deep. He made himself ignore it.

"You need a dishwasher in this place," Cait murmured as she watched him work.

"We have one," he said with a quick upward glance. "You're looking at him."

Her gaze lighted for an instant on the swell of his forearms where his wrists disappeared into the water. "Do you hire out?"

"Nope."

"Too bad," she murmured. He worked with an economy of motion that fascinated her. Every movement was precise, the way it must have been in surgery.

Age had given his body a heaviness of bone and muscle that suited him, yet he moved like a much younger man. A man accustomed to a physical life.

There was an earthiness about him now, a quality of simplicity and patient endurance of life's trials, yet a strength so deeply rooted he had no need to flaunt it.

Tyler finished with the last glass and pulled the plug from the bottom of the sink. His hands seemed very dark against the thick white suds that still clung to them. As dark as they would seem against the untanned skin of her breasts, she mused.

Instantly she felt the sudden heat of embarrassment and realized that her thoughts had taken a dangerous turn. A certain amount of fantasizing was healthy, of course. But fantasizing about Tyler was dangerously foolish.

She jerked her gaze to his face and willed a teasing lilt into her voice. "If you treat me to a soda, I'll dry those for you."

"No need. I let them air dry when I have the time." He hesitated for only a moment before he reached overhead for a glass, added ice and filled it with soda from a nozzle attached to a machine under the bar. "Sorry, I can't give you a cherry. I have to bring up a new jar from the basement."

"Thanks. I like mine straight anyway."

This time she nearly had it. A genuine smile. Something warmed inside her. It was the therapist coming out in her, she assured herself. An occupational hazard all shrinks struggled with.

"Straight it is, just like the lady likes it."

He leaned over the bar to set the glass on a napkin in front of her. As he did, she noticed that tiny beads of steam from the hot water glistened like dew on his upper lip.

His shirt, too, was sweat soaked and clinging to his broad chest like a second skin. Perhaps because of the hot water, he'd rolled his sleeves above his elbows, where they banded his biceps like snug ribbing.

Cait's mouth went dry. She shouldn't have given in to the impulse to tell him face-to-face about the letter. When they were alone, it was far too easy to be aware of him as a man, as well as Kelsey's father. A very attractive, intriguing man with a hint of heartrending loneliness in his eyes.

Because she had asked for the drink, she took a sip. Tyler grabbed a towel and wiped the counter dry. Each movement of his arm pulled the cotton of his shirt tighter until Cait had a perfect mental image of the muscles of his chest.

"What's Kelsey doing today?" he asked as he wiped his face and neck with the towel. Cait caught a whiff of tart after-shave and musky masculine sweat. She found she liked the combination.

"Baking Christmas cookies at her best friend Sarah's house."

"Sounds festive."

He tossed the towel into a bin under the counter. Cait sipped her soda while he poured himself a glass of water and drank it all.

She waited for him to say something. When he didn't, she realized that his supply of small talk was all used up. Hers, too, seemed strangely depleted.

Once they had talked for hours. Now it seemed they had little to say to each other. She found that thought unbearably sad.

After finishing the soda, she pushed the empty glass closer to his half of the wide bar. She wondered if he was waiting for her to leave so that he could get on with his work. Probably, she decided. Sunday was probably a busy day at the Lucky Horseshoe.

She slipped the napkin from under the empty glass and concentrated on making perfect pleats.

"I read your letter to Kelsey last night. You said exactly what she needed to hear."

"Is that why you drove all the way here? To tell me that?"

She glanced up. His brow was furrowed, his eyes wary. These days, it seemed that he distrusted even the smallest gesture of kindness.

"Partly. I needed to get away for a while. I figured if you could drive all the way into the city to bring it to me, I could drive out here to thank you."

"A phone call would have done, but thank you."

Knowing that he had revealed a part of himself to Cait as well as to his daughter made him uneasy. That uneasiness had him walking to the end of the bar to refill his coffee cup. As he did, he cocked an eyebrow in her direction, silently asking if she would like to join him.

"No, thanks," she murmured. She was jittery enough. The caffeine would only make her squirrelly.

When he realized she wasn't going to say her piece and leave, he silently sipped his coffee and wondered if he could truly trust her.

It was her air of complete relaxation that decided it for him. Only someone who accepted him totally, without reservations or expectations, would be so at ease with an ex-convict who went out of his way to keep people as far away as possible.

"I meant everything I said in that letter, Cait," he said, choosing his words with difficulty. "I was a lousy father. No wonder Crys was able to use Kelsey against me. I wasn't much more than a stranger to her."

Her smile was understanding. "We all have regrets, Tyler. Even Crystal, I think."

Watching her, he felt as though she had touched him very gently, just as she had the night of the play. Longings surged again, stronger this time.

Dropping his gaze, Tyler studied that dark sludge in his cup before slugging it down.

"When it comes to Crys, you're more charitable than I am."

"She was the mother of your child," Cait reminded him softly.

"Yes, I know. That's why I married her." Refilling his cup had emptied the pot, and he set about brewing another. Cait watched, uncertain whether to stay or go. Tyler didn't seem unwelcoming, just preoccupied.

She drew a quick nervous breath that she covered by clearing her throat as she glanced past him toward the clock. "Well, I've taken enough of your time...."

"I made a mistake, Cait," he said before he turned toward her. "I slept with her once, just once."

"Why *did* you sleep with her, Tyler?"

He hadn't expected the question, but he should have. Cait wasn't a woman to avoid hard truths. He took his time returning to the spot where she was sitting. It didn't help. There was no easy way to tell her the truth.

"I was dead tired. I hadn't had a woman in more months than I could remember, and she made it very clear she wanted me."

Cait nodded very slowly. "You're saying that she seduced you?"

His hand bunched into a fist that he beat softly against the bar. "No, I'm saying I'd give anything if I could have that choice over again."

"If you did, perhaps there would be no Kelsey."

Uncomfortable with the depth of emotion she invariably seemed to draw from him, he shifted his gaze from her face to the garish beer sign in the window. The soft smile in her eyes stayed in his mind.

"Sometimes I think that's the only thing that kept me sane during these past years."

"Everyone makes mistakes. As you said, I made a whopper four years ago."

His blunt forefinger traced a jagged gouge in the wood separating them. He seemed to be more comfortable if he wasn't looking directly at her.

"If you had that choice again, would you make the same one?"

"I've often wondered that myself," she admitted. Usually in the middle of a sleepless night, when the shadows were darkest. "When it was all...happening, I kept asking myself how I could have been so wrong about you. Why hadn't I seen the warning signs that are always there, even though they may be subtle? Was it because you had once been my best friend that I didn't want to see such an ugly truth in you?"

Something painful ground in Tyler's chest. "Crys didn't help."

Cait sighed. "No. My sister had her own reasons for doing what she did. I'm trying to put them in the best light I can. For Kelsey's sake."

"Sometimes I think she was jealous of you."

Cait's eyebrows shot up. "Of me? Whatever for?"

"Mostly for the gift you have of making friends, I think. She didn't have all that many."

"I know. Crys always looked at every other woman she met as a rival. Except me, of course. She thought of me as the 'smart sister,' just like everyone else did."

Not that that had stopped her from taking every boyfriend Cait ever had, of course. Once she had them, she couldn't wait to drop them. Blind adoration bored Crystal. Perhaps that was why Tyler had been such a challenge.

"Tyler, let's make a pact, okay? No more talking about Crystal. Every time we do, we end up arguing and one of us goes away mad. Mostly it's you."

Something changed in his eyes. Something important.

"Does that bother you?"

She nodded slowly. "I may have a lot of friends, but you were my best friend for a long time. When you married Crys, I missed that."

Because he needed to move, he swung open the hinged bar top and came around to slip onto the stool next to hers.

"Can we work on it again, Cait? Our friendship, I mean."

She glanced down at the tiny fan she'd made. "I'm not sure that's a good idea."

"We made a start on it the other night. Remember?"

She began to unfold the perfect pleats one by one. "When I came here the first time, you looked at me as though you couldn't stand the sight of me."

"You caught me off guard," he hedged.

Her gaze came slowly to his, full of questions and yet strangely soft. He ached to hold her again, but he knew he didn't dare. Instead, he reached for her hand and balanced it in his.

"Sometimes that's when our feelings are strongest," she murmured. "When we're caught off guard."

It both surprised and pleased him that she allowed her hand to rest in his. Tentatively he ran his finger over her skin. Her fingers quivered against his. Still, she refused to retreat.

"You're the expert on feelings, not me. I just know I don't blame you anymore for what happened. Sometimes I think it would be easier if I did."

His thumb made small, caressing movements against her palm. Her skin, already warmed by his touch, now grew intensely sensitive.

"Easier? I doubt it." When he was touching her, it was difficult to concentrate on anything but the sensations running like adrenaline through her blood. "I think it's time I got out of here and let you get back to work." Just as she tried to slip her hand from his, his fingers tightened, trapping her.

"Are you afraid of me, Cait?" he drawled softly.

"No, of course not."

"Ashamed to be seen with an ex-con, perhaps?" The slight tensing of his deep voice brought back the conversation she'd had with Kelsey.

"Actually, there doesn't seem to be anyone here *to* see us."

"That's not an answer."

"I'm not ashamed to be seen with you, Tyler. Kelsey wouldn't be, either, if she were here."

The slight flicker in his gaze told her she'd hit a sore place. "I think that would hurt me the most," he said in a toneless voice.

"Don't borrow pain, Tyler. Trust that it won't happen."

"Trust." His tone was very soft.

"Yes, trust. The way I trust that you'll get a new trial and all this will be behind you someday."

She wouldn't let herself back away from the sudden ice forming in his eyes. She had a feeling too many people he encountered had done that already.

"I'd rather put my faith in Dante," he said after a long moment of tense silence. She counted it a victory that he hadn't completely withdrawn from her.

"That, too," she said with a laugh.

Steam from the sink had coaxed wisps of curl around her face. He saw himself nosing those soft wisps out of the way so that he could kiss the sweet, vulnerable curve just below the shell of her ear. Would her skin feel silky against his mouth?

His fingers were tentative as he traced the line of her cheek. It was the sweetest kind of touching, out of character for such a deeply angry, bitter man.

"You have a way of making a man feel strong and invincible just by smiling at him," he murmured, and then scowled as though the words had slipped unbidden past his guard.

"Perhaps a man is already those things and doesn't know it." Her voice was hushed, but her heart was beating rapidly. So rapidly that she felt each beat pulse through her.

His gaze dropped to the hollow of her throat, as though he, too, sensed the reaction of her body to his closeness. When his gaze came back to hers, she found she couldn't move. Nor could she speak.

"There were times..." His voice trailed off as he leaned forward to cover her mouth with his. The reaction was immediate, a swift flush of heat in her throat. Over the swell of her breasts. Deeper.

Before she knew what she was doing, she found herself leaning toward him, her hands winding around his neck. Instantly, as though he'd been waiting for her silent permission, his big hands molded her waist and pulled her to her feet.

With a sudden, draining weakness, she leaned into him, loving the hard contours of muscle and bone supporting her so securely.

He settled her more firmly against him and took her mouth again. This time his lips were hot with a hunger she had never aroused in any other man.

Desire blossomed inside her until she knew only pleasure. Her own lips grew eager. Her hands sought his shoulders, curved over his hard biceps, moved past his collar to test the warm texture of his neck before pushing into his thick, sun-streaked hair.

Too late Tyler realized that he had relied on her to stop him. His own will was gone, submerged in the wonder of her kiss and her softness.

Because she gave so willingly, he longed to give more. Because she touched so gently, he wanted to touch with reverence. Because she was so utterly feminine, he had never felt more like a man.

The sudden demand of her lips tested the last of his resolve. It had been a long time since a woman had wanted him so openly and sweetly. His hunger edged toward unbearable. His hands roamed, eager to know all of her.

Her sweater was whisper soft. Beneath its wool, her skin was even softer. Beneath his palm, beneath the lace of her bra, her nipples were like pearls warmed by the sun. And her breasts were full and heavy.

His hands shook. His hunger turned vicious, tearing at him. He knew a sudden twisting fear. She was so small, so delicate, so pliant, this woman he knew but didn't know. It would be so easy to hurt her.

When he felt the hot pressure in his groin strain his flesh nearly to bursting, he made himself lift his head and pull back. While he still could. While he still maintained a tenuous control.

"There'll be customers in here soon," he managed to rasp out.

"Customers?" She blinked at him, her cheeks flushed, her hair tousled, her lips moist and rosy from his mouth.

His smile was charmingly lopsided. "Yeah, you know. Guys with dog collars and women with tattoos. You remember, don't you? Big Mike and the gang."

"Big Mike?" Her eyes grew round and dark. "He hasn't come back, has he?"

"No, but some of his buddies have."

Cait shuddered. "When I saw all that blood..."

Tyler stopped her with a soft, moist kiss that left them both trembling. She raised her hand and touched the faint bruise still evident on his face. Very gently she let her fingers caress his hard, lined cheeks.

"Oh Tyler, I wish…I wish…I don't know what I wish."

Something painful ground into Tyler's chest. He ached to kiss her again, but he knew he didn't dare. Not when the need to have all of her was still heavy and hot inside him.

He brushed the back of his hand over her cheek. "Drive carefully," he said gently. "Sunday's a busy day on 49."

He still held her, although he meant to let her go. Now, with her soft mouth trembling and her eyes searching his, he wasn't certain he could.

"I'd better go. Kelsey will be worried."

"Can't have that."

She seemed so fragile, standing there with her hair disheveled by his hands and her mouth red and wet from his kisses. He felt the blood begin to pound in his chest. He knew she expected him to walk her to the door. If he did, he wasn't sure he could let her walk through it. He dropped his arms and took a swift step backward.

"Give Kelsey a kiss for me. She doesn't have to know who it's from."

"I will," Cait promised. She was still shaking inside as she retrieved her purse and slung it over her shoulder.

Was this why she'd come? she wondered as she walked to the door. To find out if the rush of pleasure she'd felt at the first brush of his mouth over hers had been a fluke? A creation of her vivid imagination? Desire still hummed in her veins, leaving no doubt. Whatever Tyler had aroused in her, it wasn't a fluke.

Before she stepped into the fresh air, she turned to wave goodbye. He was standing where she'd left him, watching her.

"One more thing, Tyler," she said softly. "Merry Christmas."

Chapter 8

It wasn't as though she'd never been kissed before, Cait thought as she stretched her legs under the warm covers. She had, and very thoroughly, by each of the two lovers she'd had over the years.

Both were older, and both were thoughtful and tender in bed. She had nearly married the second man. Perhaps she should have, she thought now.

Perhaps then she wouldn't lie awake nights wondering what it would be like if Tyler was there with her, using that lean, powerful body to pleasure her.

In her mind's eye she saw him undressing her, his strong, callused hands stroking reverently over her breasts until the tips were pointed and aching. And she saw his hands move lower, across her belly to her thighs. She saw the desire rising in his eyes.

The image was vivid enough to make her mouth go dry and her palms grow moist with the need to feel the sinewy strength beneath his taut warm skin.

She saw herself tracing the corded veins winding down his arms. Exploring the warm, broad expanse of his chest. She knew that the hair on his chest was a soft golden brown. She had seen it curling damp against his skin when he'd been wearing surgical scrubs. Perhaps there was gray mixed with the gold now.

Would it be soft? she wondered. Would it twine lower, to disappear into the coarser hair around his belly button?

Cait inhaled sharply and closed her eyes. "Remember what happened last time you fantasized about Tyler Mc-Clane," she muttered as she tried to rub the heat from her cheeks with her palms. It didn't help.

Tyler pushed one fist under his pillow and tried to summon the familiar numbness that had sustained him for so long. The illuminated dial of the clock taunted him almost as much as his body did. In another hour it would be dawn.

He closed his eyes and tried to will himself into unconsciousness. But that was worse. He kept seeing the soft glow in Cait's eyes before he'd kissed her.

No other woman had ever looked at him with quite that blend of honest emotion and subtle sensuality. Her mouth had a way of smiling at him, even when she was speaking of the most somber matters. And her chameleon eyes were bold and yet shy at the same time.

He liked the way her breath caught just before she laughed. And he liked the way her eyes took on a special softness when she was speaking of his daughter. A man could withstand a hell of a lot if he had a woman like Cait beside him.

In prison, denying his physical needs had become a habit imposed on him by circumstance. A habit he hadn't been all that inclined to break since he'd been out.

But the need he felt for Cait was more than purely sexual. Somehow it was all mixed up with his emotions. Try as he might, he couldn't separate the longing for her warmth and understanding from the urgent, near-constant craving for her body.

And at the moment it was her body he longed to feel pressing soft and pliant against his. He knew the sweetness of her smile but not the sweetness of her body. He knew the warmth of her laughter but not the hot feel of her passion.

Just the thought of sheathing himself in that living warmth
brought a surge of blood to his loins. A moan escaped his
control. Shuddering, he laid his hand on his body. Instead
of the slick hardness of his own flesh, he felt the warm satin
of hers.

His thoughts splintered.

He groaned. His breath came faster.

She had such a sweet mouth. He longed to feel it warm
and yielding under his. Just as he longed to feel her body
against his again, opening to receive him. Letting him fill her
until they were welded together.

His body engorged, stretching the skin until it burned. He
longed to feel her hand on him. Stroking.

He longed to be touching her in the same sweet way. His
body convulsed, and he cried her name. But there was no
one to hear. He was alone.

The phone by the bed rang, waking him. Tyler had one
arm wound around his pillow. The blanket was twisted
around his naked loins. His face was pressed into the thin
mattress. He decided to ignore the shrill summons. The
phone kept ringing.

"Damn," he muttered as he gradually became aware that
the caller didn't intend to hang up until he answered. Eyes
still closed, he rolled over and fumbled for the phone.

"Yeah?" he muttered into the mouthpiece.

"Lord, Ty, you sound like a hibernating bear. Think I'll
call back when you're in a better mood." It was Dante, and
the bastard was laughing.

"Screw you, Dante." Tyler gave a yawn before opening
his eyes. Sunlight poured through the tears in the window
blind, striping the floor. The air in the apartment was cold,
shivering his bare chest.

"What time is it, anyway?"

"Almost noon. Time for all good boys to be up and at
'em."

"The hell it is. This is my day off."

Dante's laughter rolled down the line. "You have a wild
night or something?"

"Or something."

"Anything you want to talk about?"

"No."

Dante was silent for a moment. When he resumed speaking, Tyler heard a subtle shift in his voice—from teasing to serious.

"I got an answer from Lamont."

Tyler sat up abruptly. The blanket cut into his groin. He flinched and jerked the thick material free. "And?"

"He's amenable to a new trial."

Tyler closed his eyes, giving in to raw emotion. But when he spoke his voice was flat. "When?"

"Couple of months. Depends on his calendar." Dante cleared his throat. "There's a condition, though."

"Name it."

"Kelsey has to testify."

Tyler slumped against the cheap headboard and stared at the ceiling. The crack in the dingy plaster had gotten longer. "Did you hit him with the idea of a sworn deposition?"

"Yeah, as hard as I could. He wants a chance to cross-examine."

"What about O'Connor? Can't she just paraphrase Kelsey's words?"

"She says she can't. Professional ethics again. Even if she could, Lamont wants more. The courts are really sensitive about cases like this right now. He's covering his ass. In a way, I don't blame him."

Tyler glanced at his only photograph of his little girl. If Kelsey testified in open court, the press and TV reporters would have her picture on the front page and the nightly news until her face was as obscenely familiar as a rock star's. A feeding frenzy at its worst, the kind that could destroy a sensitive child like Kelsey.

Tyler ran his hand over his morning beard. News like this he didn't need. "Putting my daughter on the stand again wasn't in the plan, Jess."

There was a pause, then Dante sighed. "You should have let me go after her at the trial."

"She was five years old. You would have destroyed her."

"Now she's nine. You're still protecting her," Dante shot back.

"Isn't that what a father's supposed to do?"

"C'mon, Ty!" Dante's voice took on an impatient edge. "I know she's your daughter and you love her. But she *lied* about you. Because of her and her mother, you now have about as much chance of being a doctor again as I have of growing another arm."

"There's got to be a way to make Lamont accept a deposition. Find it."

"And if I can't? Are you willing to give up your only chance to protect a child you hardly know?"

"That's enough, Dante."

"Think about it, Ty, when you're downstairs pouring drinks and lighting tourists' cigarettes."

He hung up without waiting for an answer.

Nurse Pamela Strickland pulled the syringe from Tyler's arm and removed the tube of dark red blood before tossing the used needle into the special trash receptacle.

The parole board frowned on a convicted felon working in a saloon. Abuse of alcohol and street drugs was one of the prime causes of recidivism. Because tending bar was the only job Tyler could find, however, Shuffler had reluctantly agreed to his taking it—providing Tyler submitted to random tests.

Tyler hated every minute he spent in Dr. Delgado's office. The smells, the sounds, even the row of diplomas and licenses on the wall, aroused painful memories of the things he had lost.

Sometimes just hearing the murmur of voices in the next room, knowing that it was Dr. Delgado and one of his patients, had him drenched in sweat and missing medicine so much it took all his control to keep from bolting.

At first Mrs. Strickland had treated him coolly, the way most folks did when they discovered where he'd been and why. Over the months, however, he and the feisty nurse had become friends of a sort.

"Got all your shopping done?" she asked as she wrote his name on the paper taped around the vial.

"Haven't even started." Tyler rolled down the sleeve of his flannel shirt and buttoned the cuff.

"Me neither. It seems to get harder and harder every year, doesn't it?"

"That's what they tell me."

Mrs. Strickland slipped the vial into a padded envelope and added it to the bin for the lab in Sacramento. From there the results would be sent to Harvey Shuffler.

"Know of any good sales?" she asked as she secured the flap of the envelope with tape.

"Sorry. The guys at the Horseshoe mostly talk about cattle and feed prices."

"And women, too, I suspect," she added with a twinkle in her eyes.

"That, too," he acknowledged as he got to his feet and slipped into his jacket.

"Mrs. Turner over at the drugstore said that Randolph's Mercantile is having a good sale. Fancy toys and expensive books, mostly, but some clothes. Maybe I'll stop on my way home tonight." She wrote out his bill and handed it to him. "Doesn't seem right that you have to come here and let me practice my technique on you, and then have to pay for it, too."

Tyler folded the bill and shoved it into the back pocket of his jeans. "It's better than the alternative."

Sympathy softened the nurse's blunt features. "That's true enough."

They exchanged goodbyes and he left.

The morning was raw. Ice glistened in the puddles along the street. The weatherman was still predicting a white Christmas for the skiers. So far, with one week to go before the Christmas Eve crush, the resorts were anxiously watching the sky and making their own.

Tyler tugged his Stetson low over his forehead before heading south along the main drag. He walked swiftly, with long strides. He was the only one who seemed to be in a hurry. The other pedestrians he encountered seemed con-

tent to saunter along the streets. Some window-shopped.
Others chatted. A few strolled hand in hand, so close their
breath mingled.

"Mommy, Mommy! Look at the dolly. Isn't she wonderful?" The child's happy cry was like a hot lash across Tyler's
back. Someday, perhaps, it wouldn't hurt so much.

He slowed his steps. A dozen yards ahead of him a little
girl dressed in pink from the fluffy topknot of her stocking
cap to the toes of her tiny boots was gesturing excitedly with
a pink mitten toward the window of the Mercantile. Her
parents exchanged indulgent smiles and let her lead them to
the glass.

Inside was a charmingly arranged tea party. Three stuffed
bears were being served tea by a china doll with golden curls
and a perfect porcelain complexion.

"Can I have her, Daddy? Can I, please?"

"You have to ask Santa about that," her father said as he
glanced at his wife with eyebrows raised.

The mother gave a quick shake of her head before she
smiled down at the child between them. "Santa already has
your list, remember?"

The little girl's expression drooped, then brightened. "I
know! I'll send him a fax."

The young couple laughed and shared a loving look. The
father hoisted the excited little girl onto his shoulders before linking hands with his wife. Still laughing and talking,
the three of them moved on.

Tyler watched for a moment, then averted his gaze. When
he reached the window, however, he stopped and studied the
old-fashioned scene. He didn't need a collector's eye to
know that everything was old and extremely valuable. The
toys were antique, and so were the furniture and china.

A quick glance at the price tags told him that the dolly so
admired by the little girl in pink cost more than he made in
a week.

He started to walk away but found himself held by the
small pine tree behind the table. Hanging by golden rib-
bons from the thick branches were a dozen or so ornaments
of blown glass. They were simple in design and winked in

the light like fragile ice crystals. Easily destroyed, like trust.
He turned away and headed for his truck.

In less than an hour it would be Christmas Day.

The house was quiet. Kelsey was asleep. Cait was in the
den, curled up in front of a dying fire.

The logs in the grate had burned to embers. Her wine-
glass was nearly empty. She had just finished playing Santa.
Mounds of gaily wrapped presents were piled under the tree,
waiting for Kelsey to tear into them in about seven hours or
so.

Cait drew her knees to her chest and circled them with her
arms. It had taken patience, but Kelsey was finally excited
about Christmas. Tyler's letter had helped tremendously.
Kelsey kept it under her pillow.

The week before Christmas had gone quickly. They'd
hung pine-bough bunting on every available surface and
placed dozens of bayberry candles around the house. This
afternoon they had baked dozens of sugar cookies. Everything was perfect.

Wasn't it?

Not daring to answer that question, Cait roused herself
and slowly got to her feet. She stood for a moment, stretching out the kinks. Then, after checking that the fire screen
was in place, she moved toward the tree. The dozens of tiny
white bulbs on the tree cast a lovely glow throughout the
room, and she hated to turn them off. To be safe, however...

The doorbell startled her into a sharp gasp. Her hand
went to her throat as she spun around. It was far too late for
a casual caller.

The bell rang again, a shrill summons in the silent house.
Heart pounding, she hurried to answer it.

"*Tyler.*"

She had to angle her gaze a few inches higher to find his
eyes. They seemed very dark in the glow from the porch
light.

"Merry Christmas."

He was bareheaded, and his hair was tousled, as though combed frequently by his fingers. The collar of his jacket was pulled up. His cheeks were ruddy from the cold.

She glanced toward the street. His truck was parked a half block away, on the other side of Citrus Avenue. She cleared her throat.

"Merry Christmas. You're out late."

She saw the present in his hand then. It was wrapped in plain green paper and red ribbon. The bow was huge but slightly askew.

Tyler saw the direction of her gaze and held the box forward. "From Santa for Kelsey," he explained with a brief smile.

Murmuring her thanks, she took it from him and discovered that it was lighter than it looked.

"I love the bow," she murmured, flashing him a grin. "Did you tie it yourself?"

He nodded. "Took me a couple of tries, though. It's not exactly the same as a surgical knot." She heard no self-pity in his tone, only dry humor.

"I doubt that Kelsey will notice."

"If she does, blame it on Santa."

"Good idea."

Silence fell. Tyler noticed that she was wearing her hair down again. In the glow of the light, the soft dark strands had a subtle shimmer, as though the summer sun had been captured there. He shoved his hands into his pockets and glanced toward his truck.

"Well, I'd better go. Like you said, it's late."

The lonely look around his eyes told her that he wasn't quite as nonchalant about this as he wanted her to believe. His wounds went deep, and he had borne them alone for a long time.

She glanced down at the package in her arms. "Santa usually puts the presents under the tree himself, you know."

Wariness, especially of unexpected kindness, ran deep in him. Harsh experience had taught him to distrust the motives of those offering it.

"Does he?"

"Of course, silly. Everyone over the age of six months knows that."

Something flashed in his eyes like a sliver of light in the darkest dark. Before she could change her mind, she stepped back. At the same time, she pushed the door wider.

"Come in and have a cup of coffee to warm you before you make that long drive home." His hesitation was slight, but she noticed.

"Please," she said with her most coaxing smile. "I'd enjoy the company. It can get awfully lonesome talking to kids day after day."

His eyes lost some of their guarded strain. That he could understand. It was the same with talking to cowboys and bikers night after night.

"Thanks," he said as he stepped over the threshold and walked past her.

His first impression was serenity, the kind that settles in a house where people love each other. He'd never felt it in any of the places where he'd lived. He'd given up expecting it.

Cait juggled the present in one hand as she turned to close the door. He reached out to take it from her. As he did, he smelled the warm, feminine fragrance that seemed to cling to her skin.

His reaction was immediate and insistent: an urgent resurgence of the need he'd worked day and night to banish. He made himself ignore it, just as he had to ignore the rest of the frustrations in his life.

"Nice," he said, glancing at the ivory walls and burnished wood of the massive staircase and hand-carved doors. None of the furnishings he could see in the living room and dining room looked coordinated or even planned. Somehow the eclectic mixture of valuable antiques, vibrant colors and whimsical memorabilia seemed to work.

"It is now," Cait said with a pleased glance around. "When I moved in, it was a wreck. Hazel helped me with the hard stuff, like paint and wallpapering and stripping that darn staircase. I can't tell you how many times I wanted to chuck it all and just paint the darn thing over and forget it."

He frowned. "Why didn't you?"

"Because something told me that I would find a real
treasure under all those protective layers. And I did." She
grinned. "Solid oak. The kind you can't find anymore. I
knew it was there all along."

Her eyes smiled into his, pleased as a kid with her first A-
plus. She was either a naive fool or a hopeless romantic. Not
that it mattered which. The world was a dangerous, cruel
place for either. Sooner or later, even the strongest broke.
Someday Cait was going to find that out. He hoped she
would survive the knowing. Irritation moved through him,
coupled with another emotion he didn't understand.

"What if you were wrong? What if you'd done all that
hard work and found nothing salvageable under all those
layers? Then what?"

Cait knew exactly what he was saying and why. "Ah, but
I didn't, did I?" she said with a swift, telling glance toward
the rich, gleaming hardwood. "Besides, a shrink comes to
hate words like *what if* and *should have* and *but*. I prefer
absolutely, positively and *anything's possible*."

His eyes narrowed. "Anything's possible? As in miracles?"

"Absolutely!" Her laughter was soft and full of fun.
"Know something else, Dr. McClane? Under all that cyni-
cism you cultivate so carefully, you believe in miracles, too.
Otherwise you never would have become a healer."

She touched his cheek lightly. "Mmm, you feel cold.
Come on into the den. The tree's there, and there might be
a few coals left of the terrific fire Kelsey and I made while
we had eggnog and cookies."

She swept past him and headed down the wide hallway to
the last room on the right. He glanced at the door she'd just
closed and knew that was the direction he should take. Little by little she was drawing him into a way of life he had
longed for for so long. Deliberately or not, it was working.

"Yo, Santa?" she whispered from the end of the hall. "In
here."

Tyler glanced at the package he'd tucked under one arm. Hell, he couldn't very well stand there with the damn thing all night.

Cait waited until she was certain he was on his way to the den, then ducked into the room to wait. She thought she looked too much like a guard standing in the doorway, watching him. He'd had enough of that, she knew.

She expected them now—the swift assessing glance, the rapid attention to potential danger, the deeply ingrained caution in every new situation. She waited patiently until his gaze found hers, and then she waved a casual hand toward the tree.

"I was just about to turn off the lights, even though I really didn't want to. I'm glad you rang when you did, so I can enjoy them a bit longer."

It was huge, her tree. Big enough to fill one corner of the room. The branches sagged under ornaments of all sizes and shapes. Some were definitely handmade. Others looked as though they belonged in earlier times. Everywhere he looked he saw something that roused his curiosity or made him want to laugh.

Studying the huge tree and the room that held it, Tyler realized that the tug of some deeply buried longing was strongest in him here. Perhaps because the room was so like her—cozy, welcoming, with just a few startling touches of eccentricity to keep him intrigued.

The smell of some spice lingering like a warm mist was like her as well, filling his senses with a seductive feeling of well-being.

"Very nice."

Cait heard the clipped tone he used when he was keeping his emotions under tight rein, and smiled. "Did you ever get a tree for the Horseshoe?"

"A small one." He shifted the present from one arm to the other. "We decorated it with beer cans and bottle caps."

"I love it," she murmured. "It sounds perfect." She gestured toward the pile of presents under the lowest branches. "Just put Santa's present anywhere."

His eyebrows lifted, and he whistled softly. "Looks like Aunt Cait bought out at least one toy store."

"At least."

They shared a smile. Cait felt herself drawn to the slow warmth that seemed to kindle in his eyes whenever his control relaxed even slightly.

"Make yourself at home. I'll make some coffee."

"Need any help?"

"No thanks." Her throat took on a sudden tension that was reflected in her voice.

Tyler watched her leave before he put the package in an unobtrusive spot toward the rear. He was coming close to feeling like a fool. What difference could one present possibly make to a little girl with such a haul?

None, that was what.

After shucking his jacket, he threw it onto the nearest chair and walked to the fireplace. Resting one forearm on the mantel, he stood looking into the nearly dead embers. No warmth came from the grate. No cheery light.

Loneliness settled hard and sharp inside him. He was an intruder here. A man with sense would have sent the damn present instead of bringing it. Hell, maybe he shouldn't even have bought the damn thing. Crystal had always accused him of being too sentimental.

"Build it up again if you'd like," Cait said from the doorway. She walked toward him, two steaming mugs in her hands.

"It's fine. I won't be staying long."

She set both mugs on the coffee table and settled into one corner of the sofa with her shoes off and her stockinged feet curled under her. He took the chair opposite and reached for his mug.

"Are you working tomorrow?" she asked as she sipped slowly.

"No, although I have a feeling there'll be some grumbling 'long about noon from some of the regulars."

She smiled at that. Watching, he noticed that the coffee had left a sheen of moisture on the soft curve of her lower ip. The thought of transferring that moisture from her mouth to his had his senses screaming.

He swigged down half his coffee in one swallow. The brew was exotic and steaming. It warmed him all the way down.

"So, is Kelsey excited about tomorrow morning?" he asked, glancing at the tree again. Here he was, damn near middle-aged, and yet just sitting across from her had him feeling as awkward and shy as a kid on his first date.

"Lord, is she ever! She kept asking me all sorts of questions about Santa. Like what had I heard on the TV about the weather conditions over the North Pole and what kind of a snack the reindeer like best. Which happens to be carrots, by the way. That sort of thing. But then, I imagine that's old stuff to you."

He glanced toward the mantel, where a glass of milk sat next to a plate containing cookies and carrots. Before he could stop it, a look of pain crossed his face.

"I left that to Crys. The tree, the shopping, wrapping the presents. I was too busy." He watched the smile leave her eyes and felt sick inside.

"I'm sorry, Tyler. You missed so much."

He leaned forward to set his cup on the low table. "More than I know, I think," he said as he rose and grabbed his jacket. Cait rose, too.

"Thanks for the coffee." He didn't dare touch her. If he did, all his hard-won control would shatter like an icicle slammed against cement.

"Anytime. And thanks for delivering Santa's special present."

She glanced over her shoulder at the tree, and her hair shimmered into graceful movement, like a dark rich waterfall. He wondered what it would feel like brushing over his bare chest.

"No problem. Tell Kels Merry Christmas." He halted as a look of chagrin crossed his face. "I guess you can't do that."

"No, because she might wonder why you can't come to see her. I wouldn't want to lie, but—"

"But you don't want to remind her of the trial and sentence and possibly add to her guilt."

"Exactly. You should have been a shrink."

"Words are your thing, not mine."

"Besides, dealing with emotion scares the dickens out of you." Cait's smile was gently chiding.

Tyler tugged on the flyaway end of one of her curls and grinned. "Back off, Doc. I'm not one of your patients."

Her smile turned warm, as warm as the rush of tenderness he couldn't seem to control.

"Don't worry. I wouldn't take you on even if you asked, which you won't, of course."

He heard the slight catch in her voice as her words came tripping too fast. He might not be a shrink, but he knew Cait better than she thought.

With a stranger, her words were precise and carefully modulated. With him, too, when they'd first met. It had taken him a long time to win her trust, but when he had, she'd held nothing back. It was then that the words had come pouring out, along with the emotions that damn near smothered him sometimes. It was still there. The joy for life that was such a part of her.

The tug came more strongly. Knowing he had to resist, he stepped back and allowed her to precede him.

Cait hummed "Jingle Bells" to a western beat as she led him to the door of the den. She didn't want to think about him driving all those long cold miles alone while she was tucked safely into a warm bed.

He stayed one step behind her as she led the way to the foyer. Or so she thought until she had her hand on the doorknob. It was then that she realized he had stopped, apparently caught by the sight of Kelsey's pink-and-white parka hanging by its hood from the newel post.

As she watched, he reached out a big hand to free the sleeve that was trapped in the armhole.

"My little girl is growing up," he murmured.

Cait moved silently to his side. "She's almost as tall as I am. In a few years, maybe less, I'll be the shrimp around here." A frown bunched above her nose. "Now that's a ghastly thought, isn't it?"

"My mother was tall." His voice was carefully controlled again.

"Any sisters? For comparison, I mean?"

"No, just me. Way I heard it all my life, one McClane kid was enough."

Cait imagined him as a little boy. The dark gray eyes would have been as full of mischief as they were now of intelligence. And his body would have been in constant motion, fueled by a seemingly inexhaustible abundance of energy. As for his temper...

She shook her head mentally. No doubt he'd flown off the handle as quickly and easily as his daughter did when she was overly tired. As for that streak of bullheaded stubbornness, that must have come in the genes along with the unusual gray eyes and thick golden hair. Those two were more alike than either knew.

Her gaze moved past his hard profile to the dimly lit landing at the top of the stairs. "I usually check on her before I go to bed." The words were out of her mouth before she had time to carefully consider the consequences. "In fact, I was just going to check on her when you arrived. Perhaps you'd like to tag along." She climbed the stairs at a measured pace. The decision had to be his. All she'd done was open the door a tiny crack.

His heart slammed like a fist into his rib cage as he stood for a moment, watching her, hearing Dante's repeated warnings echo in his head. If he got caught...

Seconds later, he fell into step beside her near the landing.

"This is her room," Cait whispered as they paused in front of the door. "She helped me decorate."

Cait pushed the door wider, allowing the light from the landing to spill into the bedroom. As always when she looked into the innocent face of her adopted daughter, she wondered what she had ever done to deserve such a blessing.

"She's asleep," she mouthed to Tyler, who suddenly seemed to need a deep breath. She could only guess at the emotions he must be feeling. The thoughts that had taken the color from his face and shadowed his eyes.

"I'll wait here," she whispered as she stepped back.

Tyler entered alone and walked slowly toward the bed. Kelsey was curled on her side, with her face half-buried in the pillow. One small hand hung over the edge of the bed. Her cheeks were flushed. Her expression was serene.

The steady cadence of her breathing told him that she was deeply asleep. *Baby*, he thought. *Kelsey*.

Slowly he moved closer, afraid to breathe. As though sensing his presence, Kelsey sighed deeply and burrowed her cheek deeper into the pillow. Tears threatened to choke him, but he swallowed them away. A man his age didn't cry. But, dear God, he hurt.

Knowing that he shouldn't, he laid his fingers lightly against her cheek. He felt life in the warmth of her skin.

Almost half his life had been spent trying to preserve or prolong the tenuous thread of that precious warm life. Sometimes he'd won; sometimes he hadn't.

But, God help him, he'd tried. Just as he'd tried to take care of his little girl the best way he knew how. Then.

In that he'd failed. It would always be an ache in his gut. *Forgive me, baby*, he told her silently before he turned to leave.

Cait was waiting for him at the bottom of the stairs. She had Kelsey's parka draped over her arm and a soft look of understanding in her eyes.

"Still sleeping?" she whispered when he reached the bottom step.

"Didn't stir once."

"I didn't think she would."

He cleared his throat. "You were right. She's going to be tall."

"I usually am. Right, I mean."

She curved her lips into a sassy smile, but inside she was quaking. Pain, rigidly denied but far too real, shimmered like dark, opaque flecks in his eyes. His shoulders, usually so stiff and straight, seemed bowed by a great weight.

"I never knew I could miss her so much," he said with one last glance over his shoulder.

"It's that way with a lot of things in life, I've found."

"Yeah." His shoulders slid backward, and he straightened. Without speaking, he moved to the door. She moved with him. This time it was he who opened the door.

The air rushing in was cool and smelled of smoke.

The house across the street blazed with light, spilling an almost surreal glow into the street. Tyler didn't seem to notice. Instead his gaze, narrowed now and troubled, was focused on her.

"You know you could be in big trouble if it ever got out that you let me see her," he said with a burr of warning.

"Some things are worth the risk."

A flicker of emotion crossed his face. "I'm not sure I agree with that."

"But that's because the scars you carry are still too fresh. They'll fade in time—if you have faith."

He shifted until his back was against the door. Light from the overhead fixture deepened the lines gouged so starkly around his eyes.

"Faith." His inflection gave the single word an obscene twist. "Now there's a catch-all concept. Guy finds himself in a cage with no way out. Hell, don't worry about it. Just have faith. Doctor's got a kid who's terminally ill and he's fresh out of things to try. No big deal. Just have faith."

Cait felt his frustration. She let Kelsey's jacket fall to the floor so that she was free to rest her palms on his shoulders. He stiffened as though in pain, but he didn't pull away.

"I hate to tell you this, Tyler McClane," she murmured with a rueful smile. "But only a man whose faith was once terribly strong could be so bitter when he loses it."

His smile was crooked. "Do you have an answer for everything?" he asked with a strange, almost wistful note in his deep voice.

"Not everything. If I did, I would know what to say to you when you get that haunted look in your eyes. Like now."

As though it were an omen, the bells of Saint Stephen's began tolling in the distance. "It's Christmas," Cait whispered.

Using his shoulder for support, she went onto her tiptoes and brushed a kiss across his cheek. His jaw was slightly raspy where his beard grew thickest. As she suspected, his skin smelled like the wind.

His hands came up to frame her face. Perhaps they even shook. "Merry Christmas, Cait," he said in that deep rumbling voice that invariably excited an answering rumble inside her.

"Merry Christmas, Tyler," she murmured on a thick breath. "I wish you could be here to see your little girl open her present."

"God, so do I." His face twisted. Somehow Cait was in his arms and his face was buried in the curve of her neck. Nestled tightly against him, Cait felt the tremors take him as he fought to contain his anguish. She buried her face against his shoulder and wrapped her arms around his lean hard torso.

He cried brokenly, as only a strong man can cry. Tears wet her neck and pooled in the hollow of her throat, but still she held him, her own tears running unheeded down her cheeks.

Gradually he regained control. The shudders lessened. His back stiffened. Cait felt his strength returning, along with, she suspected, a large measure of rough masculine embarrassment.

"Sorry," he said as he lifted his head. "I didn't mean to lay all that on you."

His hands curled gently around her upper arms, as though he couldn't make up his mind if he wanted to draw her close again or push her away.

"I think you've needed to do that for a long time."

His mouth softened. "Maybe, but it wasn't a great idea in the cell block where I lived."

She laughed softly. "I think you're probably right."

He started to back away, but she stopped him with a hand on his shoulder. "Hold still a minute."

Smiling, she wiped away his tears with her fingertips. "There. Now you won't get frostbite."

His hand caught hers before she could withdraw it. Turning his head, he kissed her wrist where the skin was thinnest and the nerves most sensitive. Her pulse shot into the danger zone.

"Are you nervous because I kissed your wrist or because you want me to kiss you again?" he asked softly.

"Both, I think," she admitted.

"I promised myself I wouldn't. For both our sakes."

"I promised myself I wouldn't let you," she murmured, but his mouth was already seeking hers.

This time his mouth wasn't patient. His lips were hard and demanding, urging a response from hers. One hand circled her shoulders, holding her close.

The other caressed her face with the absorbed slowness of a man long blind. His callused fingertips sent small pulses of pleasure singing through her.

Her lips softened, eager for his. His mouth gentled but remained wedded to hers. His hands slid to her shoulders, and he pulled her closer. As he did, a tremor ran down the hard length of his body.

He drew back, looked at her through narrowed lashes still spiky from his tears. There was hunger in his eyes now instead of a bottomless pain. The same hunger that thrummed in her veins like a wild fever.

"You know that I want you." His voice was made husky by the need to speak of his feelings. "That I've always wanted you."

"Yes, I know."

She reached up to caress his face. His skin had a different texture from hers. More resilient, more masculine.

She knew him now. His loneliness and his despair. His silent courage and his carefully hidden sensitivity. It wouldn't take much more for her to fall in love with him again. Perhaps she already had. At the moment, she didn't care. Tyler needed her tonight as no man had ever needed her. And she needed him.

"Let's go back to the den," she whispered through lips that were still moist and full from the pressure of his. "The door locks."

Chapter 9

She was standing with her back to the fire he'd just finished rekindling. She watched without speaking, as though fearful of breaking the spell. Her look was expectant, without hesitation. Every time she blinked, her lashes cast spiky shadows onto her cheeks.

Her skin seemed like the finest satin, and her hair had the luminous quality of fine sherry. He lifted a strand and rubbed it slowly between his first finger and thumb.

"In prison I used to wear myself out so I would be too tired to dream. Sometimes it didn't work. I would dream then. It was always the same dream. About making love. To you."

He brushed the back of his hand over her cheek. "When I woke up, I still wanted you so much I thought I would go crazy." His fingers clenched around a handful of thick, soft hair, and his chest heaved.

"God help me if this is just another dream," he whispered in a tortured voice.

Cait laughed softly and ran her finger over his mouth. "It's no dream."

His hand shook as he touched her face again. It didn't seem possible that this was real. Too many times she had come to him in his dreams with this soft glow in her eyes.

"I didn't plan this," he murmured as he leaned down to brush a kiss across her parted lips. "I...don't want to make you pregnant."

Lashes lifting, she drew back. Of course he would worry about that, she realized with a rush of compassion. He'd been trapped once. He didn't intend to be trapped again.

"It's not a problem, I promise."

He pulled her close again and pressed his mouth to her throat. "God, I need you," he whispered against her skin.

Her pulse hammered at the low throb of raw hunger in his voice. "And I need you," she echoed as she closed her eyes and threaded her fingers through his shaggy hair.

His kisses were leisurely, tasting as well as wooing. His mouth was hot, but his lips were soft and seeking. Hers were eager under his and deliciously moist after his tongue had slid languidly over her lower lip in a long, erotic tasting.

His hands roamed with equal absorption. His lazily stroking fingertips were sensitive to the slight change in texture in the silk of her skin. They tested the fragile line of her jaw. Traced the sleek elegance of her neck. Lingered with maddening slowness over the tender triangle at the base of her throat.

Her breathing accelerated. Her mouth felt hot and full. Her skin was so sensitive that the whisper of the fire's heat was erotically painful. She pressed closer, desperate to be touched even more intimately.

His hands skimmed over her waist to cup her buttocks. His tongue seduced her lips until they parted eagerly to let him plunge deeply. He kissed her thoroughly, masterfully, until both were breathing hard.

Even as he dragged his mouth from hers, his hands were already working the buttons of her blouse. As he slipped it from her, his face was taut with a longing he was powerless to mask.

Her breath caught as he stripped off her bra, revealing the paler skin of her breasts. The nipples were already taut, pulling tiny puckers in the dark circles surrounding them.

"Your breasts are like warm marble in the firelight," he murmured as he treated himself to a long, searching exploration of each with his mouth and tongue.

By the time he lifted his head, her skin was moist and hot where he had kissed her. Her nipples ached from a shivering need to be touched again.

Her own hands were impatient as she pulled his shirttails free of the low-riding jeans. Even as his fingers were dipping beneath the soft elastic of her slacks, hers were ridding him of his shirt and reaching for the heavy buckle of his belt.

Tyler felt himself losing control. Just the feel of her knuckles against him as she worked the buttons of his jeans was driving him to a throbbing, insistent madness.

He covered her hand with his and eased it away from his fly. "Better let me do that," he said in a heartfelt growl. "Or I'm liable to embarrass both of us."

The whisper of her laughter was as soft as a moan as she slipped her hand from under his. "Hurry," she murmured. His deep chuckle warmed her as sweetly as the fire, and she found that she was the one who was hurrying.

It was no more than seconds before they were both naked. His skin was very dark, except for the familiar pattern over his groin where his swimming trunks had ridden. Her skin was uniformly lighter than his, her tan a pale version of his deep bronze.

His gaze roamed hungrily. His face was set, but his eyes were alive, yearning.

"I swear, no dream was ever like this." She heard reverence in his voice, and a tightly controlled yearning.

Her own voice was thick as she whispered his name. Without clothes, his body had the sculpted symmetry of classical male beauty.

Bone and muscle and sinew combined perfectly to fashion a man whose might was obvious. A man of long, sinewy thighs and powerful calves. Of spreading, hard-packed shoulders and a lean tapering torso.

Even the thin lines of healing flesh slanting over his right shoulder and curving low on his hip added to the image of indomitable strength.

But it was the potent shaft of his virility that drew her gaze. It rose hot and heavy and ready from a nest of tightly curled hair of pure gold.

"Oh, Tyler," she whispered.

Her gaze came up to find his. Wry amusement softened his hard mouth, but the fire in his eyes smoldered even more hotly. "It's been a long time for me," he said with a rough-hewn shyness she would scarcely have expected from a man of his virility. "Don't expect too much."

The firelight played over her slumberous eyes and soft smile.

"If you're worrying about me, don't."

Her voice was warm and soothing, like balm on an un-healed wound. Still, he found himself as nervous as a bridegroom. She was so small, so very feminine. What if he hurt her? What if he couldn't make himself wait long enough to satisfy her? In his dreams, every man is a perfect lover. It was a different story when a man hadn't held a woman in his arms like this for more than five years.

Still, because he would surely go mad if he didn't, he ran his hand down the smooth, sleek length of her. Over the waist that seemed impossibly small to the enticing curve of her belly. His fingers lingered, testing the satiny warmth.

Cait's fingers dug into his shoulders. Her husky, almost breathless moans were driving him beyond what little con-trol he had left.

Conscious of the blood hammering in his throat and pooling like liquid fire in his groin, he slipped two fingers inside her, between the soft folds covered by whorls of silky hair. She was wet and ready and so very soft.

With a cry she began moving against his fingers. His control shattered, and he withdrew his hand. Before she could protest the loss, he thrust into her until she had all there was of him. He caught her moan of pleasure with his mouth, determined to satisfy her first.

He strained to move slowly. To savor the hot slickness of her against his throbbing flesh. His breath shuddered in and out, drawing her delicate scent into lungs tortured to near bursting.

She kissed his neck, his shoulder, his jaw. He kissed her lips, her throat, her breasts.

Suddenly she was the impatient one, matching each of his thrusts with a wild arching of her pelvis. Answering her, his movements became frantic. Out of control. He fought to stave off the explosion until he knew she had climaxed, but it had been too long for him.

Something broke free inside him, like the last opening of his cell door. His body convulsed into hers. Pleasure mingled with a pain so intense he was unable to bite back the shuddering groan that came from deep inside.

At almost that same moment she cried out, a low keening sound of release. Spent, he buried his face in the curve of her shoulder and held her tight. The tiny shuddering aftershocks of her body felt so good. Knowing that he had pleasured her gave him a measure of peace that had eluded him for far too long.

Still drifting, Cait closed her eyes and gently stroked the bristly hair at the nape of his neck. His skin was wet with sweat and hot to the touch. But the tension that had been such a part of him was gone.

"I'm too heavy," he muttered, stirring.

"Not for me." She kissed his shoulder. "You're the best blanket I've ever had."

She heard him chuckle and smiled. "I like that," she murmured against his hot skin.

"Like what?" He sounded drowsy and yet aroused at the same time.

"Your laugh. I missed that."

He raised his head and kissed her soundly before rolling away. Before Cait could begin to feel abandoned, however, he slipped an arm around her shoulders and settled her against him.

"Sure you're not cold?"

"Positive. The fire is lovely." Lying close to him, having him under her power for even this short time, was the closest she had come to bliss in all her thirty-six years.

Totally content, she nestled close and let her eyes drift shut. His hand stroked her arm, and his chest rose and fell evenly beneath her.

"Is the floor too hard?"

"Not to me, although I admit making love on my grandmother's favorite rug is a new experience for me."

"For me, too." His hand came up to smooth the wispy hair away from her cheek.

She opened her eyes and looked into his face. His hair was tousled from the play of her fingers. His expression was indulgent. He looked like a man who was extremely pleased with himself and the woman in his arms.

"Was it worth the wait?"

His laugh rumbled. "You know it was."

"I knew it would be like this," she murmured.

He raised his eyebrows. "You did, did you?"

"Mmm. You're not the only one who had dreams."

"Tell me," he ordered in a husky voice.

"Only if you tell me yours first."

"No way." His chuckle, more unrestrained this time, rumbled in her ear. "I know how you shrinks operate. You'll find all kinds of hidden meanings in every little detail."

"What little details?" Her fingers played with the damp hair on his broad chest, and his muscles rippled in a reaction he couldn't control. Sinuously, like a cat stretching after a nap, she rubbed her leg against his.

"Stop," he growled.

Cait glanced up in time to catch an expression of desperate vulnerability.

"Not until you talk, buster." She blew a kiss against his shoulder.

"There was more than one dream," he hedged.

"How many?" She bent her knee and began rubbing it over his thigh. His heart beat faster, and he shuddered.

"Too many to talk about." His voice was raspy, and his expression turned intense.

"Were you always making love to me?"

"I told you I was."

Her fingers meandered caressingly along the line of silky blond hair bisecting his chest. The hard flat muscles of his belly rippled, then grew rigid when her fingertips burrowed into the coarser, thicker thatch of hair below his navel.

She had never been so bold, so exultantly confident in her own femininity. Her hand searched lower until she found the warm male flesh nestled in the hair. His skin was hot and smooth.

"Were we naked?" she asked as her fingers encircled him. His body surged against her hand, growing hotter and harder until he more than filled her palm.

"Cait—" The word ended on a groan, and he closed his eyes. "God, I can't take much more...."

Cait raised herself on one elbow so she could watch his face. She'd never seen him so emotionally exposed. Knowing that she was the one who had brought him to this point was a more powerful stimulant than any drug.

"Shall I tell you about my dream?" she asked, continuing her caresses.

"No more," he managed to get out. He was helpless, and they both knew it.

A heady excitement ran through her, bringing a flush to her face and a pounding in her veins. She loved the feel of his hardening flesh against her hand. She loved the rasp of his breathing and the musky heat of his body.

"It's always by the ocean. On a very secluded, very private beach I've found."

Her suddenly rapid breathing made it difficult to speak. She paused to slide her tongue along her lower lip. When Tyler groaned, she saw that he had been watching her. The hot hunger in his eyes momentarily took her breath away.

"We've been sunbathing, so our skin is very warm," she continued in a voice that was suddenly husky. "There's a breeze. It smells of the sea."

His hands clutched at the short nap of the rug. His head arched back. Teeth bared in pain and ecstasy, he began moving against her caressing hand.

"I'm sleeping and so relaxed," she whispered, her breath catching. "And then you lean over to kiss me awake. Like this."

As soon as her lips touched his, Tyler lost the last semblance of control. He pulled her on top of him, and his arms locked around her. His mouth, hot and hungry now, wouldn't be denied. He took all that she offered. Demanded more.

She answered willingly. Now the fury was in her. Desperate, moaning pleas came from her throat. By the time he raised her hips and settled her over him, she was nearly insensate.

Bracing her hands on the rug by his shoulders, she arched her back and began moving, quickly finding her own rhythm. As he began to move with her, accommodating her pace instead of his own, she knew finally, unequivocally, desperately, that she never wanted to let him go.

Kelsey and Cait, both in robes and slippers, were sitting in the midst of a mound of wrapping paper and bits of ribbon so vast it all but obliterated the pattern of the rug.

The tree lights winked like gay stars. In the grate, a cheery fire burned. Outside, the sun was valiantly struggling to emerge from the low-lying clouds.

"One more for Kelsey from Santa," Cait murmured as she leaned forward to hand the child the last present.

Tyler's.

Kelsey took it eagerly and without even noticing the lopsided bow, ripped off the ribbon and tore into the paper.

Even as Cait smiled to herself, she felt a pang of sadness. Tyler should be here to see the glow of the tree lights reflected in Kelsey's eyes.

"Look, Mama Cait! Santa brought me a doll."

Eyes shining, Kelsey lifted the fragile Victorian doll from the nest of tissue and ran her finger over the smooth porcelain face. The long silky hair caught back in a tiny velvet bow was almost exactly the same rich golden color as Kelsey's. The doll's gown was a froth of lilac satin and lace. The tiny high-button shoes were made of soft white kidskin.

"Do you like her?" Cait asked with an anxious smile.

Kelsey beamed. "I *love* her! She's just like the ladies in the old pictures at the museum."

"That's because she was made over a hundred years ago for a little girl just like you."

"Like me?" Kelsey looked pleased. "Really?"

"Really."

Cait got to her feet and stretched her arms high over her head. Her spine was tight. Her muscles still burned with a strange deep ache. Her skin, too, was unusually tender.

Lack of sleep, she tried to tell herself. Deep down, however, she knew the true cause. Tyler's kisses had swollen her lips. His whiskers had sensitized her skin.

"I don't know about you, kiddo, but Mama Cait is hungry. How about I toast us a couple of bagels?"

Kelsey looked up from a careful examination of the doll's ethereal face. "With cream cheese?" she asked with a hopeful grin.

Cait smoothed a hand over her hips. "I really shouldn't," she muttered. "But what the heck, it's Christmas. Calories never count on holidays. It's a national law or something."

Kelsey looked intrigued. "How come you know a law for everything?"

"Simple. I'm a smart cookie."

Kelsey giggled. Outside, the church bells began pealing. The sound triggered a rush of sadness. Merry Christmas, Tyler, Cait thought silently.

"So, how about that breakfast?" she murmured as she smoothed Kelsey's thick bangs.

"Okay."

Cait glanced toward the mess scattered across the floor. "Tell you what. While I do the bagels, you get busy and pick up this room. Auntie Hazel is dropping by this afternoon, and we don't want her getting lost in here."

Kelsey grinned. "It's not that bad."

"Oh, no? You can't even see the rug. There could be a treasure chest full of diamonds under there and no one could find it."

Kelsey threw her a long-suffering look, but Cait saw the reluctant acquiescence in her eyes.

"Sit here, Prudence," she said sternly to the doll. "And don't fidget," she added as she busily stuffed wads of discarded paper into one of the now-empty boxes.

"Prudence?" Cait quirked an eyebrow.

Kelsey's chin took the same obstinate tilt as Tyler's. "Don't you like it?"

Cait cleared her throat. "Well, it *is* a bit unusual."

"I *told* you. She looks like these little girls in the museum whose daddy found gold or something. Mrs. Eddington said they were triplets." Kelsey gathered up the doll's box and started to stuff it, too, with the paper.

"Oh, look! There's another present in here."

It was small, about four inches square, and wrapped in silver paper and red ribbon. There was a tiny card attached.

"To Cait from Santa," Kelsey read. Disappointment tightened one corner of her mouth before a grin chased it away. "Here, Mama Cait. Hurry up and open it."

She dropped the present in Cait's lap, then hovered nearby with an expectant look on her face. Cait drew a shaky breath. The spiky letters on the card had been printed by Tyler. The package had been wrapped by him, as well. The bow was as lopsided as the one she had admired.

"Mama Cait!" Kelsey wailed plaintively. "Don't be so poky."

Cait smiled, but her fingers were impossibly clumsy. No doubt because they were shaking, she realized as she stripped off the ribbon and ran a nail under the tape securing the paper. The box was plain. Inside, something was wrapped in tissue paper.

"Phooey. It's just another ornament," Kelsey said with a grimace of childish disappointment.

Trying to ignore the flutter of nerves in her stomach, Cait unwrapped it slowly and held it up to the light. It was a perfect globe of the thinnest glass, hand-blown by an expert. Inside was a candle with a flickering flame. It was exquisite.

"Here's another card." Kelsey dug it from the box, held it up and read loudly, "Santa grants every good boy and girl one special wish." She frowned. "What's that mean, Mama Cait?"

For a moment the lump lodged in Cait's throat prevented speech. "It means that this is a wishing candle," she murmured past the thickness.

"A wishing candle? What's that?"

"Just what it says on the card, darling." Cait took the card from the child's hand and scanned the familiar printing.

"If you've been good all year, at Christmas Santa makes your fondest wish come true."

"Who says?" Kelsey demanded.

Your daddy, Cait told her silently. Only he wasn't your daddy when he told me that.

"Someone I used to know. A long time ago."

"Before I was born?"

"Yes."

"A boyfriend?"

"No, just a friend." Cait ran her finger over the smooth glass. "A dear friend."

Kelsey cocked her head to one side and squinted into Cait's downcast face. "Do you miss your friend like I miss my friends in Hillsborough?" she asked with a child's directness.

"Yes," Cait admitted through a sudden rush of tears. "I miss him very much."

After slipping the card into the pocket of her robe, she went to the tree and hung the wishing candle on one of the upper branches. The glow from a nearby bulb turned the delicate glass into a rainbow shower of color.

"Finish tidying up, darling," she said without turning. "I'll be in the kitchen." Before Kelsey could ask her any more painful questions, she left the room.

By the time Cait reached the kitchen, tears were running down her face. She dashed them away with the back of her hand and poured herself a cup of coffee. The hot liquid helped soothe her throat but only made the flutters in her stomach worse.

It had been Christmas Eve, she remembered as she stood in front of the window and watched her neighbor's cat stalk an indignant mountain jay.

Both she and Tyler had drawn the short straws and were on duty. Around midnight, they had shared a pot of coffee and a piece of fruitcake.

Before they'd eaten it, Tyler had produced a tiny red candle he'd cadged from the kitchen and stuck it into the cake. Over the flame, he had smiled at her in a way she had never seen before.

"When I was a kid, my grandmother used to make me a wishing candle every Christmas. Sometimes it was the only present I got, but I didn't care."

"What's a wishing candle?" she had asked, just as Kelsey had.

His gray eyes had taken on a warmth that she'd never seen before. "Santa grants one special wish on Christmas Eve, but only if you've been very good. Have you been very good, Cait?"

"Very," she'd murmured.

"Then you may have one wish."

She'd glanced down at the flame flickering between them. One wish, or a dozen. They would all be the same. More than anything in the world, she wanted to spend the rest of her life making Tyler happy.

"Have you ever had a wish come true?" she had asked him.

He had smiled then, the first fully relaxed smile he had ever given her. It had transformed the harsh angles of his face and softened the flint in his eyes to a beautiful velvet gray.

"My wishes were always the same. That I would some-day be a doctor. But not just a good doctor. The best!"

The fervor in his voice had been as mesmerizing as that rare off-center smile. Cait had almost told him then that she loved him. But something had held her back. Three weeks later she had introduced him to Crystal. She had never seen him smile like that again.

Tyler turned off the shower and pulled back the curtain. He was right. The phone by his bed *was* ringing. Scowling, he grabbed the towel from the rack and padded naked into the bedroom. He caught up the phone in midring.

"McClane." He cradled the phone against his shoulder and wrapped the towel around his waist.

"Merry Christmas."

Just the sound of Cait's voice had his heart slamming against his rib cage. "Merry Christmas. How do you feel?"

"Tired but wonderful. How about you?"

"Lonely," he said before he realized he was revealing more of himself than he should.

"Me too."

He could almost see her sitting at her desk with her eyes taking on that sleepy, sated look and her lips parted in a smile that was just for him. She would never know how precious one of the smiles could be to a man who had lived without friends for so long.

"How's our little girl?" He shifted the phone to the other ear and sat down on the edge of the bed.

"Spoiled and loving it." Her soft chuckle made him smile. "And she loved the doll Santa brought her."

"Did she?"

"Yes. She's named her Prudence."

"Good Lord," he muttered. "Where did she get that?"

"From the Golden State Museum. Her class took a field trip there in the fall. Apparently she took a liking to a pic-ture she saw there of three sisters. One was Prudence. You can probably guess the other two."

Her voice had a slightly husky quality that made Tyler think of rumpled sheets and sleepy Sunday mornings. Even as he raked his water-slick hair away from his forehead, he felt the blood pooling in his groin. Somehow he kept his voice even. "Hope and Charity?"

"Close. Faith and Patience."

"I guess she has her reasons."

"One can only hope."

He smiled in spite of the black mood settling over him. "As long as she has you, she'll be fine."

"Tyler, about the candle . . ." Cait paused for a moment, and he could almost see the smile curving her mouth. "I love it. Thank you."

He had to take a deep breath to still the violent need to ask her to meet him. He wanted her. Here. In a motel. Anywhere.

He rubbed his hand over his belly. The tension increased. "You never did tell me what you wished for the last time," he said into the sudden silence.

"That's because it never came true."

Once he would have told her to be patient. That wishes sooner or later come true, just as his grandmother had promised. Now he knew better. "In that case, I hope that this time it does."

There was another pause before Cait answered. "So do I."

In the silence of his room, her voice seemed to whisper in his ear, arousing memories of the soft moans she'd made when they made love.

There were so many things he wanted to say. So many things he should have said years ago. But a man only had one chance at genuine happiness.

"Well, I'd better let you go," Cait said when the silence stretched.

"Merry Christmas, Cait. And thanks for calling."

"You're welcome. And Tyler?"

"Hmm?"

"I miss you." She hung up.

Lying back, he rested his head on one arm and stared at the network of cracks in the ceiling. His eyes burned. His throat hurt.

How many nights had he lain in just such a position, staring at the bunk above his, thinking about the woman he'd let get away?

Nights when he'd gone over the hours they'd spent together in minute, intricate detail to keep from begging them to let him out. Nights when he'd planned exactly how he should have made love to her. Nights when he'd longed to hear her voice so desperately that he'd nearly gone mad with it.

But those had been mind games to pass the endless hours. This was real. Cait was real. And she was very close to falling in love with him. He'd felt it in her kiss and heard it in her voice when she'd teased him so seductively.

The terse expletive he uttered summed up his mood. He was as caged as he'd been in Vacaville, and it was his own damn fault.

He had wanted her so desperately that he'd ignored all the reasons why it would never work between them. Reasons that were now crowding him hard. Good, valid reasons. His criminal record, the disgrace that would stain her, too, if her name was linked to his, the restrictions that governed damn near his every waking moment.

The judge's sentence.

"... *Furthermore, it is the decision of this court that you relinquish all parental rights to the child known as Kelsey Caitlin McClane. And that you refrain from contacting said child in any way at any time for the rest of your natural life or hers....*"

His life or hers.

He shouldn't even have been in the same city with her, let alone the same house. And that meant he and Cait would have to sneak around to make love. She deserved more, much more.

Closing his eyes, he tried to ignore the familiar ache settling in his chest. His scientific training had taught him that hearts don't really break. But sometimes a man could hurt so much it felt like it.

He repeated the crude curse and clenched his teeth. He had to stay away from her. He had no choice. But God, it was going to hurt.

Chapter 10

"Fifty-eight minutes until the new year," Cait muttered as she scooped clam dip onto a potato chip.

"Whoopie-doo," Hazel said, twirling her finger in the air.

"Excuse me, but do you think we might manage a little more excitement at this gala?" Cait said before popping the sloppy chip into her mouth.

"Sorry, pal. This is as excited as I get these days."

The two women were sitting in Cait's den, sipping brandy and eating junk food. It was an annual ritual that had started years earlier when they'd both found themselves alone on New Year's Eve.

The TV was tuned to the frenetic activities in New York's Times Square. The sound was muted. From the CD player nearby, classical music played, substituting for the inane commentary of the semihysterical host surrounded by overdressed revelers. Kelsey had been asleep for hours, with Prudence tucked under the covers with her.

Cait rested her feet on the coffee table and stared glumly at the reindeer prancing across the instep of her socks. "Do you think we're getting old?"

"Not me. I plan to be thirty-eight for at least twenty more years."

Cait reached for another chip. "I don't know, Hazel. Maybe we should be out doing something fun instead of sitting on our duffs watching other people celebrate."

Hazel looked through the brandy in her glass at the silent images on the TV screen. "I'll tell you one thing, you couldn't pay me to be in that crush."

"Me, either. I get squirrelly in big crowds."

Hazel swirled her brandy before taking a tiny sip. "My outrageously expensive training and God knows how many years of clinical experience tell me we have a woman here in desperate need of some intense therapy. The kind that only a semihandsome, major-sexy, cowboy-type guy can administer."

Cait shifted her gaze to the fragile glass ornament shining like the finest crystal in the glow of the lights. "He hasn't called once since Christmas. Not once."

"Maybe he's been busy."

The teasing glint faded from Hazel's eyes. She was the only person who knew the intimate details of Cait's Christmas Eve. Her instincts warned her that Cait was going to end up desperately hurt. Her common sense told her it was for the best. But her romantic heart ached for her friend.

"I've called him twice. Both times Angie came back to tell me he was busy and could she take a message."

"Cait, did you ever think that he's trying to protect you?"

"Protect me how?"

"From the scandal that would surely ensue if the media discovered that one of Sacramento's most prominent psychologists was sexually involved with a convicted child molester who also happens to be the father of her adopted daughter."

"Hazel!"

"At the very least your career would take a severe beating. At the worst it could be destroyed. Is an affair with Tyler McClane worth risking everything you've worked for?"

That and much more, she thought, and glanced at the wishing candle again. "I think I'm falling in love with him. Besides, when he's acquitted, all that will change."

"*If* he's acquitted. Nothing's settled yet."

Cait took a quick swallow of brandy. It burned all the way down, reminding her of the hot flush that bloomed on her face whenever she remembered the feel of Tyler's mouth on hers.

"He's suffered for years with shame and degradation he didn't deserve, because he was innocent. He's always been innocent. Right now he needs a friend. He picked me. *That's* what matters to me. Not the opinions of narrow-minded busybodies."

"Whoa, lady. I really *am* on your side, you know."

Cait managed a sheepish smile. "Sorry. I just hate to see him suffering."

"You know something? I do, too. That's why, with your permission, I intend to recommend that his parole be amended to include temporary visitation rights. Kelsey wants to see her daddy."

"Ty, call for you," Angie said as she placed the receiver on the bar.

"Man or woman?" Tyler asked as he drew a draft from the tap.

"Don't worry. It's not her."

Tyler served Ben Hadley his fourth of the night and wiped his hands on his jeans before taking the receiver. It had been a long day. The Horseshoe was crowded and had been all day. The noise level battered at his already-raw nerves.

"McClane."

Dante was on the other end of the line, and he was all business. "There's a chance you might get temporary visitation rights."

Tyler turned his back on the patrons at the bar. His throat was suddenly tight. "When?"

"Fielding said that the hearing is set for Thursday at four."

"Cait called you?"

"Yeah, just now. Said she'd called several times and hadn't been able to reach you. Seemed reluctant to leave a message about something so personal, so she called me. Thought I might want to be there to represent your interests."

"Hell, yes. I'll be there, too." Tyler glared at his reflection in the mirror. His face had the washed-out look of a man in shock.

"The hearing is closed, Ty. I can attend. You can't."

"Why the hell not?"

"Rules."

Tyler gave a short, succinct opinion of those rules. "Then I'll wait in the hall, or in the men's room, or a damned broom closet. But I intend to be there."

Dante remained silent. Tyler scowled. "What, no argument?"

Dante chuckled. "Not from me, buddy. I know better than to argue with you when you use that tone of voice."

"Good thinking. I'll meet you at the courthouse on Thursday."

Dante grunted. "There's one more thing."

Tyler heard the subtle change in Dante's voice and took a tighter grip on the phone. Behind him, men he had come to like but not really know stared at his stiff back with open curiosity.

"Go on."

"I think I might have been wrong about Caitlin Fielding. I'm beginning to think she just might be on your side."

Standing with his back to the wall, Tyler saw Harvey Shuffler a moment before the overweight parole officer saw him.

"What's he doing here?" Tyler demanded of Dante, who was next to him.

"Ms. Grimes requested his input," Dante muttered out of the side of his mouth as he and Shuffler exchanged nods. Shuffler merely glanced at Tyler, who met his cold-fish stare without any expression at all.

"Input on what?"

"On your parole record. It *is* spotless, isn't it?"

"Yeah, but I wouldn't put it past the bastard to lie," Tyler said as the parole officer opened the door marked Children's Protective Services and walked in.

Dante muttered something that Tyler didn't catch. At that moment Cait and another woman were stepping from the elevator at the end of the corridor.

It was always the same when he saw her. An easing of thought. A quick rush of adrenaline. An overpowering need to walk into her arms.

As she approached, she was talking to her friend in that quick, eager way that she had. Her hands, as always, accompanied her words with expressive gestures.

He noticed that she was wearing her hair up again. For courage, he knew. This time, too, he noticed the dark, wispy curls lying soft and tantalizing against her slender neck. What he noticed most, however, was the pale fullness of her mouth. Her very sexy, very soft mouth.

Today she was dressed in pink, but not the insipid color that most women wore. Her suit was a deep rose that probably had a fancy name he didn't know. Whatever it was, he liked it. And he liked the way the soft material showed off the enticing curve of her breasts and the swell of her hips without being blatant about it.

"Easy, boy," Dante muttered in a nearly inaudible aside.

Tyler felt heat sear his jaw. Before he could tell Dante what he could do with his advice, however, Cait had approached and was making the necessary introductions.

"Dr. Hazel O'Connor, Tyler McClane, Jess Dante."

Hazel turned to Tyler first. Her handshake was firm and sure as she murmured with a smile, "I'm glad to meet you, Dr. McClane, since I feel as though I already know you in many ways."

Cait's colleague had an open, friendly face and intelligent eyes. She was also looking at him without censure, something that was rare these days.

"Dr. O'Connor," he said with a smile that came more easily than he'd expected. "Thank you for all you're doing for my daughter."

She answered him with an understanding nod before turning to Dante. "Mr. Dante. We've spoken on the phone so often that I found myself very eager to put a face to the voice."

"Dr. O'Connor."

Tyler liked the way the slightly formidable woman managed Dante's awkward left-handed handshake without the slightest flicker of reaction. Dante noticed, too. His usual reserve with strangers was nowhere in evidence as he and the psychologist began discussing the hearing.

Listening but not participating, Tyler told himself to relax. His palms were sweating. His throat was dry. Vascular signs of intense nervousness. Along with an accelerated pulse.

Those things would gradually dissipate.

Not so his intense awareness of the woman next to him. He desperately needed one of her smiles. He needed *her.*

Her scent reminded him of the night she'd lain in his arms. Not even the classy suit could make him forget the silk of the skin underneath. Of her hot, moist softness closing around him.

The muscles of his arms strained against the need to hold her again. He shoved both hands into his pockets. It didn't help.

"So, are you nervous?" Cait asked him in a low tone.

"Terrified."

"Me too. Teri Grimes is about as warm as a gestapo agent."

Tyler felt an ominous tightening in his gut. "Sounds like she should be a guard at Vacaville instead of a social worker for kids."

"Don't worry. Hazel and I can handle her. We've had a lot of practice." Cait's eyes crinkled into a grin.

He noticed that she was wearing a hint of makeup that somehow made her eyes darker and her lashes spiky. But it was the steady calm shining from the depths of those eyes that he noticed most. Noticed and hung on to.

"How's Kelsey?" he asked after a moment of silence that neither seemed inclined to break.

"I think she said about two words to me this morning, so 'm not quite sure."

"Does she understand what's going on today?"

"She knows that the judge is going to decide if you can ome and see her on a regular basis. Sarah's parents are di- orced, so Kels knows all about visitation days."

"Is she scared, do you think?"

"More contemplative, I think, although she's told me nore than once that she wants to see you again. Even so, his is all pretty overwhelming for an almost-nine-year-old."

"For an already-forty-one-year-old, too."

This time the silence held. Even Dante and Hazel had run ut of conversation. Fighting a need to pace, Tyler unbut- oned his jacket and shoved his hand into the pocket of his lacks.

"Looks like you and Dante have different tastes in ties," Cait murmured, flipping the pointed end with her forefin- er. It was just an excuse to touch him, but he didn't have o know that. "Is it new?"

Tyler wished she wouldn't look at him in that slightly earsighted way. It made her eyes take on the slightly drowsy ast of a woman eager for love.

It came again, the quick, hard tug of desire. He had nanaged to back down on his hunger for her, but now, sur- ounded by people and worried sick besides, he felt the ur- ency building again.

He tried to distract himself by concentrating on the pat- ern of the tie. He'd bought it in a hurry on the day of Kel- ey's school play. It wasn't one he particularly liked, but he adn't wanted to embarrass Kelsey, even though no one in he audience could know who he was.

"Everything is new," he said. "Crys threw away just bout everything I owed after the trial."

Cait realized that he was wearing the same clothes he'd vorn to the play. The blazer, a classic navy blue, had diffi- ulty accommodating the wider-than-average breadth of his houlders. His shirt, a pristine white that made his tan even nore dramatic, was crisp with starch and stretched across a elly that she knew to be lean and fit. His trousers, though wool and pleated, did little to hide the power in his long, sinewy thighs.

Cait squared her shoulders and ran her tongue along her lower lip. She was nervous and trying hard not to show it. But Tyler noticed, and frustration settled like a stone in his gut.

He should be the one doing battle for her, not the other way around. Hell, there were a lot of things he should be doing, like using a scalpel instead of a damned corkscrew. And sleeping next to her warm pliant body instead of alone.

Restlessness gripped him again, the same restlessness that had nearly driven him crazy in prison whenever he thought about a life without a purpose. He felt emasculated at the very thought of never practicing medicine again.

"Uh-oh, there's Teri's secretary." Cait touched his arm and drew his attention toward the office. The woman standing there was dressed in gray flannel. Tyler's gut twisted when he saw that she had a humorless face and perfect posture.

"Dr. Fielding? Dr. O'Connor?" the woman called. "Ms. Grimes will see you now."

Cait gave her a wave and a grin. "Thanks, Marge."

Hazel cleared her throat. "Here's hoping," she said as she walked toward the office. Cait started to move away as well but stopped when Tyler laid a hand on her arm. Dante shot a quick look at both Tyler and Cait before following Hazel.

"I'll be right there," Cait called after them.

Tyler realized his hand still rested above her wrist and made himself withdraw it. Her warmth stayed with him.

"Cait, whatever happens, I want you to know that I'm grateful for all you've done for Kelsey. And for me."

Her gaze searched his face. "I should have done this four years ago. I'll always regret that I didn't."

The soft tremble in her voice had his jaw tensing. "Take my advice and put it behind you. Regret's a damn heavy load to carry."

"That's what I keep telling myself, too. But I still feel guilty."

Cait saw something flicker in his eyes. A moment's reflection told her that it was more than mere sexual hunger.
It was a rigorously disciplined self-denial. And a terrible
sadness that slipped inside her and made his pain hers.

"Keep your fingers crossed," she whispered as she went
on tiptoe and kissed him hard on the mouth.

Stunned into speechlessness, Tyler watched her hurry
away from him. Even when the door closed behind her, he
was watching.

Two hours later Tyler was again leaning against the wall
and wondering if his stomach could tolerate another cup of
coffee from the canteen.

He had just decided that it wouldn't when Harvey Shuffler pushed open the door opposite and stalked over to him.
The man's face was livid. One eyelid had taken on a nervous twitch.

"Maybe you have those two female doctors conned,
McClane, but you don't fool me."

Tyler kept his face expressionless. "I want to help my
daughter."

"Don't give me that. You want to sleep with her the way
you did before."

Tyler knew a moment of rage so savage he couldn't
breathe. He went icy inside. His hands balled into white-
knuckled fists.

"Go ahead, *Dr.* McClane," Shuffler urged. "Take a
swing at me."

Tyler thought about all the times he'd had to swallow his
anger. The days and nights he'd lived with a knot in his
belly. Remembering, he took a deep breath the way he'd
learned to do, followed by another and yet another until he
had mastered the rage.

"Not a chance, *Mr.* Shuffler."

Shuffler's expression turned ugly. "You think you're so
damn clever, acting like some upstanding guy who's been
given the shaft, when all the time you're sick inside. But
sooner or later you'll slip up, and then you're mine."

"I know the rules."

Shuffler sneered. "Yeah? Well, here's another one fo
you. You're not to see your daughter without Dr. Field
ing's permission and only in her presence or Dr. O'Con
nor's."

Tyler's face went stony. "Your idea, no doubt."

"No, Dr. Fielding's." A gleam slithered into Shuffler'
washed-out blue eyes. "Looks like the lady shrink doesn'
quite trust you as much as she lets on."

"That's my problem, not yours." Tyler's voice wa
sheathed in steel.

Shuffler's face splotched beet red. His expression turne
mean. "McClane, you step out of line just once and you'
know what a problem really feels like." He poked a flesh
finger into Tyler's chest. "That's a promise," he hissed be
fore he turned and stalked away.

Tyler saw Cait then. She was so close that he knew she'
heard every word. He forced himself to face her and brace
for her reaction to his humiliation.

"You know something? That man is a real pig," sh
muttered as she walked toward him. Her eyes were lighte
from within with anger. Her mouth was formed into an ex
pression of disgust. He had never wanted her more.

"That's a polite way of putting it, I guess."

Cait laughed. "Are you all right?"

"Now I am."

For a moment they stood motionless. She sensed hi
frustration and his anger, but there was little she could d
to help.

"Jess and Hazel are hammering out the specifics wit
Teri, but it looks as though you'll be able to see Kelsey a
least once a week. Perhaps more, if we can arrange it."

Tyler had trouble filling his lungs. "Starting when?" Hi
throat burned.

"Starting now, actually. Uh, I'll call you and we can mak
plans."

"Whatever you say."

"Well, that's a first," she teased. "Maybe I should hav
that written down and notarized."

"Too late."

He watched her eyelashes sweep up and down and wondered why he hadn't noticed how thick and lacy they were. Or why he hadn't realized that they were a shade darker than her hair.

"You look whipped," he said, glancing over her shoulder toward the end of the hall, where Shuffler was repeatedly jamming a thumb into the elevator button. "Was it that rough?"

"Not so bad. Hazel and Dante did most of the talking." She made a face. "And your *buddy,* the pig person."

His eyes crinkled a split second before he laughed. Cait saw a rare glimpse of the man he had once been and felt a slow rolling deep inside her. Like a wave building to tidal proportions.

"One thing he's not, and that's my buddy."

Cait sobered. "No, he's not. He tried his darnedest to convince Teri to deny visitation rights unequivocably."

"So he said."

"Have you done something to make him mad?"

His brows made a hard line over his nose. Even so, his mouth was surprisingly relaxed, as though he were still smiling inside. "Jess asked me that, too. I can't come up with anything specific."

She brushed a piece of lint that only she could see from his lapel. "He reminds me of a lot of bullies I've known. All talk and no guts."

"He doesn't need guts. He's got the rule book to hide behind."

His hand came up to fold around hers. Cait liked the way her hand felt in his. Dainty, warm and very safe. She liked the way he smelled and looked. Most of all, she liked the way his mouth gentled just before he kissed her, the way it was doing now.

Her lashes fluttered shut, and she raised her face to his. He noticed the freckles then. Tiny ones the color of antique gold. His head lowered. A split second before his mouth found hers, his gaze flicked to a spot behind her.

"Company," he grated.

She opened her eyes and blinked. "Hazel?"

"And Jess. My timing's always been rotten," he said with a smile that seemed rueful and supremely masculine at the same time.

"How's your timing on Saturday?"

"Why?"

"Come to lunch. Just the three of us. You and me and Kelsey." His fingers pressed tighter, and he swallowed hard.

"What time?" His voice was scratchy with emotion.

"Eleven." She drew a deep breath and reluctantly slipped her hand from his. "You know the address."

Cait's heart was thudding almost as loudly as the knock on her front door. She allowed herself a moment of panic, then straightened her shoulders. There was nothing she could do about the rush of heat to her face, however, or the erratic way she seemed to be breathing.

"Morning," Tyler said when the door was open and they were face-to-face.

"Good morning."

He had brought flowers. White carnations. Her fingers brushed the back of his hand as she took them from him and raised the cool, lacy blossoms to her nose. They smelled of cinnamon.

"I've always loved carnations," she murmured, a smile in her eyes. "Thank you."

"I haven't bought flowers for a woman in a long time." One side of his mouth moved. "I hope it hasn't gone out of style."

"Not with me," she said softly. "But then, I've been told I'm a closet romantic." She dimpled. "I suspect that really means I'm hopelessly old-fashioned."

"Guess that makes me old-fashioned, too, since I brought them." He touched one of the blossoms, the one closest to the silky skin beneath her chin. It was the next best thing to touching her.

"You're right on time." She opened the door wide and stepped back to allow him to enter.

"Actually, I was an hour early. I've been walking around the block to work up my courage."

He was ashamed of the kind of father he'd been. He just wasn't all that sure how to become a better one.

"You're here. That's what counts," she murmured as she closed the door.

Tyler worked on steadying his nerves as he followed her down the hallway to the kitchen. He hadn't even been this dry mouthed and scared when he'd taken his state boards.

"I'll just put these in water, and then we'll go outside. Kelsey and Prudence are making sure the birds don't get *all* the tortilla chips."

She opened the junk drawer and searched through the jumble for the scissors.

Tyler prowled the kitchen, absorbing a part of Cait's life that he'd never known before. Like the rest of her house, the kitchen was pleasantly cluttered and splashed with sunshine. Kelsey's school papers and an assortment of snapshots of her and her friends covered almost every square inch of the refrigerator door.

One corner had been turned into a cozy breakfast nook, where the mismatched cushions on the benches looked inviting. There was a bay window, too, that looked out over a well-tended rose garden complete with birdbath and hummingbird feeder.

"Someone must like birds."

"I do, except when they decide to take a bath at the crack of dawn." Cait stopped her search for the scissors to glance toward the window.

"There's this very independent mockingbird who just loves to sing in his shower. I wouldn't mind much, but I'm absolutely convinced he's the only off-key mockingbird in California. But we're discussing it."

She laughed. The sound was soothing, like a sudden cool breeze on a steamy day in high summer. Tyler had liked the sound of her laugh before he had liked her. Just as he'd been seduced by her personality before he had serious thoughts about her admittedly very seductive body.

"Aha, I knew it was here," she muttered as she drew the large shears from a nest of odds and ends.

Tyler stood in the doorway and watched. One by one she snipped the ends from the crisp silver-green stems. She worked quickly but carefully, as though preparing the flowers was the more important thing in the world.

She hummed as she worked, and her eyes had the same soft look of pleasure that he couldn't seem to get out of his mind. He unzipped his jacket and turned back the cuffs. The house wasn't warm, but suddenly he was sweating.

"Something smells good," he said, because the silence was suddenly too tense to handle.

"Chocolate cake." Cait threw the scissors into the drawer and raked the cuttings into her hand before tossing them into the trash basket under the sink. "It's Kelsey's favorite," she added with a soft smile. "But then, you know that, don't you?"

"Mine, too."

I know, Cait thought as she stretched toward the top cupboard for a vase. But the crystal container remained a fraction of an inch beyond her reach, no matter how tall she tried to make herself.

"Here, let me," Tyler muttered. As he reached past her to fetch the vase from the shelf, Cait was intensely aware of the strong, male body so close to hers.

For an instant she considered turning into his arms, but the memory of her unanswered phone calls stopped her. Later, when they were alone, they would talk. She would, anyway. In the meantime, she busied herself with the flowers.

"Tyler, there's something...about the conditions Ms. Grimes imposed," she said into the fluffy blossoms. "I heard Shuffler tell you that it was my idea."

He waited until she looked up at him, then used the back of his hand to brush her hair away from her flushed face.

"It's okay. I'm not upset. Shuffler laid it on thick to get a rise out of me, but I understand. You were right when you told me I should be glad someone is fighting to protect my daughter."

"Is that what you think?"

He nodded. "It's not easy to trust a guy with my record."

Cait drew a sharp breath. "Oh, Tyler!" she exclaimed softly. "That's not it at all. I could see that Shuffler had just about convinced Teri to rule against you, that's all. I had to think of something, anything, to make sure that didn't happen."

"I'm glad you're on my side, Cait."

"Is that why you haven't taken my calls? Because you thought I didn't trust you?"

His brow knotted, as though he were in pain. His gaze dropped, then rose to search her face before settling on her mouth.

"I never should have touched you. It put us in an impossible place."

Cait took a deep breath. The hungry way he watched her told her that it wouldn't take much to fan the smoldering desire in his eyes into flames. But that would be the worst kind of manipulation, the kind Crystal had practiced so well.

"Why don't we just concentrate on being friends, then?"

"I'm not sure that's possible."

Her chest felt tight from the strain of holding in her emotions. "Shame on you, Tyler McClane. Don't you know that anything's possible if it's what you really want?"

"Is it?"

Her breath trembled in and out. "Remember the wishing candle?"

Cait gave him a quick smile, and he saw that her eyes looked golden in the sun. A longing to belong in this place came without warning. A man could be happy here—if he belonged. He felt a hard ache settle in his chest.

"If you're ready, I'd better go out there and face my daughter," he said with a quick look at the door leading to the patio.

"Yes, you'd better. Poor Kelsey's been up since six, making sure things were perfect for our picnic."

Carrying the flowers, Cait led the way through a small utility room to the back door. Outside, the sun was shin-

ing. Busily foraging birds stopped occasionally to sing from
the sheer joy of the day. Winter mums were blooming in
sturdy redwood planters bordering the brick patio.

There was a large redwood table in the center. Plates,
glasses and silverware were piled at one end. At the other
end were trays of raw vegetables and chips next to a terra-
cotta bowl of salsa. Another small table held napkins, place
mats and condiments. Sodas were cooling in a nest of ice in
a bright red chest.

Near the chest were another, smaller table and chairs.
Kelsey's Christmas doll was seated on one of the chairs. A
much loved pink plush rabbit with chewed ears sat on the
other. A miniature china pot and two cups were neatly arranged between them.

Tyler saw only Kelsey.

Dressed in purple sweats and bright pink sneakers, she
was standing by a grill at the far side of the patio. Her hair
was tied into a thick ponytail by a matching pink ribbon.

His heart began a slow painful thudding in his chest. So
tight were his muscles that he had trouble drawing enough
air into his lungs.

Now that he was face-to-face with his daughter, he realized that he didn't know the first thing about talking to a
nine-year-old.

The closing of the door drew her attention, and she
turned. Her mouth trembled before she clamped her lower
lip between her teeth.

"Hello, Kelsey," he said very quietly. "Uh, it's a nice day
for a picnic." He glanced upward at the blue sky. A few
puffy clouds rode high and lonely on the horizon.

Kelsey sidled to the miniature table. As she busied herself pouring Prudence's tea, she kept sending curious
glances toward the big man with the nice face who didn't
smile much and looked like a cowboy.

Mama Cait had said he was her daddy, so she knew he
had to be. But the memories she had of Daddy were of a
man in a stiff white coat who didn't talk much and was always in a hurry.

"Prudence hates picnics," she said when both tiny cups had been filled. Tyler noticed that her gaze never quite settled on his face. The distance between them seemed to stretch forever. But he had to try.

"She does? Why?"

"She says they're too common."

"Prudence is a very proper lady," Cait explained gravely to Tyler as she walked past him to carry the flowers to the table.

"I can see that," he said with equal gravity. "No doubt she prefers high tea."

"No doubt," Cait murmured with an encouraging smile.

Tyler drew a deep breath before turning again to his daughter. "What about you, Kelsey? What do you think about picnics?"

Kelsey shrugged. "They're okay, I guess."

Cait winced mentally at the singular lack of enthusiasm in the child's voice, even though she knew that it was prompted by fear and anxiety. One look at Tyler's face told her that he was struggling with exactly the same emotions.

"Well, I love picnics," she said with a defiant grin as she pulled out a chair and sat down. After plucking a carnation from the vase, she waved it in the air like a baton. As she'd intended, both Kelsey and Tyler stopped eyeing each other warily and turned in unison to look at her.

"Okay, pay attention, you two. We have to get organized here." She noticed that both Kelsey and Tyler wore identical looks of surprise and grinned.

"Kelsey, you set the table. Tyler, you see to the coals."

"Oh sure, give her the easy job," he muttered, but his heart was thudding heavily.

"C'mon," Cait scolded. "You were raised on a ranch. Surely you know how to cook out?"

"Yeah, but we used mesquite logs and a spit. I don't know anything about these wimpy charcoal things."

"What do you think, Kelsey?" Cait prompted. "You want to trade jobs with your daddy?"

Kelsey eyed him uncertainly, but some of the pinched tension eased from her face. "No way."

"Sorry, Tyler," Cait told him with a look that was anything but pitying. To hide her grin, she lowered her head to the carnation and treated herself to another sniff of its spice.

"Yeah, so I see."

He saw too many things. The graceful arch of her neck when she drew closer to the flower. The soft rise of her cheek.

Did she know that her skin seemed as touchable as the pure white blossom? he wondered as he walked to the cooker and regarded the hunks of charcoal turning gray around the edges.

"Why do I think I'm not going to like this?" Tyler said to Kelsey, who was watching him with open curiosity now.

"'Cause you're probably not," the little girl said with the first sign of a smile he had seen.

"Don't look so uptight, Tyler," Cait said with a wink at Kelsey. "Daddy looks as though he's about to be staked out over an anthill, doesn't he?"

Kelsey giggled. "Maybe I *should* trade with him."

It was such a small thing, the subtle hint of teasing in her voice, but Tyler felt as though he had just passed the first hurdle.

A quick glance in her direction told him that Kelsey was no longer watching him as though he had just stepped from an alien space ship.

"Forget it, kid," he said with a shake of his head. "You had your shot at this prestigious job. Now it's mine."

Cait saw the little girl's mouth twitch and wanted to hug the father. No one watching him now would see a single sign of the humiliation he had suffered because of this small, shy child. Nor would they have an inkling of the emotional torture he had endured because of her innocent mistake.

"I like that attitude, Tyler," she said as she selected a plump carrot stick from the tray. "Shows a lot of class don't you think, Kels?"

"I'm not sure." The child finished laying out the last of the silverware before moving toward her father again. "What if he ruins our picnic?"

"Hey, have a little mercy here," Tyler told her before darting a frowning glance at the coals. "I'm new at this."

"We can tell," Cait muttered. "Can't we, Kels?"

Kelsey giggled again. "We sure can."

Tyler felt his throat close. No matter what happened after this, he would still have the gift of his daughter's laughter to add to his pitifully small collection of memories.

Conscious that both Kelsey and Cait were watching, he stood with his hands on his hips and evaluated his options. An oven mitt hung from the grill's handle, along with a long fork with two tines.

"Help me out, Kels," he pleaded in an exaggerated whisper. "What the dickens do I do next?"

Kelsey seemed to have forgotten her earlier wariness as she said, "You sorta spread them out in the bottom."

"Uh-huh. Spread them out in the bottom." He eyed the fork and mitt warily. "How?"

"With that," Kelsey said, pointing to a sad-looking twig with one singed end propped against one of the wooden planter boxes.

"Mmm, very clever. The latest in high-tech implements, I take it."

"I beg your pardon," Cait said with an affronted toss of her head. "I'll have you know I made that wonderful implement myself."

He was acutely aware of the encouragement in her eyes and the hard thump of his heart beneath his sweatshirt. "I beg pardon, ma'am. I stand corrected."

Tyler wiped one hand on his jeans before retrieving the makeshift poker. One eyebrow lifted as he turned toward Kelsey. "This thing really works, huh?"

Kelsey bobbed her head. "Most of the time."

"Now what?" he asked Kelsey.

She grabbed the oven mitt and held it out to him. As she did, she moved closer and said in her bossiest tone, "Now be very careful, or you'll burn your hand the way Mama Cait does sometimes."

"Oh, yeah? What does she do then?"

Kelsey dimpled. Leaning closer, she whispered, "When she thinks no one is listening, she says a lot of really bad words."

Tyler's gaze slanted toward Cait. "Shame on you, Mama Cait," he chided.

"It's cathartic," she said with a wave of her half-eaten carrot. "You should try it sometimes."

"What makes you think I haven't?"

With Kelsey's help, he did as he was told. Now and then the child issued an imperious command. The father patiently obeyed.

Cait nibbled on the end of her carrot stick and watched the slanting sunlight play over the strong bones of Tyler's face. She was beginning to like him very much, especially when he allowed himself to be teased the way he was now.

Who do you think you're kidding? she thought. It was more than liking. She had fallen in love all over again.

"C'mon, you two slowpokes," she said past the sudden sweet lump in her throat. "I spent all morning slaving in a hot kitchen to make the world's greatest hamburger patties. I don't know about you, but *I* would like to eat at least one before the sun goes down tonight."

Kelsey giggled and sneaked a peek at her father before protesting to Cait, "If you spent all morning in the kitchen, how come you were taking a bubble bath when I got home from Sarah's house?"

Cait knew that she was turning pink and hoped Tyler didn't notice. "So I spent a few minutes in the tub. Big deal," she muttered, but inside she was smiling. Maybe they didn't know it yet, but father and daughter had just taken a very large and important step toward each other.

Chapter 11

"How about pepperoni and mushrooms?" Tyler suggested over the top of the menu he had damn near memorized.

"Yuck," Kelsey muttered. "I hate mushrooms."

"Okay, scratch the mushrooms. How about pepperoni and black olives?"

This time Cait made a face. "I hate black olives."

Tyler closed the menu and folded his big hands carefully on top of it. They were very clean, with very short nails and prominent knuckles.

"Green olives, then," he asked with a glint of challenge in his eyes.

Cait managed to keep a straight face. "I hate those too."

"Why am I not surprised?" he muttered in an exceedingly dry tone that Kelsey seemed to find hilarious.

"We usually have pepperoni and anchovies," she said between giggles.

Tyler sat back and shook his head. "God help me and my unsuspecting stomach."

Kelsey and Cait exchanged looks. "Poor Daddy," Kelsey murmured as she reached over to pat his hand. "Just wait and see. You'll like it."

He found himself looking at Cait. She was smiling, but her eyes were shiny with unshed tears. He tried to return her smile, but he couldn't.

It had been three weeks since he'd received permission to visit Kelsey. He had seen her every Monday after his appointment with Shuffler and twice on successive Saturday mornings.

This was the first time she had called him Daddy.

Tyler usually left Cait's house well before Kelsey's bedtime. This Monday night, however, they had gotten involved in looking at some family albums that Cait had taken from Crystal's house after her death. Before they knew it, it had been time for bed.

Always the opportunist, Kelsey had talked Tyler and Cait into going through the biggest album one more time before she had to settle down.

It was the first time Tyler had been in her bedroom since Christmas Eve. Cait was there, too, perched on the other side of the bed. To a stranger's eye the scene would seem routine—a mother and father tucking in their child for the night. To Tyler it was a miracle that he didn't quite trust, even now.

"How old was I in this picture?" Kelsey pointed to a color print on one corner of the page.

"Three, I think," he told her after studying the faded likeness. "You were furious because your mother wouldn't let you wear your cowboy guns to nursery school."

"Cowboy guns? I had cowboy guns?"

"Yep, with genuine fake mother-of-pearl handles."

Kelsey's eyes grew bright with excitement. "Where are they now?" she asked with touching eagerness.

"I don't know, baby." He had a damn good idea, however. Crystal had been furious when he'd given their adorable and very feminine child the guns he had always cherished.

"There's another box of your mother's stuff in the attic," Cait told the child with a smile. "Tomorrow we'll see what's in it, okay?"

"How about right now?"

Cait tousled the child's silky hair. "Enough stalling. It's nearly twenty minutes past your bedtime."

"Just another five minutes, please?" Instead of turning her hopeful look on Cait, however, she turned to Tyler.

"Okay with me—if Mama Cait agrees."

Kelsey's pleading gaze swung toward Cait, who chuckled. "She knows a soft touch when she sees one," Cait told Tyler with an affectionate shake of her head.

He raised one of his eyebrows in the wry, extremely masculine gesture she was coming to know intimately. "Who, me?"

"Yes, you, Tyler McClane," she insisted. "You would spoil her rotten if I let you."

"What's wrong with five minutes, anyway?" he asked with a grin.

She glanced at Kelsey's bedside clock. "Nothing's *wrong* with it," she told them both. "Unfortunately, we've used it all up arguing."

Kelsey protested profusely. Tyler groaned and tried to look indignant. Cait simply grinned. With a dramatic sigh, Tyler closed the album and placed it on the nightstand before he got to his feet and smiled down at the dainty little girl.

"Sorry, baby. Looks like she's outfoxed us again."

"Darn," Kelsey muttered through a grimace of disappointment.

"School tomorrow, remember," Cait said as she lifted the blanket and waited for the little girl to scoot deeper into the warmth.

"Night, baby," Tyler said with a smile. "See you next week."

"On Monday, for the movies," Kelsey reminded him solemnly.

"Monday, for the movies."

A gleam came into Kelsey's eyes. "Can Sarah come, too?"

Tyler felt his gut knot. How did a man tell his daughter he could be arrested for even speaking to her little friend?

"Not this time, baby."

"Next time?" bargained Kelsey.

"Kelsey, sweetie, don't badger your daddy," Cait chided gently. "He wants to spend time with you."

"And you, too. Right, Daddy?"

Tyler's gaze shifted toward Cait and held, longer than politeness allowed. But he found that he liked the level way she looked at him, even when the strain around her eyes told him that she was upset. And he liked the way her eyes smiled an instant before her lips did.

"Right," he said very softly, very firmly. "I come to spend time with both of you."

Cait felt warmth flutter through her as she bent her head to kiss Kelsey good-night. "Night-night," she murmured as she smoothed the coverlet to Kelsey's chin.

Kelsey wound her arms around Cait's neck and gave her a bear hug. "Night-night, Mama," she murmured. "Today was fun, wasn't it?"

"It sure was," Cait said with a smile. "Did you remember to thank your daddy for taking us for ice cream?"

"I forgot," Kelsey whispered before darting a glance over Cait's shoulder. "Thank you for the ice cream," she said in a dutiful tone.

"You're welcome, Button."

Kelsey's small mouth grew thoughtful. "My nose didn't really look like a button when I was born, did it, Daddy?"

He touched the tip of her nose with his fingertip. "Maybe not, but it sure was cute."

Kelsey giggled. "Night-night, Daddy." She lifted her arms toward him for the first time. As he gathered her close to his chest, Tyler felt something tear inside him, releasing a flood of deep feeling that was nearly too much for him.

"Night-night, Button. Sleep well."

Even though his voice was low and even, it had taken on a definite hoarseness. And his broad back was stiff with the emotions he was fighting.

Cait fought down the urge to rest her hand on the proud angle of his neck and let him know without words that he wasn't alone. But she didn't dare.

This was a battle Tyler had to fight alone, and she had to let him. Turning her back, she walked to the window and opened it an inch or so.

As she did, she gazed at the sky. The stars were unusually bright, and the air had a soft feel to it. A night for lovers, she thought as she drew the drapes closed. She turned to find Tyler smoothing Kelsey's hair.

"I wish you could be here in the morning when I wake up, like other daddies," Kelsey said in a drowsy little voice. Already her thick blond lashes were drooping.

Tyler struggled to keep his emotions under control. So do I, baby, he thought. You don't know how much. It wasn't only the desire to be there for Kelsey that tore at him, however. It was also the idea of having a family life again, a real family life, without restrictions and limitations and rules. A life where he could be as affectionate with his daughter as he wanted without worrying about what others might think.

He sensed movement beside him and glanced sideways to see Cait standing there. More than those things, even, he wanted a life with this woman. With the woman he should have made his wife a long time ago. He felt his face freeze.

"I'll wait for you downstairs," he said as he brushed past her.

Cait knew a moment of surprise. She had expected him to say goodbye and leave. "I'll just be a minute."

Cait sat on the side of the bed and listened to the quiet thudding of his boots as he went down the stairs. Nothing was easy, she thought.

She and Tyler both loved Kelsey. Kelsey loved her Mama Cait and was very quickly coming to love her father. The problem was between Cait and Tyler. Every time they were together, the tension between them grew worse. Even though he hadn't touched her once since that day in the kitchen, she was more aware of him than ever.

She knew that staying indoors too long made him edgy. That he was very careful never to be alone with Kelsey, even though the two of them had never said anything more about the conditions governing his visits. And she knew that he never talked about his years as a doctor, even if she or Kelsey brought up the subject.

Those things she knew because she cared about him. Because she loved him, she wanted him to make love to her again. And she wanted to make love to him.

Fighting a smothering frustration, she leaned over to brush a kiss on Kelsey's forehead. The little girl stirred but didn't wake. As always, Cait left one small light burning before she left the room.

She found Tyler in the den. He was standing by the fire watching the flames. In the orange glow his cheeks looked gaunt. His mouth had taken on the hard, forbidding line that she hadn't seen in weeks.

"I think Kelsey's down for the count," she said as she slid the double door closed behind her and turned the key in the lock.

"Does she still have nightmares?"

She crossed the room to close the drapes and switch on the desk lamp. "Very rarely, and usually only when she goes to bed overly tired," she said as she settled herself into a corner of the couch.

His head came up, and he turned to look at her. "Like tonight?"

"No, but she was getting there." He nodded but said nothing. Cait ran her hand along the top of her thigh. "Would you like some coffee before you go?"

"What I'd really like is a double Scotch."

Cait glanced at the eighteenth-century hutch that doubled as a bar. "Help yourself."

"No, but thanks for not reminding me that I would be breaking parole as soon as I took the first sip."

Cait shifted her gaze to the flames. They ate at the logs with an insatiable appetite that wasn't to be denied. "Is it so bad, being on parole, I mean?"

"Not as bad as prison."

"From what I've heard about our wonderful penal system, I'm not sure anything could be as bad as that."

"You're wrong." She looked up in time to see his face twist.

"Tell me."

Tyler drew a deep breath. Cait couldn't seem to look away from the emotion building in his eyes.

"Not being able to practice medicine. That's worse." He spread his hands and looked at them. "Knowing that every day I lose some of my skill. That there are new procedures I don't know, new techniques I might never know."

"What happens if you don't get your license back?"

"I don't know, Cait," he said in a tired voice. "I don't think about it much anymore. I can't. I would go crazy if I did."

She sensed that he was drawing inside himself again, shutting her out. Not this time, she thought. Without taking time to worry about the consequences, she left the sofa cushions and went to him. He stiffened when her hands found his shoulders and rested there, but he didn't move away.

"Try to be patient. It'll work out. You'll see. After you're cleared the way you should have been at the first trial, the rest will fall into place."

"There's something else, Cait. It's about the trial." He moved away, breaking the contact of her hands.

"What about it?" She tried to ignore the sudden dread making a hole in her stomach.

"Jess wants Kelsey to testify again. For me, this time. Lamont insists on it, and Jess seems to think she's my only hope."

Cait went very still. The familiar shapes and colors of her favorite room seemed to sharpen until they seared her eyes. "Jess may be right."

He stared at the fire. His back was straight. Asking for anything was difficult for a man with his pride.

"Do you think she can handle it? Do you think she can get up on the witness stand one more time?"

Cait took a moment to think. "I don't know, Tyler. I'm not sure Hazel knows yet. She's made terrific progress, especially in these last weeks. But I know her nightmares were all mixed up with her memories of the trial, too." Cait noticed that the room seemed very quiet all of a sudden.

"I don't want her hurt, Cait. I can't stand that."

"I know. And I can't stand to see you hurt," she whispered softly. "You don't deserve it. You never did."

It took him a moment to master his emotions. He was having to do a lot of that lately. When he had himself under control again, he turned to face her. "I can take it."

"So can Kelsey."

"She shouldn't have to."

"You can't protect her from the consequences of her own actions, Tyler. You shouldn't even try."

He leaned against the fireplace, arms spread, and crossed his ankles. A contemplative look tightened his face as he stared at the scuffed toes of his boots. "It's damn hard being a parent."

"You know what? I think every parent I've ever had in my office says that to me sooner or later."

He saluted that with a brief glance. "Have *you* said it?"

"Just about daily when Kels first came to live with me. Now I have it down to once or twice a week."

He grinned, but his eyes were bleak. "Sometimes I think I'll never get the hang of it. Like tonight. I know I'm too easy on her, but our time is so limited."

"You're afraid she won't love you if you deny her something she wants or discipline her for misbehaving."

"Yeah, that's about it."

Cait strolled toward him, her arms crossed. "I felt the same way, even though professionally I know very well the dangers of raising a child without limits."

His grin was crooked. "Sometimes I think about getting into the truck and heading for Mexico. No more Shuffler, no more Horseshoe, no more worries that I'm a worse father now than I ever was."

"Why don't you?" Cait asked softly.

He shrugged. "I've asked myself that more than once. If it weren't for Kelsey..." He left the sentence unfinished as he turned to look at her.

Cait smiled. "Even if it weren't for Kelsey, you wouldn't run."

He raised his eyebrow very slowly. "No?"

"No. You're not a quitter, Tyler," she murmured with deep conviction. "No matter how stacked the odds might be against you, you don't give up."

She took his hands in hers and kissed each callused palm in turn. His fingers clenched around hers.

"You may not be able to practice medicine anymore, but you're still the same man who wanted to make a difference. Try to be patient. If it can't be medicine, you'll find another way to contribute. I know you will."

The lines around his mouth deepened. "You almost make me believe."

"Believe it. I do."

Tyler wondered if she knew how much he wanted to kiss her. Now and every time he saw her. He released her hands and used his to frame her face.

"Every day since Christmas, I've thought about you and remembered and wanted you again. And every time you called, I wanted to rip the phone out of Angie's hands so that I could hear that husky little catch you get in your voice when you start talking too fast."

"I don't!"

"Oh, yes, you do, my Cait." He tilted his head to one side, lined up his mouth with hers and kissed her with the greedy thoroughness of a man who'd denied himself for too long.

Cait's knees nearly buckled at the hot, sweet pleasure filling her. Even while her mind was exulting, however, her hands were burrowing under his sweatshirt to find the warm skin beneath.

Finding it, she ran her hands up and down the small of his back, exciting quick shuddering ripples, as though his body were a slave to hers.

"You're punishing me, is that it?" he gasped against her neck. "For not taking your calls."

"That's it," she murmured into the fleece of his faded sweatshirt. Using her fingernail, she slowly traced the bumpy line of his spine. This time the shudders shook his entire body.

"God, Cait, you don't know what you're doing to me."

"Tell me," she whispered against the unruly silver of his hair.

"Driving me damn near insane, that's what."

He loosed the top two buttons of her shirt before slipping his hand inside to cup her breast. Instantly, like damped coal burning into flame, her nipple hardened and puckered, sending a shiver of hot pleasure through her.

"That's not fair," she cried in a breathless rush against his shoulder as she arched into his touch. His fingers lightly pinched the throbbing bud until the inner shivers became a shudder of need.

Her hands tugged at his hair, forcing his head up. At the same time her hand sought his belt buckle.

This time she loosened it quickly and was already working on the second tiny metal button of his fly when a groan exploded from him.

"No more talking," he muttered as he pulled her into his arms again. Just the touch of her kindled a heat in Tyler that approached pain. He knew what was happening. He was letting himself need her more than any man should need a woman.

But he no longer had the will to deny himself. She was with him, even when he was alone. It was she he reached for in the middle of a troubled sleep, even though he knew she wouldn't be there. And it was her face he automatically sought wherever he went.

"Then kiss me," she murmured.

"God, you're pushy," he complained hoarsely, but the sudden emotion in his eyes made her go weak inside. She offered her mouth eagerly. Just as eagerly, he took it.

His hands shook as they stripped the silk shirt from her shoulders. Her bra, a silly little thing of lace and silk, followed.

Answering her small, urgent moans, he drew back and let her push his sweatshirt over his head. Pulling back then, he shed his boots, his jeans, his briefs. Eagerly she rid herself of her slacks, her shoes, her panties. When he drew her down to the floor, she went willingly.

The rug's pile against her bare back was evocatively familiar. So, too, were the soft hiss and warm breath of the fire. The musky scent of passion.

Unwilling to wait any longer, she laced her hands through his shaggy hair and pulled his mouth down to hers. No longer content to be wooed, she moved under him, caressing him with her breasts, her cheek, her hands. He rasped out his pleasure so deeply that his neck corded.

For so long he'd been dead inside. With Cait, he was coming alive. It scared him, even as it made him want her more and more.

His skin became slick with sweat that soon coated her. Her heart raced under his hands. His beat just as furiously, pumping blood to the most sensitive part of him until his flesh was hot and distended and ready.

When he couldn't stand it another instant, he nudged her thighs aside and tested her readiness. A groan escaped his lips when he discovered just how much she wanted him.

"Yes, oh, yes," she moaned. "Now, please, now."

He sank into her slowly, letting her body stretch to accommodate the engorged length of his.

"Tyler," she whispered. "It's so good, so...so very sweet."

"Oh, yes, Cait. Move with me. Stay with me, sweetheart."

When the climax came, it shuddered through both of them, leaving them spent and sated and deeply joined.

* * *

The door to Hazel's inner office was ajar, but Cait knocked anyway.

"It's Cait," she called at the same time. "I'm early."

Kelsey's session was scheduled for six, and it wasn't yet five-thirty, but Cait had been too nervous to stay home.

Twilight was settling, throwing the Sacramento skyline into silhouette. Tyler was already in town for his regular appointment with Harvey Shuffler. When Shuffler let him go, he would be coming here. Today was the day the three of them would broach the subject of testifying with Kelsey.

"C'mon in," Hazel answered from within.

Cait pushed open the door and entered. Hazel was sitting behind her desk with her stockinged feet propped on an open drawer and a cup of tea in her hand. She frowned as she took in Cait's pink cheeks and windblown hair.

"Lord," she muttered. "You look like you just slogged through a blizzard."

Cait laughed and tugged off her furry gloves. "This is California, remember? The Golden State. Land of sunshine and prosperity. We don't allow blizzards, especially in March."

Hazel made a face. "A lot of people I know have taken to calling this the granola state. You know, the land of fruits and nuts."

Cait choked back a laugh. "Behave yourself, Dr. O'Connor."

"No way! That's not any fun."

Cait shoved her gloves into the pockets of her parka and hung it with her purse next to Hazel's ski jacket on the hall tree. Then, smoothing her mohair sweater over her hips, she crossed to the credenza and helped herself to a cup of Hazel's best tea.

"Where's Kels?" Hazel asked as Cait stirred some of the steam from the brimming teacup.

"At Sarah's." She settled into a corner of the couch, slipped out of her loafers and tucked her legs beneath her. "Petra is helping them work on their Brownie badge in embroidery. She promised to drop Kelsey off here in plenty of time for her session.''

One of Hazel's strawberry eyebrows rose. ''Embroidery? You've got to be kidding!''

Cait shrugged. ''Her den mother swears it's a valid part of the program.''

''Hmm. I thought you didn't believe in stereotypes.''

''I don't.'' Cait tested the tea and and found it drinkable. She took several sips before adding, ''Next month it's my turn to teach the troop to change a tire.''

''That's more like it!'' Hazel exclaimed with a grin that reminded Cait of a mischievous six-year-old.

''Haven't you heard? Rampant feminism went out with maxidresses and man-tailored suits.''

''There's feminism and feminism, my friend. As you well know. For example, I don't see you shucking your career to be someone's domestic servant.''

Cait groaned. ''Don't start. I'm too nervous to argue.'' She plucked a Tootsie Roll from the dish on the table and shot a questioning look at her friend.

''I shouldn't,'' Hazel said with a sigh. ''But what the heck, throw me one. I'll swim a few extra laps tomorrow.''

Cait tossed her a candy before taking another for herself. ''Maybe I'll join you. I need to take off a few pounds.''

''Oh, yeah?'' Hazel paused in the act of unwrapping the candy to shoot Cait a disbelieving look. ''Where, pray tell?''

''The usual places. Hips, thighs, you know.''

Cait popped the candy into her mouth and swirled her tongue over the sweet chocolate. Suddenly another image rose to her mind. Blood surged into her face.

Her pulse sped up, gradually at first, then faster and faster, as she thought about what would happen tonight, after Kelsey had been tucked into bed.

It wasn't easy, but she and Tyler managed to find time to make love nearly every time he visited. The results were dramatic. She was blooming. He seemed much more content. Everything seemed better after they had been together. Even the lousy, unseasonably chilly weather didn't bother her.

A feeling like warm spring rain flowed through her, and she ran one nervous hand up and down her arm. Her sweater was soft under her palm, like the hair on Tyler's chest.

She curled her fingers to savor the warmth the way she savored the feel of Tyler's kiss. She glanced up to find Hazel watching her with worry clouding her eyes.

"It won't be long before Kelsey's ready to be released from therapy," Hazel murmured. "Since her daddy came back into her life, her progress has been exceptional."

Cait smiled. "He's wonderful with her, Hazel. It's like he's a different person than he used to be around her. When he's with her, she gets his constant attention. And she's beginning to tease him terribly, which is good for both of them."

Hazel's gaze flicked to the form on her desk. It was the weekly report she was required to file on Tyler with Teresa Grimes. As far as she had been able to observe, he had followed the requirements set down by Protective Services to the letter.

"If today goes well, it won't be too many more weeks before there will be no longer be a valid reason to keep Kelsey in therapy. As soon as I dismiss her, there will no longer be a valid reason to ask Teri Grimes to extend his temporary visitation privileges."

Cait slumped against the sofa cushions. "You could ask for an extension—just until Tyler's trial. After that, it'll be academic, I'm sure."

Hazel sighed. "Sometimes I think Rebecca of Sunnybrook Farm has been reincarnated in you, Dr. Fielding."

Cait laughed, dissipating some of the tension that had suddenly filled the office. "No way. You should hear me swearing at those idiot drivers out there."

"The visitation was always meant to be temporary. The only reason we got it pushed through at all was because of Kelsey's fragile emotional state. Helping her outweighed the potential of risk in Grimes's mind."

Hazel pushed the files aside and rested her chin in her palm. "Suppose, for the sake of argument, I did ask for an extension? What grounds could I give?"

"Humanitarian reasons? Sheer kindness?" Her lips curved upward. "A favor?"

"Teri Grimes? You must be kidding," Hazel scoffed. "If her intentions weren't so admirable, I would be hard-pressed to be civil to the woman."

"I know what you mean. But then, after the hearing last month when I practically bullied her into granting Tyler access, I have a feeling she's not very disposed to be civil to me, either."

"To either of us. Don't forget, I was right in there pitching when Tyler's PO was coming on like a gold-plated idiot."

Hazel took a bottle of aspirin from the drawer and shook three into her hand. Cait watched as she washed them down with the last of her tea.

"How about for the well-being of the patient, then? You could describe how lost and even abandoned Kelsey would feel if all of a sudden Tyler stopped coming to see her. Use her marked improvement since Tyler's come back into her life to support the argument."

Hazel tossed the aspirin bottle into the open drawer and closed it with a hard shove. At the same time, impatience flashed across her normally placid countenance. "Cait, the woman has a degree in clinical social work. Even if I were inclined to try to snow her, which I'm not, she'd see right through my argument."

"How could she? It's the truth. Kels really will be terribly upset to lose her daddy again."

"Perhaps, for a while. But I'm sure we're both skilled enough to minimize the damage."

Minimize the damage? Cait thought with sudden outrage. This was her daughter's happiness Hazel was discussing so clinically. And hers, too, if she was honest with herself.

Heat rose to her face, but she forced herself to keep the hot, angry words inside. When it came to professional

ethics, Hazel was as immovable as the granite hills surrounding the city. Logic was the only way to budge her.

"Okay, what if I try to convince her?"

"She'll ask my opinion. I can't lie."

"For Pete's sake!" Cait exclaimed. "I'm not asking you
to lie. I'm asking you to grant me the professional courtesy
of allowing me to present my opinion as a consulting therapist."

"In this case, you're the mother. Not the consulting."

"I'm both. And my opinion is as worthy of consideration as yours."

"In my opinion, your opinion is biased."

Cait's hands made small fists. "In *my* opinion, you're
overstepping the bounds of professional courtesy."

Hazel slapped her hand against the desk. "Now just a
minute, Cait—"

"Mama, are you and Auntie Hazel fighting?" It was
Kelsey who spoke.

Taken by surprise, both Hazel and Cait turned startled
eyes toward the door, where the bright-eyed little girl was
standing hand in hand with her father.

"We met in the elevator," Tyler said quietly when Cait's
gaze swung to his.

"How much did you hear?" she asked quietly.

He smiled, but his eyes remained shadowed, the way they
always did after he'd spent time with Harvey Shuffler.

"Not enough to worry about."

"Are you mad at Auntie Hazel, Mama?" Kelsey asked
again as she gave her mother a bear hug.

Cait kissed Kelsey's smooth cheek and discovered that it
was cold against her lips. "Not mad, sweetie. Auntie Hazel
and I are having a difference of opinion over something, but
that doesn't mean we're mad at one another. We're still
friends, just like you and Sarah are still friends when you're
having a difference of opinion."

Kelsey's brow puckered. "You mean a fight, right?"

Tyler's laugh rumbled across the office. Cait scowled, and
Hazel looked bemused before their eyes met.

"Told you she was bright," Hazel muttered before she burst into laughter. Cait joined her. The tension dissipated.

Kelsey's head swiveled almost comically as she looked from one to the other. "Did I say something funny?" she asked, turning to her father for the answer.

"No, baby. You said exactly the right thing. Auntie Hazel and Mama are laughing because they realize all of a sudden that they're really on the same side and shouldn't be shouting at each other."

"I don't shout," Cait muttered.

"Could'a fooled us, huh, Kels?" He winked at his daughter.

"Yeah, could'a fooled us." Grinning, she took Tyler's hand and led him toward the sofa where Cait was curled.

"You sit here, next to Mama Cait."

Tyler's gaze sought Cait's over Kelsey's head. As she smiled her forgiveness at him, he realized how much he needed this woman. Not just the intense physical pleasure she gave him, but for the stability she brought to his life.

"Okay with you if I sit here, Mama Cait?"

Cait heard a low rumble of amusement in his voice. And something more, something only she would recognize. Hunger. The same hunger tugged at her as she patted the cushion next to her. "Okay, Daddy."

The sofa springs dipped under his weight, throwing Cait's thigh a few inches closer to his. They weren't touching, but Cait knew exactly how hard and resilient his body would feel next to hers.

"And what about you, Miss Kelsey?" she asked as the little girl stood watching them, a huge smile on her face. "Where will you sit?"

"I'll sit on Daddy's lap, just like Sarah does when her daddy tells her a story."

The little girl started to plop herself onto Tyler's thighs, but he curled his arm around her waist to stop her. It was nearly killing him to have to ask permission to hold his own child, but he knew that he had no choice.

"Maybe we'd better ask Dr. O'Connor if that's where she wants you," he said with a casualness that was anything but real. "After all, it's her office."

Kelsey looked puzzled, but she obediently swung her gaze to the woman behind the desk. "Okay, Auntie Hazel?"

Hazel smiled at her patient. "Do you like sitting on your daddy's lap?" she asked calmly.

Kelsey's mouth drooped. "I don't remember."

"You don't remember?"

"Uh-uh. I was too little when I lived with him and my first mommy, wasn't I, Daddy?"

"Yes, sweetheart," he said in a gentle voice that only his patients and Kelsey had ever heard. "You were just a very little girl then."

"And you were a doctor and very important and sometimes you were too busy. But not like now, right, Daddy? Now you're just a bartender."

"Right, sweetheart. Now I'm just a bartender and not busy at all."

Only a trained observer could have heard the bleak frustration in his voice. Only a trained observer would have seen the helpless agony that flashed for a moment in his eyes. Hazel cleared her throat and avoided Cait's gaze.

"It's fine with me, Kels, if you want to sit on Daddy's lap. In fact, it might be a good idea, because he and I and Mama Cait want to talk to you about something really serious and really important. Okay?"

Kelsey looked startled at the words "really serious," but her expression cleared as she climbed trustingly into Tyler's lap and snuggled against his wide, strong chest.

"Okay," she said with an open smile. "I'm ready."

Chapter 12

Tyler came awake in an instant. Someone was downstairs in the bar.

Even as he was pulling on his jeans, he was moving. After inching open the door to the stairwell, he paused to listen. The stairwell was dark. Below, on the landing, he saw a flash of light. At the same time he heard muffled footsteps.

Arms spread, he braced both hands against the dusty walls of the stairwell and took the sagging stairs one riser at a time. He was nearly to the bottom when he smelled it. *Gasoline.*

He inhaled swiftly, and as he did, he heard the sound of splashing. The bastard, whoever he was, was intent on torching the Horseshoe.

Tyler moved silently on bare feet to the end of the hall, where he halted to sweep his gaze around quickly. There was very little light to aid him. What little there was came from the reflected glow of the beer signs in the window and the small light burning behind the bar.

It took him a moment or two to discover a man's shadowed figure near the entrance. An object he took to be a gasoline can stood near the man's feet. Near the center or the room, chairs and tables had been piled together into a makeshift pyre.

Before Tyler could react, the intruder lit a match and threw it. The gasoline exploded, sending flames roaring high enough to scorch the ceiling. In a split second the room was bathed in brilliant yellow light.

The arsonist, on his way to the door, paused to admire his handiwork. Even as Tyler recognized Big Mike Bronsky, he was running.

Alerted, Mike whirled, his hand going to the knife in a sheath on his hip. At the same instant Tyler launched himself in a flying tackle toward the man's gut. His forearm caught Mike full in the face, snapping his head back. Both men crashed to the floor.

Tyler landed heavily with his body sprawled across Mike's. In the light from the blaze, he saw that Mike was unconscious, down for the count.

Uttering a blistering obscenity, he levered himself to his feet. Already flames were spreading in a jagged circle wherever the gasoline provided fuel. Floor tiles curled and melted, releasing a noxious stench. Heat scorched his face and bare chest.

Using his forearm to shield his eyes, Tyler sprinted through the edges of the inferno and headed for the extinguisher behind the bar.

He jerked it free, released the seal and directed the spray toward the worst of the blaze. Sparks flew. Flames sputtered. Tears streamed down his face, carving tracks in the soot. Working furiously, he gasped for air in the thick smoke.

Ten minutes later, the fire was out. Tyler was still high on adrenaline, but not so high that he didn't feel the pain from an angry burn on the back of his right wrist, the one he'd used to coldcock Mike. The man himself was still unconscious, lying in a heap near the entrance.

Coughing uncontrollably, Tyler made his way past the biker to the door and flung it open to admit cool fresh air. Arms braced, he lifted his face to the night and drew in large gasps until the heat searing his lungs eased. Gradually the stinging tears ceased and his breathing returned to normal.

He took stock then. The shabby street was deserted. The few businesses that still remained were shut up tight. Nothing stirred. If anyone had seen the fire and reported it, the siren for the Volunteer Fire Department would be howling.

Tyler turned slowly, pondering his options. Behind him, he heard the sound of foamy fire retardant dripping from the remnants of the tables. There wasn't a peep from Mike.

He left the door open and switched on the light. Mike didn't stir. A quick but skilled glance told Tyler that the man was still breathing and nothing seemed broken. He walked closer and prodded the big man with his bare foot.

"Hey, Bronsky," he ordered without bothering to disguise the anger that still pulsed through him. "Wake up."

The big man groaned, but his eyes remained closed. Tyler heaved a sigh and bent to check the biker's vital signs. His breathing seemed regular enough and his pulse was strong. But one pupil was dilated.

Possible concussion, Tyler registered before the impact hit him. No matter what Mike's intentions had been, he'd ended up injured, perhaps seriously.

Tyler had no choice but to call an ambulance. As he picked his way through the blackened and smoldering debris en route to the telephone behind the bar, he realized that the town marshal was certain to become involved. Which meant that Shuffler was sure to be contacted.

He ground his teeth at the thought of the hassle that would mean. And the publicity. He would be lucky if he didn't lose his job. Hell, he would be lucky if he didn't end up back in prison again.

He was reaching for the phone when he realized that he had more trouble than he knew. His wrist wasn't only burned. It was broken.

"Whadya do, McClane, bribe that hick marshal not to bring charges against you for assault?" Harvey Shuffler pinned Tyler with eyes that were little more than slits.

Tyler kept his gaze steady and his temper under tight control. Shuffler had been primed and ready for him when he'd arrived for his regular appointment. For the past hour the squat parole officer had been trying to shake his story.

"I told him the truth," Tyler repeated one more time. "He believed me."

"You're just damn lucky that guy Bronsky had more gas cans in his van. Otherwise, you'd be behind bars right now, waitin' for a revocation hearing."

Shuffler leaned back and began cracking his knuckles one at a time. His cubicle had no ceiling, and the noise from the other offices droned all around. Tyler waited. Under the plaster cast applied by the emergency room doctor, his wrist was hot and throbbing.

Across town, Cait and Kelsey were expecting him to take them out for pizza and a movie, after which Kelsey was to sleep over at Sarah's.

Knowing that they were waiting, perhaps worrying, had his gut in a knot and his frustration level boiling. He could barely stomach Shuffler, but the rules said he had to be polite. They didn't say he had to like it.

He glanced at the clock on the cubicle wall before saying in an even tone, "If that's all, sir, I'm late for an appointment to see my daughter."

"No, that is not all," Shuffler spat out. "You sit there and wait till I'm done with you." Shuffler finished with one hand and started cracking the knuckles on the other.

Suddenly he leaned forward to hiss into Tyler's face, "You're hiding something, buster. I can smell a lie, and the smell is on you."

"I'm not lying."

Shuffler's lips curled. "But you're hiding something, aren't you?" he said slowly, narrowing his gaze even more. "Something you don't want me to know. Now what do you suppose that could be?"

Tyler schooled his features into blankness. Shuffler was like an old coon dog he'd had once. Tenacious, but thickheaded.

"You hate me, don't you, McClane? And you hate having to answer my questions."

Tyler summoned an image of the look of happiness in Cait's eyes when he walked through her front door. If he made a mistake now, he might never see that look again.

"The rules say I have to answer them, so I do."

"Rules, hah."

Shuffler leaned back and studied Tyler's closed expression. His own expression was one of calculated cruelty. "You always follow the rules, don't you, McClane?"

"As much as you do," Tyler said evenly. The rules forbade this kind of harassment. Shuffler knew that as well as he did. Shuffler also knew that Tyler didn't dare report him.

Shuffler's eyes turned mean. "I hear you're going to get a new trial in six, seven months. That right?"

"Yes."

"Word is, the lady shrink who has custody of your kid is all of a sudden on your side. That right?"

"Yes."

"The same lady shrink who went with her sister to turn you in, right?"

"Yes."

"Makes a man wonder why, doesn't it?" Shuffler's mouth twisted into a smirk. "Course, it wouldn't look too good to the jurors in the new trial if your parole were to be revoked, would it? I mean, it would say a lot about the kind of man you were, right? If you were caught breaking the rules, I mean?"

"Depends on the rule."

"Bull! Man who breaks one rule usually breaks others. The jury would have to know about that, have to take that into consideration when they deliberated."

Pain shot up Tyler's arm, and he realized he was clenching his fingers around the rough edge of the cast. Slowly he eased open his swollen fingers. The pain lessened. Beneath the plaster, his skin still felt clammy.

Shuffler stood, signaling that, at last, Tyler was free to go. But as he got to his feet, Tyler realized that the man wasn't quite through with him.

"Take my advice, McClane. Call off the new trial."

Tyler's stony gaze angled down into Shuffler's. "Why should I do that?"

A muscle spasmed at the corner of the parole officer's fleshy mouth. "Because there's not a guy living who can keep from breaking one of the rules of his parole, not even you, Mr. Big Shot Surgeon. All I have to do is look long and hard enough and I'll find a violation. It's up to you whether or not I start looking."

"Is that a threat?"

"You might say that, yeah."

It didn't add up, Tyler thought. The man reeked of hatred, the kind that had nothing to do with his job. Hatred he could handle. Not knowing why it was directed so violently at him was something else.

"Why, Mr. Shuffler?" he demanded softly. "How come you're so intent on putting me back in prison?"

Shuffler's face suffused with color until it was beet red. "Because I've met your kind before."

"My kind?"

"Yeah, your kind. Successful, a paragon of virtue in public, a sadistic son of a bitch in private."

"Wrong. You don't know me."

"Hell, I don't! I was raised by a guy like you. He happened to be a dentist, not a doctor, but he had the same arrogant opinion of his own importance."

Tyler frowned. "You hated him, I take it."

"Yeah, I hated him, and so did my baby sister."

Now it made sense, Tyler thought with a sinking feeling. Too much sense.

"He molested her?" he guessed tonelessly.

"He sure as hell did! Didn't even wait till she was out of the crib." A terrible pain flashed for an instant in Shuffler's eyes, giving Tyler a glimpse of a man he'd never seen before. In spite of his disdain for the man, he couldn't help sympathizing.

"And you feel responsible?"

"For years I told myself it couldn't be true, what my sister claimed. Not my father, the man I idolized."

Shuffler was breathing hard, and his lips were white. Ty-r wanted to tell him to sit down before he risked a stroke. He didn't dare.

"I'm not your father," he said instead. "And I did *not* molest my daughter or anyone else. I swear it."

Shuffler's face twisted. "Yeah, so did my old man. Right up to the day my sister slashed her wrists on her sixteenth birthday."

Kelsey opened the door before the doorbell had even stopped pealing. "Daddy!" she exclaimed. "Me and Mama Cait were worried about you!"

"Sorry, baby. I got tied up."

He bent to gather her into a hug. She planted a big kiss on his cheek before snuggling against his shoulder. "That's what Mama Cait said probably happened, but I was afraid you'd had an accident or something."

"I'm always careful," he said into the baby-fine silk of her hair.

"Promise?"

"Promise."

He released his daughter and straightened. Cait stood with one hand on the newel post. As soon as he saw her smile, he relaxed. It was always that way. Some old-timers swore that prison paranoia never left a con, even when he'd been out for years.

He wanted to touch her so badly that he ached with it. At her insistence, however, they were careful not to show overt signs of affection in front of Kelsey. He understood her reasoning, even agreed with it, but it was damn hard on him at times.

He found himself smiling and realized that just the sight of her took some of the edge off his black mood. She was dressed casually in jeans and a sweater, the way he liked her best. Neither was provocative or deliberately sexy, which was why they seemed to be exactly that.

"What happened?" She allowed her gaze to settle for an instant on the cast half-hidden by his shirt cuff.

"There was a fire at the Horseshoe."

"A fire!" She grabbed his unhurt arm. "How? W anyone hurt? Are you all right?"

He rested his hand against her cheek. "It was nothing s rious. We lost some furniture and a lot of floor tiles, that all. I just got a little too close when I was putting it out."

Her fingers touched the cast. "That looks broken."

"It is. A simple fracture. Be in a cast a month, that's all.

Her gaze searched his face. Her lips trembled. Her mout was dark with worry. "But—"

"Stop worrying, Mama Cait. I'm not about to let a litt trouble keep me away from my two favorite ladies."

Kelsey beamed. "How come there was a fire, Daddy?"

"Somebody wanted to cause trouble, that's all."

"Who?"

Tyler's glance angled for an instant to Cait's face. "Yc don't know him."

"Do you?"

"Yes."

"What's his name?"

"Mike."

Cait gasped. "Oh, no," she breathed. "Not him again.

Kelsey's head swiveled toward the soft sound of h mother's distress. "Do you know that man, Mama Cait?

Cait recovered quickly and made her voice carefully c sual. "I've met him once or twice, yes."

Kelsey's gaze Ping-Ponged back to her father. "Are yc sure you're okay?"

Her eyes were round with worry. Her lips trembled. T simple expression of her caring nearly ripped him apart.

"Yes, baby. I'm fine."

Kelsey's eyes cleared. "Then can I be the first one to wri my name on your cast?"

Cait's lashes fluttered open. The clock said two-fiftee still the middle of the night, but the lamp by her bed was st burning. It took her a moment to realize why. When she di heat flooded her face and a drowsy smile curved her lips.

Slowly she turned her head. Tyler was sprawled on h back with his face turned toward her. His hair was a ha hazard tumble of wheat-and-silver strands that she knew would be soft to the touch.

His arm, the one with the cast now sporting Kelsey's name spelled out in red felt-tipped pen, was flung over his head. Even relaxed and unmoving, the sculpted muscles and corded sinew looked capable of impressive power. Or, she knew now, incredible gentleness.

Emotion blurred her gaze as she followed the line of his arm to his wide shoulder and from there to his face.

Sleep had eased some of the lines bracketing his mouth, but not all. She had a feeling nothing ever would. Suffering such as he had endured usually left behind telltale signs. In time, the harshness might fade and his smile might flash far more readily. Or so she fervently prayed.

She herself was deliciously sated, like a cat basking in the sun on a spring day. Her nipples were still slightly swollen from Tyler's kisses, and her body ached in special, intimate ways.

It was the first time he had been in her bed. Since Kelsey wouldn't be returning from Sarah's slumber party until midmorning, it was also the first time they'd had the freedom to make love without worrying about being interrupted.

Still, it wouldn't be long before he had to leave. The workers were coming at seven to begin repairs on the Lucky Horseshoe, and he had to be there to let them in.

Slowly, so as not to wake him, she inched closer until she felt the warmth of his breath on her face. His mouth was slightly open and far more relaxed than it had been since he'd arrived hours earlier.

The covers were bunched below his waist, as though, in his sleep, he had gotten too warm. His bare chest seemed very dark against the pale yellow sheet. Tiny male nipples nestled in swirls of silky hair invited the exploration of her tongue one more time.

Cait slid her hand along the mattress until it was close enough to his chest to feel the heat that emanated from him. Smiling, she reached out to touch him—not to arouse, she told herself, but simply to reassure herself that he was really there. Before her fingers brushed his skin, however, he suddenly groaned and turned onto his side.

Cait froze. Was he in pain? Maybe he was hurt more seriously than he knew. Even a simple fracture was vulnerable to infection.

As though he'd sensed her worry, his eyes opened and looked into hers. Instantly he seemed wide-awake and alert. There was no sleepy fluttering of his thick lashes, no yawning, no easing into consciousness the way she had to do before she could function.

Cait was astonished, but perhaps she shouldn't have been. As an intern and then as a resident he had spent years on call. And when the call had come, more often than not, as a surgeon, he would have had to act quickly and decisively. Some habits were hard to break, even though they were no longer necessary, she told herself as she fought a pang of sadness.

"Hi," she said softly.

"Hi, yourself." His good arm hooked around her bare back, trapping her. She used her shoulder to caress the flare of his biceps, which hardened instantly, thrilling her with the tremendous strength of him, strength that he always held in check when he was holding her.

"Mmm, I like having you in my bed."

"Oh, you do, do you?" He began stroking her spine.

Cait smiled at the quick, urgent desire that invaded her breasts and weakened her thighs.

"Mmm." Her voice instantly kindled smoldering heat in his smoky eyes.

"Mmm what?" His fingers made sensuous forays over the curve of her buttocks.

"Mmm, I think I like that even better." She leaned close enough to brush a kiss over his mouth. "And I like the way you smile at me right before you make love to me. You should do that more often."

His mouth took on a vulnerable softness. "Smile at you or make love to you?"

"Both." She pressed closer until she could feel the eroti-
lly rough rubbing of his chest hair against her nipples
rough the silk teddy.

His hand cupped the back of her head while his mouth
ok hers repeatedly. At the same time he pulled her lower
the pillows until she was lying prone and quivering in the
ddle of her own bed.

His chest loomed over her, a magnificent living sculpture
muscle and bone and sinew. But it was the hunger in his
es that enthralled her. It was the hunger raging in her own
dy that had her reaching for him. He came to her in-
ntly.

His breath was warm on her neck as he pressed arousing
sses into the hollow of her throat. She gasped as his tongue
pped into her ear. Leisurely he explored the small folds
fore retreating, leaving her trembling and wanting.

"More?" he whispered in a voice so husky it enchanted
r. At the same time, he moved and she felt the pressure of
hot arousal against her thigh.

She shifted until she could rub against the hot hard flesh.
e skin stretching so taut there was as soft as velvet, one
nature's contradictions. His body shuddered as though
had just been lashed hard. His arm tightened around her
til her face was pressed to his chest and his thigh trapped
s.

"God help me," he muttered against her throat. "I want
make it good for you, but—"

She kissed his nipple and watched it harden. Her fingers
oked the line of his back, testing the change in texture
m smooth to hair rough. Her hand dipped lower, mold-
g over the tight, hard-packed muscle. He shuddered again,
is time against her breast.

His mouth wet the silk of her teddy as his tongue lapped
st one nipple into a painful tightness, then the other.
easure ran like warm water along the midline of her belly
the exquisitely sensitive mound between her legs.

His mouth was hot and wanting on her skin, alternately
pping and kissing her until she was engulfed in hot, flam-
g need.

"You feel so good," Tyler murmured against her sk
"So good."

He was nearly drowning in sensations. His musc
burned with the effort of holding back. His breathing w
an agony clawing at his chest. Sweat beaded his forehe
and dampened his torso.

He wanted this night to last forever, but the hot pressu
in his loins threatened even his powerful control. Bendi
again to take her mouth, he slipped his hands under the si
veil keeping her skin from his and slipped it over her hea

Using his tongue, he tasted the salt around her nipples a
the sweet moisture pearling beneath her breasts.

Lost in the swirl of sensation and need, Cait let her fi
gers clutch at his neck, his hair, his shoulders. The heat
his body and the musk of his arousal were nearly driving h
mad.

She writhed desperately, driven by an insatiable need. S
tried to speak, but the hot sweet need running through h
made her breathless. Instead, with shaking fingers, she s
her hand along his hard flank to the velvety hardne
pressed against her thigh.

The sweet pressure of her fingers against his distend
flesh undid him. Fiery need clawed into him until he w
powerless to resist.

He tried to tell her that he needed her so much it sca
him, but the words were locked behind the tension in l
throat. Instead, he lovingly spread her legs and position
himself above the soft, quivering mound that was so eag
to welcome him.

She tossed her head from side to side on the pillow. H
eyes were closed, her lashes dark against her flushed chee
her lips parted and swollen from his. Her breath came
husky gasps.

Bracing himself on his good arm, he eased into her
slowly as his screaming nerves would permit. He kept l
own eyes open and riveted on her passion-softened fe
tures. As he filled her to his full length, his name trembl
on her mouth so caressingly that it brought a lump to l
throat.

Her lashes fluttered open, and her passion-drenched gaze sought his face. He became a man enthralled, driven by the urge to mate. He held himself tightly within her, rocking back and forth to the rhythm of her small, eager responses.

He was utterly sensitive to her, moving to her direction, subjecting his own body to hers. So fierce was his concentration that he knew a split second before she did when the tension burst inside her, sending her head arching backward and her nails raking his shoulders.

Even as he cried out her name, he poured himself into her in a torrent of hot, desperate need that was at the same time incredibly sweet.

Holding her, caressing her, he felt the aftershocks take her in gentle, shuddering spasms. As he bent to kiss her again, a feeling he didn't recognize surged through him, gentling him.

He rolled to his back and folded her against his chest. With his good hand he pulled the sheet over their sweat-slicked bodies and rubbed his face against her soft, hot cheek.

Cait snuggled closer, too spent for words. Beneath her cheek, his heart thudded in a powerful rhythm that even now had only slowed a few beats from its frantic, sex-driven pounding.

The motion of his hand slowly running up and down her spine was seductive and soothing, as soothing as his deep, even breathing and the rich, potent scent of him still clinging to her skin.

He didn't have to be a doctor to win her respect. Or rich. Or any of the things he thought women wanted. She smiled, but deep inside a small niggling thought took root and refused to be dislodged. What if he didn't win an acquittal? it prodded. What if the judge never changed his sentence? What then?

She shivered so violently that Tyler's arms closed tightly around her. "Cold?" he murmured in a drowsy voice that brought tears to her eyes.

"Mmm," she answered, snuggling closer. "Go to sleep, darling. We have three more hours."

Chapter 13

"Smells like a damn camp fire in here." Dante cast critical look at the half-completed repairs and grimaced "How can you stand it?"

Tyler rested his sore forearm on the bar and shrugged "You can get used to anything, if you have to."

Dante's gaze came back to his face. "How long before the repairs are finished?"

"Three, four days. By Tuesday for sure."

Dante toyed with the half-full glass of beer in front him. "Courthouse scuttlebutt says the county DA's gonn come down heavy on your buddy Bronsky. Breaking an entering, arson, attempted murder."

"So I hear."

"He talk to you about testifying?"

"Yes, last night. I said I would."

Dante's expression said that he'd expected as much. "D you tell him about the attack outside Cait's office?"

"No."

"Might make a difference in proving motive."

"Seems to me that's pretty much proven already." Tyler folded his shirtsleeve another turn. As he did, he saw the crawling signature on his cast. *Kelsey Caitlin McClane.*

Crystal had wanted to call their baby Caitlin. He had refused. Caitlin McClane aroused images of someone else in his mind. Images he had vowed on his wedding day to banish forever. Now, however, they were back to tantalize and torment him all over again.

Dante reached over the bar to snag another fish taco. Because Tyler had spent all his free time with Cait and Kelsey, he and Dante hadn't had dinner for several months. Both men had missed the hours they'd spent together, though neither would admit it to the other.

"You got a reason to be so generous toward a man who tried to burn you alive?"

"I don't want Cait involved in any of this. She'd have to be if the DA started nosing deeper." Tyler slugged down half the contents of the drink he'd fixed earlier.

"For God's sake, Ty—"

Dante caught the swift, cold look Tyler was aiming his way and scowled. "I hope the lady knows how much you are about her," he muttered before washing down the taco with the rest of his beer.

Without commenting, Tyler refilled Dante's glass.

"How's Kelsey?" the attorney asked.

"Good. She turns nine on Saturday."

"So I've heard at least a dozen times." Dante took a hefty swallow before wiping the foam from his upper lip with his tongue.

Tyler flexed his fingers against the plaster cast. The pain was minimal now, but the damn thing was beginning to itch. "I asked Shuffler last week for permission to attend the party tomorrow. The bastard still hasn't given me an answer."

"Be patient, Ty. He doesn't have a valid reason to deny permission so he's just trying to make you sweat before he has to give in."

Tyler glanced toward the door he kept open most of the time now in an attempt to air the place. From the looks of

the deeply blue, cloudless sky, it was a glorious day out
side, and it suddenly occurred to him that it was spring. The
hills weren't yet green, but wildflowers were blooming.

He found himself wondering if Cait would like to walk th
hills with him someday soon. When he was free to ask he
for a date without worrying, that is. When he was free to d
a lot of things.

"Jess, tell me the truth. Am I just kidding myself, think
ing I might be able to practice medicine again? If we win ii
court, I mean?"

Without seeming to, Dante studied Tyler's harsh profil
in the mirror behind the bar. The past weeks had change
his friend. Mostly by tempering some of his bitterness, bu
in other ways, too. He didn't seem as restless. His eyes ha
more expression.

"I don't know, Ty. And that's the truth. Cases like thi
depend too much on the human factor."

Tyler's brows pulled into a frown. "What the hell doe
that mean?"

"In a way, the licensing board is a lot like the parol
board. Sometimes they have too much latitude in interpret
ing the facts and not enough sense to interpret them prop
erly."

"Meaning?"

"Meaning that their personal biases can sometimes get i
the way. We could go in there with irrefutable evidenc
proving that you were shafted by your ex-wife and still ge
one stubborn, opinionated jerk who's already made up hi
mind and refuses to change it under pain of death."

"Like that bastard Shuffler."

Dante nodded. He knew all about Ty's continual hassl
with his parole officer and the reason behind it. "One thin
I've learned, buddy," he murmured into his beer. "Life ain'
always fair."

Dante didn't so much as glance at the neatly pinned empt
sleeve of his sweater. He didn't have to. Tyler knew exactl
what he was thinking.

Dante turned his glass around and around, trying to fin
a way to bring up a touchy subject. Push Tyler McClane to

far and he withdrew to a place where not even God himself could reach him. And yet this was too important to bury. Finally he told himself that he had to risk Ty's wrath, no matter how icy he became.

He took a quick swallow of beer before saying softly, "You're sleeping with Cait Fielding, aren't you?"

"Is there a reason for that question?" Tyler's voice was clipped.

"Yes, and don't bother to tell me to mind my own business. In case you've forgotten, getting you acquitted *is* my business."

"So?"

"Do you have any idea what Lamont would do to her if he knew?"

"Kelsey's willing to testify. Hazel will corroborate her story. You don't need Cait's testimony."

"The hell I don't. I'd sell my Mercedes for at least one more corroborating witness."

"Cait's still a credible witness."

"Like hell. Not if the two of you are sexually involved."

Tyler walked to the end of the bar and poured himself a cup of stale coffee. It burned his throat and churned in his gut.

It had been four days since he'd seen Cait. Four days since he'd held her and kissed her and listened to her quiet breathing in the healing silence of her bedroom.

He missed her like hell. He thought about her almost constantly. Not even the hard physical labor he'd put in on the repairs helped. The worst times were at night. The loneliness crowded him badly then, just as it had in prison.

"I think she's falling in love with me."

When Dante blistered the air with a creative curse, Tyler realized to his chagrin that he'd spoken his thought aloud. "Yeah, I know," he said with a crooked grin. "The lady deserves a lot better."

"I hope to hell the lady knows what she's taking on."

Tyler thought about the soft, sweet passion in her eyes and wanted to groan in frustration. A fair number of women had wanted him, but none had ever made him feel as special and strong as Cait could with just a smile.

That realization had him lying awake for the past three nights, wondering how he could find the strength to walk away from her if he lost in court again.

Tyler drained his cup and set it on the sink before returning to his customary spot near the end of the long, scarred bar. Opposite, Dante watched him with brooding eyes.

"How about the lady? How do you feel about her?"

Tyler stared at the shallow groove worn in the wooden flooring behind the bar where countless guys like him had walked while tending to the customers out front. It wasn't a bad life for some guys. For him, it was just another kind of prison, one he wouldn't ask anyone to share.

"Don't worry, Jess. Until I know if I have a future or not, I can't afford to feel anything."

Dante sat without moving for an instant, his thoughts turning his eyes very dark and still. And then, with one swift movement of his strong hand, he lifted the glass to his mouth and drained it before slamming it onto the bar again.

"Hit me again, buddy. I feel the need to get very, very drunk this afternoon."

Tyler glanced at his unfinished drink. "You and me both," he said with a short laugh as he reached for Dante's glass.

"Go ahead, McClane," called a voice from the doorway. "I would purely love to see you drunk on your ass. So would the parole board."

Tyler stood motionless, watching Harvey Shuffler amble into the Horseshoe as though he owned the damn place. Dante muttered an obscene opinion of the fat man's sexual proclivities under his breath before swiveling to watch his swaggering approach.

Tyler wholeheartedly agreed with his friend and looked forward to the day when he would be free to tell Shuffler to go to hell.

"This is a surprise," Tyler said when Shuffler was close enough for him to smell the sweat staining the underarms of his limp white shirt.

"Rules say I have to make occasional surprise visits to the parolees under my jurisdiction."

"So they do." Tyler glanced at the bottles arrayed on glass shelves behind him. "You want a drink?"

Shuffler glanced at the half-full glass near Tyler's loosely coiled fist. "Maybe I'll just finish this one," he said with a sly look. He lifted the glass and sniffed. A frown crossed his face before he took a tentative sip.

"Tonic," he muttered with a sneer. "Damn sissy's drink."

He slammed the drink to the bar and glared across its expanse at Tyler's carefully expressionless face.

"Think you got me, don't you, McClane? Think you put one over on me, huh?"

Tyler leaned against the counter and crossed his arms over his chest. "I don't think you know my attorney, Jess Dante."

Shuffler's gaze touched Dante's face briefly before angling brazenly to Dante's empty sleeve. "You're the race driver, right?"

"*Ex*-race driver."

"I hear you scored McClane here a new trial. Promised the judge new evidence, right?"

Dante raised one devil-black eyebrow. "That's privileged information."

"Nothin's privileged when it comes to one of my parolees, counselor."

"A matter of opinion, Shuffler."

"Correction, counselor. It's a matter of law. Just like your buddy here, I'm an expert on the rules." Shuffler slanted Tyler a hooded glance. Tyler stared back at him without reacting.

"Let me give you some advice, Shuffler," Dante said in a voice that was suddenly sharp and commanding. "Keep whatever you've heard about this case to yourself. And I mean all to yourself. Otherwise you just might be opening yourself up to a charge of obstructing justice."

"Let me give *you* some advice, counselor. Don't count on this case ever getting to trial."

Tyler heard a new confidence in Shuffler's voice and went cold inside. Nothing showed on his face, however, as he asked Shuffler if he'd like to take a look around. "As part of your inspection," he added.

"Nah, I've gotten everything I needed this trip." He grinned to himself, as though he found his own words particularly amusing. Tyler fought a quick battle with his pride and lost.

"What about Kelsey's party?"

"Oh, yeah, I almost forgot," Shuffler replied readily, as though he had been expecting the question. "I've got your request on my desk. Been meaning to call you about it."

Tyler waited, but inside his temper was prodding him.

"Aren't you going to ask me what I decided?" Shuffler asked when it became obvious that Tyler wasn't going to speak.

Tyler caught the warning look Dante sent him and managed to rein in his rage. "What have you decided?" he asked in a flat tone.

Shuffler smirked. "Go ahead and go, McClane. Have a *wonderful* time."

With a nod toward Dante and another smirking smile, Shuffler ambled off. A few seconds after he'd disappeared through the open door, Tyler heard the sound of a car being started in the parking lot, followed by the receding drone of a badly tuned motor.

He and Dante exchanged looks. "That bastard was enjoying himself," Tyler muttered.

Dante's eyes narrowed. "It's almost like he knows something we don't and can't wait to spring it on us. Or rather, on you."

"He's bluffing."

"I don't think so." Dante frowned. "Did you tell him that there were going to be other children at the party?"

Tyler nodded. "Cait even gave me the names."

"Who else is coming?"

"Dr. O'Connor and Kelsey's regular baby-sitter."

"No one else?"

"As far as I know."

Dante's mouth flattened. "I don't like it, Ty. That guy is trouble with a capital *T*."

"Yeah, and he's all mine for another seven months at least."

Dante drummed his fingers on the bar. In his eyes, the look of suspicion deepened. "How would you feel about missing the party this year?"

Tyler's head came up, and his eyes slitted. "I've missed too many already."

"Kelsey would understand."

"No she wouldn't. Neither would Cait."

Dante heard the warning in his friend's voice and backed off. It was becoming more and more apparent that Ty had a blind spot when it came to the two females, mother and daughter, who had become his family in every way but legally.

Even as Dante turned the conversation to something else, he made a private vow to do some checking into Harvey Shuffler's comings and goings. Two could play that bastard's game.

It was already close to midnight. If he didn't leave now, he wouldn't get to Sutter Creek before dawn.

"Sweetheart, have a heart. It's a long cold drive."

"Just one more kiss."

Tyler groaned, and Cait's mouth became fluid under his. He ran his tongue over her curving bottom lip. She tasted of the rich Beaujolais she'd had after dinner.

He wrapped his arms around her shoulders, holding her tight, and buried his face in the curve of her neck. She buried her face against his shoulder and held on to him. She felt him smile against her skin.

"I can't seem to get enough of you," he murmured. Trembling, she drew back and waited until he opened his eyes to look with fevered hunger into hers.

"I wish you didn't have to go."

"So do I." Tyler ran his hands through the thick, shimmering length of her hair, trying to repair the damage his

fingers had so recently caused. "And right now, before I
forget everything but making love to you."

"Mmm, sounds promising." She turned her head to
brush a kiss over his wrist.

"No more, woman. Remember, I'm five years older than
you. I need my rest."

Cait smiled, wanting to tell him that she would take him
with or without the sex. "Then give me a hug, old man, and
get out of here before I remember a lady never seduces a reluctant man."

"Reluctant, hell," he muttered as he pulled her into his
arms and kissed her temple. "I'm damn near numb. After
all those years of celibacy, a man needs time to build up his
stamina."

"You're certainly working on it," she whispered into the
worn collar of his jacket. The laughter she felt rumbling in
his chest warmed her almost as much as his body heat.

"Maybe tomorrow, after the party, we can work on it
again."

"You're on," she murmured as she drew out of his arms.

Tyler tugged his hat over his brow and reached past her
to open her front door. The air was spring soft and smelled
of the daffodils in the planter box on the steps. A crescent
moon was just rising over the trees.

"Drive safely," she murmured as she fussed with his collar.

Tyler glanced down at the arousal that refused to subside. "Slowly, anyway."

Cait laughed. "Come early tomorrow. I'm going to
need—" She was interrupted by the sound of a child in distress.

"Kelsey!" Cait cried. "It must be another nightmare."

Tyler slammed the door and was up the stairs first, with
Cait right behind him. This time Kelsey was sitting up in a
tangle of covers, but the terror in her eyes was achingly familiar.

As soon as Tyler came through the door, she lifted her
arms to him. "Daddy, Daddy," she wailed.

He crushed her against him. Sobbing, she buried her face
the crook between his neck and his shoulder. Tyler tossed
f his hat before lowering his head to hers.

"Easy, baby," he murmured as his big hand rubbed her
ck. "Don't cry. I've got you." With the hand in the cast
awkwardly pulled the bright coverlet over the child's bare
s and smoothed it tight.

Kelsey shuddered. "I h-hate dreams, Daddy. I wish I'd
ver have another one."

"Not all dreams are bad, baby." Tyler's gaze met Cait's
er the child's tousled head.

"Mine are."

"Mine were, too, for a long time. But now they're not.
t when I have you and Mama Cait to make me feel good
side."

Kelsey was crying steadily now, her tears wetting his neck.
ler held her close and whispered soothing words. Min-
s passed while, gradually, the sobs lessened to an occa-
nal hiccup.

"Better now?" Tyler asked. She shook her head but
dn't look at him. "What's bothering you, baby?" he
obed gently. "Maybe I can help if you tell me what it is.
at's what daddies are for, you know. To keep the bad
ings away."

Slowly Kelsey raised her head and looked at her father.
You'll be mad," she muttered in a low, halting tone.

Tyler smoothed her hair. "No, I won't."

"Even if it's... awful?"

"Especially if it's awful."

Kelsey ducked her head against her father and sobbed as
ough she were being beaten. Even as Tyler soothed her, his
ze swung to Cait's.

"Kelsey, talk to us, sweetie," Cait whispered as she sat
wn next to Tyler and stroked the little girl's leg.

"I c-can't. Daddy'll hate me for sure this time." Cait bit
r lip and gave Tyler an agonized look.

"Please, Kelsey," Tyler said very softly. "It hurts me
en you won't talk to me."

Kelsey blinked. "Please, don't make me tell," she blurt
out. "Please don't. I know I should, and I want to, bu
c-can't, I just can't."

She crumpled into Tyler's arms, a small shivering bund
in pink. "Tell?" he asked in a too-quiet tone. "Tell wh
Button?"

"T-tell the judge and those men that I lied. Plea
Daddy, I just *can't*."

"Then you don't have to," he said gently.

"Don't say that," Cait whispered to him. "She's j
nervous. She'll be fine, won't you, Kels?"

Kelsey shook her head. "P-people who lie have terri
things happen, just like my mommy."

Cait felt a chill. Crystal was dead because she'd had t
much champagne and driven recklessly. "Kels, sweet
that's not true. Mommy's car hit a slick patch on the str
That's why she's dead."

"No, no!" Kelsey cried. "She's dead 'cause she was ba
and if I tell everyone how bad I really am, something te
ble will happen to me, too. Just like Mommy."

Tyler and Cait exchanged agonized looks. To an adu
mind, Kelsey's reasoning was flawed. To a child's it v
unerringly logical.

Tyler closed his eyes on a wave of pure rage. Crystal h
won again. Without meaning to, she'd had the last word

"Baby, listen to me," he murmured close to Kelsey's e
"I give you my word. No one will make you testify if y
don't want to. Not me or Mama Cait or Auntie Hazel."

"You won't be mad?" Kelsey mumbled haltingly.

"None of us will be mad. I give you my word."

"You won't h-hate me?"

Tyler's control nearly shattered. His chest heaved, and
jaw clenched. It took several long deep breaths before
could speak calmly. "You're the best thing that ever ha
pened in my life, Kelsey McClane. I loved you when I s
you, and now that I know you better, I love you even mo
Nothing you could do will ever change that. Nothing."

Kelsey's head rose slowly. An expression of uncertainty pinched her features, but the abject misery was gone from her eyes. "Maybe w-when I get older I could do it. Okay?"

"Sure, baby." Tyler's hand shook as he ever so gently wiped the tears from his daughter's cheeks. "Maybe in a few years. But let's not worry about that now. Right now, let's just make a deal that you won't ever have to testify. Okay?"

"Okay."

Kelsey threw trusting arms around her daddy's neck. Her daddy's arms closed around her, keeping her safe.

Chapter 14

The phone rang as Tyler was walking out of his apartment. Habit had him answering before the third ring. It was Dante.

"Thank God I caught you. We may have trouble."

Tyler glanced at the birthday present under his arm. It was a set of clothes for Prudence that he'd had made by a local seamstress.

"What kind of trouble?"

"I just found out that Shuffler paid Bronsky a visit in the county jail on the same day he visited you. According to one of the deputies there, he stayed over an hour and came out looking like a mangy old cat who'd just eaten his fill."

"Damn."

"My guess is that Shuffler knows everything Bronsky knows."

Tyler's mouth went dry, and his hand all but crushed the carefully wrapped package. "So why hasn't he used it against me?"

"Lots of reasons. He needs more evidence, the paperwork to order your arrest is going through channels, Bron-

y is demanding some kind of deal in exchange for his *s*timony against you. Take your pick.''

Tyler hated the way his insides were churning at the *t*hought of going to prison again. ''Thanks for the word,'' *h*e told Dante tersely.

''Welcome.'' There was a pause before Dante added, '*W*atch your back, partner.''

''Will do.''

''Wish the kid a happy birthday for me. And give Caitlin *a* big kiss from her old buddy Dante.''

Tyler's reply was succinct and rude. Dante hung up *l*aughing.

''Thank God for VCRs and Walt Disney,'' Cait muttered *a*s she dumped the last of the dirty paper plates into the *tr*ash. ''We have almost an hour to regroup before it's time *t*o open the presents.''

Tyler finished putting the last of the milk-sticky glasses *in*to the dishwasher and shoved the door closed. ''I'm still *tr*ying to figure out how six little girls could demolish an *en*tire cake and a half-gallon of ice cream in less than ten *m*inutes.''

Cait laughed. ''Not quite all,'' she reminded him. ''Kels *in*sisted that you have the biggest piece.''

''She's bribing me into taking her to see the circus next *w*eek.''

''What do you mean? You told me you already have the *ti*ckets.''

His grin flashed, almost as boyishly as it once had years *a*go. ''Yeah, but she doesn't know that.''

''Hmm, very devious.''

''Not at all. I'm outnumbered around here, remember? *E*specially today, with Hazel bossing me around almost as *m*uch as you and Kels. A guy has to fight for survival any *w*ay he can.''

Cait closed the lid of the trash bucket and went to him. '*'*Poor Tyler. I thought you were enjoying it.''

His fingers smoothed the hair away from her face. Be*ca*use he'd told her once while they'd been making love that

he loved her hair loose, she wore it that way whenever ┃
was expected.

"I am. As soon as the birthday girl is safely in bed t┃
night and everyone else has gone home, I intend to let ye┃
boss me around a lot more. In bed, this time."

Cait blushed. "I'm not the demanding one," she grum┃
bled, despite a rush of pleasure.

"Oh no? Could'a fooled me." Tyler's slowly archi┃
eyebrow gave him a devilish look that Cait could never ┃
sist.

"Maybe you'll be too tired. After all, you must ha┃
helped me string miles of crepe paper."

"Not to mention all the balloons you made me blow up.┃

Cait's gaze lingered on his mouth. "Hmm, I hear i┃
good practice," she murmured in her best sultry tone.

The lines around his eyes crinkled, but his eyes remaine┃
strangely watchful. "Yeah? For what?"

"Kissing, for one thing."

"Is that an order?" His tone was teasing, but Cait hea┃
an echo of his earlier bitterness.

"No, an invitation," she murmured.

"In that case, I accept." This time the smile he gave h┃
was also mirrored in his eyes an instant before his mou┃
aligned with hers.

His kiss was infinitely gentle, and yet she felt the sma┃
shudder that went through him the moment their mout┃
met. She had expected the kiss to deepen, to turn hungry th┃
way his kisses invariably did.

But this time he seemed content with gently exploring h┃
mouth with his lips and his tongue. He tasted of chocola┃
and the coffee he'd consumed by the gallons. She knew sh┃
tasted of orange soda.

His arms circled her waist in the possessive, masterful wa┃
that was familiar to her now. She arched closer until h┃
breasts were pressed against his chest.

In response his hands slid lower to cup her buttocks a┃
lift her hard against him. At the same time his tongue gen┃
ly ran over her lips until she parted them eagerly.

His tongue made slow, thrusting movements until she was nearly mindless. Slowly, sweetly, she felt her body melting into the strength of his.

When he raised his head, his face was flushed and his eyes glittered. "Later," he murmured.

Dazed by the sensations running through her, Cait managed an understanding nod. "You're right, darn it. No wonder most of the parents I see in my office have a haggard look. They're always being interrupted."

She reached up to tidy the shaggy thatch from his forehead. It seemed to have a mind of its own and resisted every effort to tame its rebellion.

"You could use a haircut," she murmured with a wifely look in her eyes that sent him reeling.

"Next week."

She grinned. "Lord, you're—"

"Stubborn. I think we've already established that."

"I think you made a mistake telling Kelsey she didn't have to testify."

"We've already established that, too." This time his voice carried an edge. Cait knew she was precariously close to pushing him too far. But this time she decided to risk his cold withdrawal.

"It could be years before she's ready to testify, years you could have spent practicing medicine."

"If Jess manages a miracle, all that will be academic. In the meantime, her phobia gives Hazel an excuse to keep her in therapy and I can keep my visitation privileges."

"What if Jess is fresh out of miracles? What if my testimony and Hazel's aren't enough?"

"They will be. They have to be."

"Tyler, please listen to me."

His finger touched her mouth. "No, Cait. I need you to go along with me on this. Please."

"But—" She was interrupted by the sudden bonging of the front doorbell.

"I hope that's not one of the mothers," she murmured as she tried to slip from his arms. But his hands tightened.

"Hazel will get it."

"Yes, but—"

At that moment the kitchen door swung open. Afte
casting an uneasy look over her shoulder, Hazel slipped in
side before closing it firmly behind her again. As her gaz
went from one to the other, Cait could have sworn that Ha
zel had just witnessed a dreadful accident.

"What is it?" she cried softly. "What's wrong?"

"That man Shuffler is at the door, with a U.S. marshal
He says he's here to arrest Tyler for violating his parole."

"I want my d-daddy," Kelsey was curled into a ba
around her pillow, crying as though her heart was break
ing. Prudence lay within arm's reach, clothed now in th
green velvet dress and bustle Tyler had given her.

"I know, sweetie. I do, too."

Cait drew a ragged breath. Her eyes burned from lack o
sleep, and her stomach was still queasy. The ice cream an
cake she'd eaten over twelve hours ago were only a distan
memory. Even though she'd fixed a snack for Kelsey an
Hazel around supper time, she herself hadn't been able t
eat more than a few bites.

Kelsey threw her pillow aside and used Cait's lap instead
"I hate that fat little man with the loud voice. He's nastie
than the bad guys on TV."

Cait couldn't have agreed more heartily. Her finger
trembled as she gently wiped the tears from the little girl'
hot cheeks.

"Remember what Hazel and I told you, Kels? That ma
was just doing his job. Daddy was the one who broke th
rules."

"But he couldn't let that guy Bronsky hurt you! Eve
Auntie Hazel said that, and you agreed."

"It's...complicated, sweetie. A lot like life, actually
Sometimes, no matter how much you want something, yo
can't seem to make it happen."

"Why not?" Kelsey's eyes were troubled.

"That's a good question, sweetie. A lot of smart peopl
have been asking it for as many years as people have been o

this earth. I'm not sure anyone has ever come up with a good answer."

"What do *you* think?" Kelsey persisted.

"I think your daddy needs us to be strong for him."

Curiosity flashed through the misery in Kelsey's red-rimmed eyes. "How?"

Cait drew a long breath. "By smiling when we go to visit him in the jail and by telling him we love him."

"Do you love him, too?" Kelsey asked as though the thought pleased her.

"Very much."

"Really and truly?"

Cait touched her fingertip to Kelsey's button nose. "Really and truly."

"Maybe you and him can get married, and then he could live here with us 'n' be here in the morning when I wake up 'n' be here at night to tuck me in."

Cait kept her features calm, but inside she felt a familiar sinking feeling. "I wish that were possible, Kelsey. Maybe someday it will be, but not now."

Kelsey frowned. "Why not?"

Cait tried to clear the tears from her throat. "Because it's very possible—very probable, in fact—that Daddy will have to go back to prison."

Crushing fear took the hope from the child's eyes. "Because of that man who put the handcuffs on Daddy's wrists?"

"Partly. And partly because Daddy really did break the rules."

"But that man was hurting him—"

"It isn't only that, sweetie. Daddy did something else he shouldn't have done." Cait drew Prudence closer until the prim little doll was sitting in Kelsey's lap. "Daddy gave you this doll, not Santa."

Kelsey looked both surprised and pleased. "I thought you did!" she exclaimed.

Cait smiled. "And all this time I thought you believed in Santa Claus."

Kelsey ducked her head. "Mommy said he wasn't real. She said only dumb little boys and girls believed in Santa Claus."

Anger swelled through Cait. Damn you, Crystal, she raged silently.

"She's wrong, Kels. Santa Claus might not be a real person who goes around putting presents under the tree, but he is the spirit of generosity and kindness and loving one another that Christmas is really about. Can you understand that?" Kelsey nodded, but her eyes were still wide.

Cait cleared her throat. "It was in that same spirit that your daddy came to this house on Christmas Eve to bring you Prudence, so in a sense she really did come from Santa."

Kelsey looked troubled. "That's not a bad thing, is it?"

Cait's gaze dropped to the valuable doll. Tears filled her eyes as she fingered the hem of the new clothes Tyler had had made. "Wanting to give you a present was a wonderful thing, sweetie. But Daddy shouldn't have brought it here to the house."

"Why not?"

"It's complicated, so try hard to understand, okay?" Kelsey's head bobbed, but she looked worried.

"When the judge sent Daddy to jail, he also told him that he could never come to see you again or phone you or be in the same place where you were without permission."

It sounded brutally cruel to her now. At the time she had fervently lauded the judge's courage. "On Christmas Eve, when Daddy came here, he didn't have that permission. So even though he had a good reason, he *was* breaking the rules, and someone found out."

Kelsey's forehead was wrinkled in concentration, but the look in her eyes told Cait that she understood. "Who found out, that fat little man?"

"Yes, eventually. But the man who told him was the same man Daddy had a fight with. The same man who tried to burn down the place where Daddy works."

"How did *he* find out?"

Cait used the sheet to wipe her eyes. They still burned, but
ot from tears.

"Apparently he'd been following Daddy again, looking
r an opportunity to hurt him. According to Mr. Dante,
addy's attorney, Bronsky saw Daddy talking to me at the
oor, and so he knew who lived in this house. And since I
e here, Shuffler figured out that you did, too."

"Like in the spy movies?"

"Exactly. So what Daddy did is called contempt of court,
d judges usually hate it when that happens."

"So the judge will send Daddy back to prison to punish
m because he was bad?" Kelsey's voice was very thin. Cait
ew that this had merely served to reenforce Kelsey's con-
ction that terrible things happened to bad people. But it
as more important that she understand what had hap-
ned in the middle of her happy party.

"It's up to the parole board now, but yes, that's proba-
y what's going to happen."

"For... for how long?"

"Mr. Dante says three years, maybe more."

Kelsey stared straight ahead, but her arms tightened
ound the fragile doll until Prudence was nearly bent dou-
e. "So... so it's really my fault this time, too, isn't it?"

"No, sweetie, *no!* Daddy wanted to give you Prudence
cause he loves you. But the mistake was his, not yours."

Cait glanced at the picture hanging on Kelsey's wall. It
as a photo of Cait, Crystal and Kelsey. For the first time
ait noticed how Crystal had put herself in the middle in-
ad of her daughter.

"If there's anyone to blame, Kelsey, it's your mother. She
as a grown-up. She knew right from wrong, but she did
rong by lying about your daddy and by talking you into
ing, too."

Kelsey stared at her. Very gently Cait pried the child's
ngers from the doll and straightened Prudence's rumpled
rb. The doll's blue eyes stared straight ahead, very much
e Kelsey was staring. Unlike Kelsey's face, however, the
oll's porcelain features still reflected serenity.

"Mama Cait?"

Cait realized that Kelsey was now looking at her. "Ye[s]
sweetie?"

"Do you think . . . I mean, maybe, if I tell those men [o]
the . . . the—" She gestured helplessly, and Cait smiled as s[he]
supplied the right words.

"Parole board."

"Do you think if I tell them that Daddy didn't do ba[d]
things like Mommy said, they might not send him back [to]
prison?"

Cait's heart seemed to stop for an instant before gallo[p]-
ing furiously. "I don't know. Is that what you want to do?"

Kelsey's head bobbed tentatively at first, then more a[s]-
sertively. "I want Daddy to come home."

"Daddy doesn't expect you to tell anyone anything. R[e]-
member the pact you made?"

"That was before."

"Nothing's changed, Kels. You'll still have to say und[er]
oath and in front of a lot of people that you lied. You mig[ht]
even get your picture in the paper, and then Sarah and a[ll]
your friends will know that you lied."

It was very clear from the sudden fear in Kelsey's eyes th[at]
that hadn't occurred to her. Cait knew she might be throw[-]
ing away Tyler's only chance. Nevertheless, she had to ma[ke]
sure that Kelsey understood exactly what testifying cou[ld]
mean to her.

"I don't care," Kelsey said with the defiant jut of her ch[in]
that she'd inherited from her father.

"Daddy might go to prison anyway, no matter what y[ou]
say."

"But he might not."

A child's thinking was so uncomplicated, Cait though[t.]
If only hers could be that way. She knew all too well, ho[w-]
ever, the odds Tyler was fighting.

If he'd been convicted of burglary or embezzlement [or]
even selling dope, the board would be more inclined to [be]
lenient, given the terrible overcrowding in California pr[is]-
ons. But sex crimes against children were universally a[b]-
horred. Rightfully so, Cait knew. But Tyler wasn't guilty[.]

"Mama Cait? You think I should testify, don't you?"

Cait dropped her gaze to her daughter's face. Yes, yes, *es,* she wanted to shout. *Because I know better than you do* *hat another stretch in prison will do to your daddy.*

"I think this decision has to be yours, and yours alone," *ie* said calmly. But inside her stomach was churning, and *er* throat ached to release the words in her heart.

Kelsey bit her lip and stared at the wall.

"Whatever you do, darling," Cait added in a firm voice, "I'll support you all the way. And I'll always love you."

Seconds clicked by. Kelsey remained frozen, deep in *iought.* Cait sat perfectly still.

"If...if I testify, will you be there with me?"

Cait's throat pinched tight, and her heart raced. Neither *f* those things was reflected in her calm tone. "Abso- *itely.*"

Kelsey took a deep breath. "I'm still scared, but I'm more *:ared* that I'll never see Daddy again."

"No!" Tyler's voice was hoarse but firm with determi- *ation.* Beyond the thick glass separating them, Cait saw his *and* clench around the phone pressed to his ear. It was *:riving* her crazy communicating with him this way.

He looked so tired, and his face was gaunt from the *veight* he'd lost in the two weeks he'd been incarcerated. She *onged* to kiss away the tension and hold him close, but *ontact* visits weren't allowed in Sacramento County Jail.

"Please, Tyler," Cait murmured into the phone on her *ide.* "Kelsey has a right to make that decision. You said so *ourself.*"

"No, Cait, and that's final."

"Why is it final?"

Tyler raked the hand that was still in a cast through his *hick* hair. He needed a haircut and a shave. The prison *umpsuit* he was wearing had been designed for a much *maller* man and desperately needed laundering.

"Because, Cait, it wouldn't do any good. No matter what *Kelsey* says, Shuffler's got me cold. I don't want her put *hrough* hell for nothing."

"That's her choice."

"It's *my* freedom that's at stake." Anger made his voi
dangerously cold.

"That's not an answer."

"It's a fact."

Cait sat back in the hard plastic chair and fought the nee
to give in to tears. Even though she'd promised herself th
she would be composed and reassuring, she was dange
ously close to breaking down.

Seeing him penned up, seeing the changes that had a
ready taken place in his face, knowing what was waiting f
him, was almost more than she could bear.

"I love you. Doesn't that mean anything to you?" sl
asked when she had her voice under control again.

"You know it does." His voice sounded raw, eve
through the phone.

"Then fight so that we can be together. Let me fig
alongside you and Kelsey. She wants her daddy home agai
And so do I."

His eyes changed, the only sign of his inner agony. A
ready he was steeling himself for a life where uncontrolle
emotions would make him vulnerable.

"It was always impossible. We were just kidding ou
selves that it wasn't."

Cait shook her head. "Not me. I believe in the imposs
ble. So did you once. You told me that's why you love
medicine so much. Because miracles happened every day.

He flinched. "Stop it, Cait. You're only making th
worse for both of us."

"Not me, Tyler. I'm still fighting. You're the one who
given up."

"I'm the only one who seems to be facing reality," he s
but shouted into the phone. This time the flash of emotic
in his eyes was harder to conceal. Cait counted that as
victory. She was playing dirty and she knew it, but she didr
care. She was fighting a desperate battle with terrible co
sequences if she lost.

She glanced around. All the cubicles were filled but th
one next to her. On the visitors' side of the glass, she sa
mostly women. Their ages varied. Economic situations, to

But the misery on their faces was universal. They had given up.

No, she thought. Never.

"This is the reality," she said softly into the plastic phone receiver that smelled sickeningly of disinfectant. "You gave Kelsey the choice of testifying or not. I thought that was a mistake, but I supported you because you asked me to. Now she's made her choice, and I'm supporting her because *she* asked me to."

His mouth twisted. "It's not the same—"

"It's exactly the same."

"She'll be hurt, perhaps irreparably." His voice was low and not quite controlled.

"Living the rest of her life with guilt on her conscience will hurt her even more."

"You don't know that!"

"In my practice I see the damage caused by guilt nearly every day. Sometimes it makes me cry because the pain has gone on so long that the damage really *is* irreparable."

"Cait—"

"Kelsey *needs* to do this, Tyler. No matter what the results are, she'll come out of that hearing room feeling good about herself."

He took a deep breath through his mouth. "Lamont will tear her to pieces."

"I don't think so, but if he does, I think she can survive."

"Damn it, I don't!" he shouted loudly enough for the sound to carry through the glass.

Faces turned her way, some out of curiosity or annoyance, others out of compassion. At the guard's station behind Tyler, a Hispanic with a florid face and hard eyes watched him warily for several seconds before shifting his gaze to the clock on the wall. Tyler had been granted fifteen minutes. Most of those were already gone.

Fearful that the guard would call a halt immediately, Cait leaned forward to gain as much privacy as she could and rushed into speech.

"I've already called Dante. He's arranged for Kelsey and me to attend the hearing tomorrow. Whether you like it or not, Kelsey intends to testify."

Tyler's strong jaw worked convulsively before he controlled the muscles of his face. But his eyes remained dark with strong emotion.

"Call it off, Cait."

She shook her head. "I can't."

"Try to understand, Cait."

He wasn't pleading, but she knew from the sudden hoarseness in his tone that what he was going to say came from that fiercely protected place inside him. "Tell me," she whispered.

His face took on an expression of terrible strain, and his knuckles whitened from the strength of his grip around the phone. "I learned something these past few months with you. That I could feel again. That I wanted to be part of the family you and Kelsey had made together. That there are all kinds of prisons."

His chest rose and fell as he drew in air. "I could accept my life the way it was when I was alone. I hated it, but I could manage. But with you..."

"With me?"

His gaze flickered like a caress over her face, and Cait felt some of the fear leave her.

"With you, I was always conscious of the things I wanted to give you but couldn't. When we went out, I wanted it to be where people could see us and know how happy we were, but I had to protect your reputation."

Cait's jaw dropped and her eyes flashed. So that was the reason they'd never gone anywhere but the local pizza parlor and a nearby ice-cream shop. "What are you talking about? You don't have to protect me from anything."

"Yeah, I know," he said, saluting her reaction with a crooked smile. "It was damn controlling and just a little sneaky, but it was all I had to give you. My protection. And now... now that's all I have to give Kelsey. If you let her testify, you'll be taking that one last thing away from me.

I'm going back to prison anyway. At least let me go back with my pride."

Tears flooded her eyes, making it difficult to see the anguished eyes boring into hers.

"Please, Cait," he whispered into the receiver. "If you love me, don't do that to me."

For a long moment she was too choked with emotion to speak. The tears ran unchecked down her cheeks. Her mouth trembled with the need to convince him.

Moment by moment, the hands of the clock were moving inexorably. Any second now the guard with the bored face would order Tyler away from her. And he would have to go.

"I do love you," she whispered in an achingly tender voice. "So much I don't have words to tell you *how* much. More than anything, I want a future for us. The three of us. And someday...someday I want to give Kelsey a brother or sister to love."

"Don't, Cait."

"You've already given us so much. Don't you realize that it's because of you that she has the courage to walk into that room tomorrow? Because of your strength and the love you've shown her. And your forgiveness."

She took a deep breath. Time was nearly up. The steel in his jaw told her that she hadn't reached him.

"As for me, you've made me feel beautiful and treasured and respected. You let me be me, even when it couldn't have been easy for you. You've given us so much. Please let us help you now. Please, darling, please."

He closed his eyes, and when he opened them, she knew she'd lost.

"It's a chance in a million, Cait. I can't let Kelsey take that risk, no matter how strong she thinks she is. I've been there. I know what those bastards can do. Kelsey could never stand up to it."

Cait saw the glint of some brutal memory come into his eyes, and she longed to break through the glass and hold him.

"I think she can. So does she. If there's a chance in a million, I want us to have it. All three of us."

Pain turned his face into a mask. He dropped his head and let the phone fall. Even if she spoke now, he wouldn't hear her.

Oh, Tyler, I love you so much, she thought. Please believe. Please try.

Slowly, as though he'd heard her thoughts, his head came up and his gaze found hers. His shadowed eyes seemed utterly black now, and his mouth was motionless. The intensity of his gaze was almost more than she could bear.

He sat without speaking, his gaze roaming her face hungrily, as though he were memorizing her features. Cait sat perfectly still, conscious that the next few moments might very well decide if her life was ever going to be complete.

When she couldn't stand it any longer, she smiled and pressed her free hand palm out against the glass. Slowly, as though he couldn't help himself, Tyler pressed his hand to hers. It was so much bigger, so much stronger, but the glass between them, cold and unyielding, kept her from feeling its gentleness and warmth.

"I love you," she whispered, knowing that he would read her lips.

His face twisted as though he'd taken a fatal blow. And his eyes narrowed, perhaps to hide the anguish he could no longer disguise. For an instant she thought he was going to repeat her words back to her. Heart racing, she held her breath, waiting.

Seconds passed. Neither moved. Cait felt herself being pulled toward the longing that shivered like tears in his eyes. Then, abruptly, he broke the symbolic contact of their hands and used his to lift the phone to his mouth again.

"Keep Kelsey out of that hearing tomorrow, Cait. Or, I swear, I'll never forgive you." Before she could react, he had hung up the phone and disappeared behind the impenetrable steel door.

Chapter 15

Tyler lay stiff and unmoving on the narrow bunk and tried to block out the sounds that were so obscenely familiar. The cell block was dimly lit, revealing row upon row of austere, narrow cages. Men slept four to a cell.

He dragged his forearms across his eyes and tried to will himself into oblivion. But it was a useless effort. Cait was still with him, her soft, anguished, pleading voice tenaciously alive in his thoughts. With every breath he took, he longed to be with her. She was as necessary to him now as food and drink and air to breathe.

He thought of her reappearance into his life and the spirit she'd shown, even when he was venting his white-hot rage at her in his office. He thought of the resentment he'd felt toward her, even as he was coming to want her in his bed.

He had fought the first wisps of feeling as fiercely as he'd once fought to become a doctor. It hadn't taken long, though, before he had realized he was coming to love her.

Tyler clenched his jaw and tried to blot the image of her shining eyes and sensuous, teasing smile from his mind. Even now, knowing that she intended to strip him of the last

of his pride, he wanted her with an intensity that filled him
with helpless fury.

It wasn't physical hunger that tormented him, however.
That he had learned to endure once and would learn to endure again. But the rest—her serenity in face of his black
moods, her quiet humor that jolted him out of feeling sorry
for himself, her sweet laughter that was a balm to his hurting soul—those things he would always crave with a sharp,
endless need.

He wanted her, but, God help him, he would never forgive her. A man who was any kind of a man at all protected
the ones he loved. She hadn't even allowed him the one
small gift he had left to give.

To some men that might not seem like much. To a man
facing a long stretch in prison, however, a man who needed
to feel strong and invulnerable and self-contained in order
to survive, it was everything.

"Nervous?"

Cait gave Dante the reproachful look his question deserved. "How about you?"

The burly attorney shook his head. "I was calmer right
before I stepped into a Formula One car for the first time."

"How was Tyler when you saw him last night?"

"Icy. He told me what happened between you. He also
told me that I wasn't under any circumstances to call Kelsey as a witness."

Cait's eyes flew fully open and she gaped at him. "You
didn't agree?"

"No, I didn't."

"Thank God." Cait slumped against the slats of the
bench.

Dante was silent for a moment, and his expression was
troubled, as though he were working up his courage. Finally his mouth firmed, as though he'd made a decision. "I
owe you an apology," he said gruffly.

"You do?" Her gaze touched his terrible tie before rising
to his face.

His grin was ragged. "Not very long ago I told Ty that you weren't his friend. I was wrong. You're probably the best friend he's ever had, including me."

Cait's throat worked. "Thank you," she whispered nearly soundlessly. "You've been a good friend, too. Not only to Tyler, but to Kelsey and me these past weeks. I don't know what we would have done without you and Hazel. When one of you couldn't be around, the other always managed to be there." She smiled. "Like today. Chicken pox, for goodness sakes."

Dante nodded. "She swore she got it at Kelsey's party. I told her we didn't need her testimony, not with Kelsey's. It didn't seem to help. She was still mad at herself."

Cait glanced past his broad shoulder to the water fountain halfway between the bench where she and Dante were sitting and the door to the hearing room. Kelsey, dressed in a new dress she'd picked out herself, was slurping her third drink since they'd arrived fifteen minutes ago.

"The kid has guts," Dante murmured with a fond smile. Kelsey had wound her way into his heart the first time she kissed his cheek and called him Uncle Jess.

"Like her daddy," Cait whispered.

Dante's big hand covered hers where it clutched her purse. "Like her mamma, too. It takes a hell of a lot of courage to go against Tyler McClane when he's in the kind of mood he's been in since his arrest." Dante squeezed her hand in understanding before withdrawing his.

Cait swallowed, but the raw taste of panic remained. "I'm not brave, Jess. I just didn't have any other choice, not when I know what will happen if he has to go to prison."

Dante glanced down at his hand without answering.

"He'll die this time. Won't he?"

His gaze flickered toward Kelsey, who was slowly walking toward them with her hands pressed together tightly and her expression solemn.

"Yes, Cait. I think he will." His gaze came back to hers. She read sympathy there and a grief that rivaled her own. "His time with you has changed him too much. I don't

think he can make himself hard and unfeeling the way h
was before.''

Cait's eyes filled with tears. "Don't say that," sh
pleaded. "Don't even think it."

"How much longer, Uncle Jess?" Kelsey asked as sh
drew close.

Dante looked at his watch. "Shouldn't be too long now
squirt. These things never start on time, though. Some
times your fanny gets darn tired."

Kelsey giggled, but her eyes remained fixed on the close
door across the corridor. Cait and Dante exchanged looks
That was the door leading to the cell block where Tyler wa
locked away.

It was almost ten minutes later when the door opened an
Tyler stepped through, followed by the same guard she'
seen in the visiting room.

"Daddy!" Kelsey jerked to her feet, intending to go t
him, but Cait caught the hem of her dress and stopped he

Tyler was shackled hand and foot. It would be awkwar
for him to hug her, even if the guard would allow it, which
she decided after a swift look at his set face, he wouldn't.

"Let me go, Mama Cait," Kelsey cried as she tried to jer
her dress from Cait's grasp. "It's Daddy."

"I know." Cait's gaze was fastened on Tyler's face. Ev
erything else blurred. The shabby, institutional furniture i
the waiting room. The guard's face. Even when Dant
hooked his arm around Kelsey to pull her against his thigh
Cait was only dimly aware. Nothing could interfere with he
need to make Tyler understand.

"Tyler," she whispered. "Please listen to me. I love you
Don't put this between us. Please don't."

He paused to look at her. Tension rode his shoulders an
whitened his jaw. She saw only his eyes. Smoldering wit
black, embittered anger too strong to be controlled, the
impaled her.

"Nothing's changed, Cait," he said in the coldest voic
she'd ever heard.

She sat stunned and hurting as he walked slightly ahea
of the guard toward the hearing room. His back was proudl

straight, his shoulders braced to take whatever punishment the board handed out. The chains hobbling his long legs rattled obscenely against the floor.

Next to her, Kelsey was crying softly. Dante's expression was frozen. Cait's gaze clung to Tyler's back as the guard knocked once, then opened the door. She was still staring long after the door had closed behind him.

Ninety agonizing minutes later, the three of them, Cait, Dante and Kelsey were back on the same uncomfortable bench.

It had been as bad as Cait had expected. Worse.

Prompted by Harvey Shuffler, Lamont had been unrelenting in his nasty insinuations that Kelsey was lying now to protect the man who was sleeping with her mother.

Tyler's face had turned stark white at that. Like sudden frost over iron, his eyes had gone cold. Cait knew that he had been ready to explode. Even though she had been across the table, too far away to touch him, she leaned forward enough to draw his quick, machine-gun gaze.

Please don't, she had signaled with her eyes. Trust me. Trust your daughter. His jaw had clenched, but he'd made no move to protest.

Dante had been superb, countering Lamont's accusations with calm rebuttals. Step by step, he'd led Kelsey through her story, pausing to let her calm herself when she seemed on the verge of panic, stopping to pour her a glass of ice water when tears flooded her eyes and her mouth trembled uncontrollably.

All through her ordeal, however, it was Tyler's face the little girl watched. Her daddy gave her strength.

Now it was all over but the waiting. Cait had never been so nervous. Her palms were sweating, and she had to keep swallowing to ease the pinched dryness in her throat.

Next to her, Dante was fidgeting with his tie, his hair, just about anything his hand could reach.

Kelsey's head was cradled in Cait's lap. Her feet rested on Dante's hard thighs. At the moment her quiet breathing and the hiss of the ventilation system overhead were the only sounds in the long, empty corridor.

"I'm so proud of you," Cait murmured, bending low over the exhausted little girl.

"Me too, squirt," Dante's deep voice chimed in. "You handled some mighty tough questions like a real soldier."

Kelsey's lashes swooped up and down. "I still don't like that Mr. Lamont," she murmured indignantly into the fold of Cait's skirt. "He was real nasty to Daddy when he was trying to explain about that man Bronsky."

"When wasn't he nasty?" Cait muttered, bringing a chuckle to Dante's throat. Kelsey grinned, too, before her eyelids fluttered closed again. Cait suspected that the little girl hadn't slept much last night.

She herself had paced the floor until well past midnight before climbing into bed to spend the rest of the night staring at the wishing candle on her bedside table.

"It just has to come true," she muttered. "It just *has* to."

"Pardon?"

Cait gave Dante an apologetic look. "Just talking to myself."

He nodded. "Whatever gets you through the night. Me, I like to pass the time imagining what I'd do to that bastard Shuffler if I ever got him alone in a dark alley."

Cait grinned at that. Perhaps that had been his intention. She had learned that under the rough exterior, Tyler's friend was almost as kindhearted as Tyler. But then, maybe that was why they were friends.

"Jess," she murmured, "what are his chances?"

Dante glanced down at his hand, which slowly closed into a fist. "Less than fifty-fifty."

"How much less?"

He shot her a rueful look. "Ty's right. You can be as stubborn as he is."

"Don't change the subject."

His expression sobered. "Twenty-five, seventy-five."

Cait slumped against the hard bench. In her lap, Kelsey slept peacefully now, but the signs of her ordeal were still visible in the paleness of her skin and the puffy eyelids.

The others who'd attended the hearing—Lamont, Shuffler, Tyler, the guard—were still in the hearing room. They'd remained after the board members had retired to an inner office to deliberate.

Kelsey had wanted to stay, too, but Cait couldn't bear another instant of Tyler's cold withdrawal. Bless his heart, Dante had opted to wait outside with the two of them.

"How long does it usually take?" she asked him now.

"Varies," he answered with a bleak grin. "I remember once it took nearly five hours."

"Five hours!" she exclaimed. "I'll be a wreck."

"Don't worry. This is pretty clear-cut. Either they believed Kelsey, in which case they'll be on Ty's side and inclined to be lenient—at least until they know the results of his new trial. Or they'll believe Shuffler and Lamont, in which case they'll think Kelsey is lying now and throw the book at Ty."

"Thanks a lot," Cait muttered through lips so dry they hurt.

"Just trying to lighten the mood," he said with a grin that looked frayed around the edges.

"There's only one thing that can do that." As though in silent agreement, they both looked toward the hearing room where Tyler waited to learn his fate. Just as I'm waiting out here, Cait thought.

Dante cleared his throat. "How about some coffee? There's a machine outside."

"God, no. I'd be sick."

"Maybe you're right," he muttered.

Cait was silent for only a few seconds before bursting out, "Why is he so stubborn, Jess?"

"He's a man. And every man needs to feel that he has something to contribute, something of value to give to the people he cares about. The last few years have left him with little more than his pride. He thinks you took it away. To a man like Tyler, that can be damn near unbearable, like stripping away his manhood."

Cait gaped at him. In his own way Dante had said the same thing that Tyler had said. "Is that what he told you?"

"No, it's what I know." He hesitated, then touched his sleeve. "When I lost this, I thought I was washed up. As a race driver, certainly, but also as a man. My wife left me because she wanted the fame and money that went with me more than she wanted me. I felt emasculated. In fact, I actually was impotent for a long time."

He paused, gathering his thoughts. A faint red tinge overlaid the olive of his skin, and his eyes were focused on some distant spot.

"Ty came to see me 'long about the time I'd hit bottom. I was broke, still weak from all the surgery, disgusted by my body. He literally kicked my ass out of bed and bullied me into admitting I was just feeling sorry for myself." He turned his head to look at her. "In a way, maybe that's what he's doing, too."

"If he saw it in you, why can't he see it in himself?"

Dante shrugged. "You're the shrink. You tell me."

Cait smiled and turned away. *Because he doesn't love me enough to fight,* she thought on a wave of pain. *Maybe he never can.*

"Uh-oh," Dante muttered. "Looks like something's happening."

The door was opening. Shuffler came out first, walking fast. Fear engulfed her. Time seemed to stand frozen. And then Tyler was striding through the door.

"The chains are gone," she murmured to Dante, who rose.

"Damn straight they are!"

"Does that mean—"

"We won," Dante murmured. "Damn it, we won!"

Tears flooded Cait's eyes. "Wake up, Kelsey," she whispered as she gently shook the little girl. "Wake up and look."

"Hmm?" Kelsey's eyelids opened slowly, as though she had been deep in sleep. Cait helped her to sit up.

"Daddy's coming," she murmured past a thick ball of relief and gratitude clogging her throat. At that, Kelsey's eyes snapped wide.

"Daddy!" she shouted.

This time, when she shot to her feet, Cait didn't stop her. With a whoop of joy Kelsey ran toward her daddy, who swept her up in his arms and hugged her hard against his heart. His head was bowed and his shoulders shuddered, as though he were having difficulty coping with the emotions moving through him.

Kelsey was laughing and crying at the same time. "Did we win, Daddy?" Kelsey cried. "Did we?"

"We sure did, thanks to you," Tyler said with deep feeling rasping his voice. Behind him, the members of the parole board were filing out in groups of two and threes, heading for the exit to the right. One or two smiled in their direction. Lamont stared straight ahead as he passed by.

"Really and truly, Daddy?"

"Really and truly." Tyler kissed her heartily before shifting her to one arm so that he could pull Dante into a clumsy hug with the other.

"Thanks, friend," he muttered.

"You ain't seen nothing yet," Dante said with a grin so wide it threatened to crack his strong jaw. "Wait till the trial. With a dynamite witness like this one, we can't lose." He planted a big kiss on Kelsey's cheek before stepping back out of the way.

There was nothing between Cait and Tyler now. Nothing but the cutting words he had flung at her. Nothing but the action she'd taken against his wishes. At the moment those things seemed as high as the tallest prison walls and just as unscalable.

"Congratulations," Cait said softly. Her cheeks were still wet, and her hair was falling from its pins. Tyler nodded, but he didn't speak. Instead, he kissed Kelsey again, then lowered her to the ground. Her hand found his, and he held on tight.

He seemed friendly enough, Cait realized, watching through her tears. Friendly, but distant. Terribly, terribly distant.

"Isn't it terrific, Mama Cait? Daddy can come home now."

"Very terrific, sweetie." Cait managed a smile, but he
hands were busy ruining her best purse. Tyler watched he
steadily but said nothing. Dante looked from one to th
other impatiently.

"C'mon, Kels," he said, holding out his hand. "Let's yo
and me go get the car and bring it around front."

"Okay," Kelsey said before wrapping her arms aroun
her daddy's lean waist in another happy bear hug.

"Hurry up, okay?" she said over her shoulder as sh
skipped beside Dante toward the exit.

"Okay," Cait called after her. She continued to watc
until Dante and Kelsey disappeared around a corner. Slow]
she turned to face the only man she'd ever loved.

"So," she said softly, "you're a free man."

"In a manner of speaking," he said at last. "My parol
is still in effect."

"There's the trial in six months."

He wanted to touch her so badly that his hands wer
shaking like an intern's as he faced his first incision. H
shoved them into the pockets of his red jumpsuit and noc
ded. "You look tired."

Cait mustered a small smile. "I haven't been sleepin
well."

"Neither have I." His voice was muted. "I kept thinkin
of you."

She took a step toward him, then stopped. "What wer
you thinking?" she asked softly.

"That I needed to hate you."

His words were softly spoken, but his mouth was hard
Hurt shivered through her, as sharp and stinging as an
blade.

"I see," she said, and her voice seemed hollow in th
empty corridor.

"I'm not sure you do."

"Then tell me." She took a step forward. He stiffened
and she stopped.

Tyler took a deep breath and cast his thoughts backwar
to a time and place he never wanted to visit again. "There
a game cons play in prison, even the guys in for life. The

pend hours on it. Mostly it's just talk. About the things they'll do when they get out. The first meal, the first drink, the first woman—things like that.''

"Did you do that, too?" Cait asked softly. In spite of the hurt still living inside her, she needed to know.

"Rarely." His voice was clipped now, as though he hated talking of such things but was determined to do so anyway. "Sometimes, late at night when it was too hot or too noisy to sleep, I couldn't seem to help myself. And then I would think about starting over with a woman who wanted me for me and not what I could give her.''

He ran his tongue over his bottom lip as though his mouth were suddenly dry, before continuing. "She never had a face or a name. How could she? The only woman I'd ever really wanted thought I was some kind of depraved monster." He took a slow, painful breath. "You, Cait."

Emotion misted her eyes. "Then why—"

"Let me finish, please."

Biting her lip, she nodded. She was afraid to breathe, afraid suddenly that he would close up again.

"I said that it was a game, and it was. That's *all* it was, because the real world is a hell of a lot different than the one a guy behind bars wants it to be."

"It doesn't have to be," Cait murmured softly.

He smiled, but there was no humor in the quick movement of his hard mouth. "Be realistic, Cait. You live in a nice house in a nice neighborhood. I live over a saloon, which, at the moment, isn't even paying me a salary."

"So?"

"So a man has to offer a woman a lot more than that."

"Who says?"

"*I* say. And you know I'm right."

This time when she went toward him, he stood stoically still and waited. When she reached for his hand, he flinched but folded his fingers over hers.

"I *know* that you'll be acquitted when you come to trial again. And that means you'll get your license to practice medicine again."

Tyler lifted their joined hands and looked down at h
carefully tended nails. They were covered in clear polish th
only seemed to make them seem more graceful. And fra
ile.

"Even with an acquittal, Jess says that at best I have
fifty-fifty chance of ever practicing again. And he's a hell
a lot more optimistic than I am."

She yanked her hand from his and propped it against h
hip. At the same time she thrust her jaw a good half in
closer to his. "So you're just going to give up? Is that it?

Anger flared in his eyes, turning them silver. "No, I'm n
giving up. I'm trying to show you why it can't work b
tween us."

"Is that supposed to make me feel better?"

"Cait, I have nothing to offer you."

She reminded herself that he'd been hurt very badl
Healing would take time, but it had to start sometime. A
it couldn't start with pity or misunderstanding.

"Thank you very much for assuming that I'm like n
sister," she threw at him with all the honest fire she cou
muster. "I can't tell you how gratified that makes me fe
right now."

There it was again, he thought in astonishment. Th
quick burst of temper from her that always caught him o
guard.

"I never said—"

"Oh yes you did. Not five minutes ago you stood there
that stupid, ugly red suit and told me in that stiff voice y
use when you're keeping everything buttoned up tight i
side that there couldn't be anything permanent between
because you were no longer a rich, prominent doctor an
of course, that means that I couldn't possibly want you."

"Cait, I—"

"Oh no! You've had your turn, Tyler. Now it's mine
Her eyes smoked, and her cheeks grew pinker with ea
word. Her scent swirled around him, filling his senses. H
heart sped faster and his respiration increased, making hi
realize just how helpless he was around her.

"I've had two lovers in my life before you," Cait rushed on. The swift surge of some volatile reaction in his eyes encouraged her. At least he wasn't still looking at her in that frozen way she hated.

"Both were prominent, successful men. Both asked me to marry them. I'm not saying that to brag or make you jealous, but because it's true. It's also true that I turned them down."

The challenge snapping in her eyes dared him to ask why. It was a dare he would be a fool to take. He took it anyway. "Why?"

Her answer was ready and sure and rocked him back as surely as a sucker punch. "Because I didn't love either of them enough to want his baby. But I want yours, Tyler. And I want you, just the way you are. Stubborn, moody, impossibly sexy and the father of all the rest of my children."

Cait knew enough about human nature to know that not even the world's best actor could fake the quick rush of color from his face. Or the sudden blank look of shock in his eyes.

"You said it wasn't a problem."

"It isn't. And I'm not pregnant, damn it. I won't ever be unless you stop standing up there on all that pride and take me home."

Not even the sudden narrowing of his gaze could hide the emotion blazing from them. "Don't I have any say in this?"

"Some, but remember, I'm not getting any younger, and neither are you. Also, Kelsey really needs a brother or sister to keep her from becoming impossibly spoiled."

He stared at her as though he couldn't believe his ears. "Don't look so stricken, Tyler," she said with a soft laugh. "This is the nineties. Single women propose to reluctant lovers all the time."

It seemed an eternity before he moved. When he did, it was to haul her against him. His mouth crashed down on hers, branding her with a wild sweet pleasure so powerful it bordered on pain.

His good hand flattened against her cheek, and she felt the wild, surging rhythm of his heartbeat through the toughened skin of his palm. Her own pulse was speeding in perfect time with the racing blood heating her own skin.

"Is that a yes?" she asked in a shaken tone.

"It sure as hell is," he grated. "And don't think you can change your mind, because as soon as I can get permission from my new PO, we're getting married." He glared at her as though he expected her to refuse.

"Okay, but I'll need time to get a knockout dress, and one for Kelsey, too, of course."

Blood was pounding in his head, making his need for her damn near unmanageable. "The day after I get the permission, no later."

"Then there's the cake and flowers and a minister. Hazel has to be there, of course. And Jess. I suppose you'll want him for your best man."

"Cait." His voice broke on her name.

She placed both hands on his chest and felt his heart sprinting beneath her palms. "Remember when you gave me the first wishing candle and you asked me what I wished for?"

He didn't answer, but she saw his eyes begin to smolder. "It's the same thing I wished for this Christmas. Would you like to know what it is?"

"I'm afraid to."

He dragged her hands from his chest and trapped them between his. The edge of his cast cut into her palm, but she didn't mind a bit. His expression was a mix of sheer masculine shock and volatile desire.

"Well, if you'd rather not know—"

"Tell me," he ordered, "before I go stark, staring mad."

Cait smiled. "Happily ever after."

He scowled. "What?"

"My wish. I wished for happily ever after for us. You and me together. For always."

Tyler couldn't remember how her arms got around his neck or how her mouth got so close to his. It seemed that she was determined to push her way into his life, no matter how many problems he might cause for her.

"You *are* going to make my wish come true, aren't you, 'yler?" she asked against his lips.

In answer his mouth moved on hers, hot and heavy, but is tongue made love to her with surprising restraint, far nore arousing than the most urgent invasion.

"I love you, Cait," he murmured as he concentrated on er lips, her throat, the soft skin in the vee of her collar. "I ove you so much. Even when I was hating you, I loved ou."

"Oh, Tyler," she whispered. "I'm so happy I could urst."

His mouth was on hers again, feverish with need. He felt er give against him, but only so far. Her hands roamed his ace, gentle yet sure. He felt something warm inside him.

"Ahem. Excuse me, folks."

Locked together, both Cait and Tyler started in surprise t the sound of the Latin-flavored voice. It was the guard e had seen earlier with Tyler. Now he stood a few feet way, the shackles and handcuffs that had confined Tyler ow dangling from his hands.

"C'mon, McClane. Tell her you'll make her damn wish ome true, whatever it is, so I can get you checked out of ere before quitting time."

Tyler turned to look at her, an expression of deep love oftening his eyes to a rare and beautiful topaz.

"You heard the man."

"Hmm," she whispered adoringly. "Are you going to do hat he says?"

His smile started in his eyes first, then spread to his eautiful, not-so-hard mouth.

"A wish for always?" he mused. "I guess I can handle aat."

Epilogue

"Daddy, c'mon," Kelsey called impatiently from t
doorway of the master bedroom.

"Just a minute, baby," Tyler muttered around the ri
bon caught between his teeth.

"Mama says you'd better get your fanny downstairs *rig*
now or you'll be in bad trouble."

Tyler tugged the ribbon from his mouth and wrapped
one-handedly around the soft foam football. With the oth
he tried to hold the wrapping paper snug against the poin
but the paper still looked lumpy.

"Hand me some more tape, will you, baby?"

"It's already covered with it. Besides, Jesse won't noti
All he wants to do is chew on the paper anyway."

"He's teething."

"He's been teething since he was three months old. Eve
toy he owns has little teeth marks all over it."

Tyler stepped back. "You're right," he said with a gri
Deftly he scooped up the lumpy football and tossed it to h

Kelsey caught it expertly, the way he'd taught her to c
and grinned. Arm in arm, they hurried down the stairs.

Cait was waiting at the bottom with a mulish look on her face. "You said five minutes, Tyler. It's been twenty."

Kelsey gave her daddy an I-told-you-so look and headed for the dining room, where Dante and Hazel, the baby's godparents, were trying to outdo each other seeing who could get the biggest belly laugh from one-year-old Jesse Fielding McClane.

"Sorry, sweetheart," Tyler murmured, trying to look suitably chastened, even as he pulled her into his arms.

"You don't look sorry," Cait murmured as she slid her arms around his neck.

"No?" He raised one silver eyebrow.

"No. You look just the way you always look when you're about to talk me into going upstairs and locking the bedroom door."

"Sounds like a damn fine idea to me." His grin came easily now, like a sudden burst of sunlight in a dreary day. Sometimes she deliberately teased him, just to see it flash.

"Tyler, stop that. We have guests."

"So?" The thought of stripping her out of her slacks and silky shirt was damn near irresistible. Even after twenty months of marriage, he still got as shaky as a teenager whenever he thought of making love to her.

"So you'll have to wait," she murmured, but her belly rubbed enticingly against the arousal she could feel beginning to throb behind the fabric of his trousers.

"Keep that up, wife, and you'll be upstairs so fast you won't have time to yell for help."

Cait's blood heated at the thought. When Tyler was in one of his playful moods, she could deny him nothing. Not that she wanted to, she realized, raising her mouth for the kiss she knew he intended to give her.

His mouth was warm and possessive, and his hands roamed freely, even though they were standing in the foyer in full view of anyone who might wander through.

Her own hands played with his thick hair. Worn shorter now, it was still soft to the touch and very sexy when her hands were finished disheveling it.

Tyler was breathing hard when he ended the kiss. "Fifteen minutes," he whispered against her throat. "One of those quickies you like so much."

"Me?" His mouth was now busy exploring her throat.

"Hmm. Remember how it was after Jess was born? You were after me at the oddest times, and then, when I finally gave in, you were always in a hurry."

Tyler raised his head to look at her. Even when he was teasing her, he always seemed to be loving her with his eyes.

"That's because your son kept me so busy I didn't have time for those long lingering sessions *you* like so much."

"Ah, the good old days," he murmured.

Cait hit him on the shoulder. "Behave yourself, buster."

"Yes, ma'am." His expression sobered, and Cait wondered if he was thinking about the years he'd spent taking orders. Even now, he sometimes woke sweating and shaking from a nightmare he would never reveal.

She made her smile gentle as she went on tiptoe to kiss him out of his sudden dark mood. She'd done that a lot at first, especially in the weeks right before the trial, when all three of them were tense and worried.

The fire in his eyes was hot, but his smile was boyishly crooked as he pulled a small package out of his pocket and handed it to her. "For you, wife."

"What's this?"

"It's a present, what's it look like?"

Cait shook the small box neatly wrapped in silver. "It looks expensive, that's what it looks like," she chided gently.

Tyler leaned lazily against the newel post and watched her tear into the wrapping with the excitement of a child. He never got tired of watching her. Sometimes at night he lay awake for hours, holding her close and watching her face as she slept.

"Oh, Tyler," she whispered as she drew the dainty, exquisitely designed pendant of shimmering silver from its nest of velvet. "Another wishing candle."

"I know it's not Christmas, but what the heck." He took the pendant from her hand. "Turn around," he ordered gruffly.

Cait obeyed, dropping her head and lifting the thick fall of her hair out of the way at the same time. Tyler looped the chain around her neck and fastened it, but before he let her go, he bent to brush a reverent kiss over the silky skin beneath the silver.

Moisture stung his eyes, and he closed them against the sudden need to tell her how precious she was to him. Ever so gently, he turned her around and kissed her. Her mouth yielded, soft and enticing as always, and a shuddering feeling of thankfulness rushed through him.

"Thank you for giving me another child to love," he said with a slight tremor in his voice. "And for giving me back my faith."

Cait's smile wobbled. He was so dear to her, her sometimes moody, sometimes difficult husband. "Thank you for exactly the same things."

He cleared his throat. "I guess we'd better join the others before Jesse gets chocolate icing all over your precious needlepoint chairs."

"The little dickens," she murmured with a tender look. "He's got a lot of his father in him."

"And a lot of his mother, especially when he doesn't get his own way."

"I'm not spoiled," she muttered mutinously. "And you know it."

"Mmm, seems to me I'm the one who's always giving in when we argue."

"That's because you can't wait to get me into bed so we can make up."

He grinned. "That's true." He wiggled his eyebrows. "Wanna have a quick battle?"

Cait's giggle was cut off by the swift descent of his mouth. His hands combed through her hair. His body rubbed against hers, heavy with the need to fill her. Moaning sweetly, Cait clung to him, testing his resolve.

"Sweetheart," he rasped with a groan, "if you don't stop—"

His words were halted by an insistent beeping coming from the tiny receiver clipped to his belt.

"Not again," Cait murmured as he muted the sound. "That's the third time this week."

"That's what you get for being married to a doctor," he teased, but his expression was suddenly strained. "Cait, if it really bothers you, I could cut down on my hours at the clinic. There's another doc coming in part-time and—"

Cait laid a gentle hand on the mouth that was so rarely hard now. "I'm just kidding, darling. I know you have to go, just as you know the kids and I will be here when you get back."

Tyler's chest rose and fell in an effort to contain the emotion building in him. "I love you, Caitie McClane," he whispered. "So much. I can't make it without you." His fingers were achingly gentle as they traced the sweep of her cheek.

"You're my life, you and the kids. No matter what happens from now on, nothing will ever be as important to me as that."

Cait's brimming eyes told him that she understood. With a groan, he lowered his head and kissed her one more time.

She would be waiting for him when he got back, no matter how late. His wife, who loved him just as he was. His wife, who had taught him about happily-ever-after. The wife he'd wished for every Christmas since he'd first met her.

* * * * *

OFFICIAL RULES • MILLION DOLLAR BIG WIN SWEEPSTAKES
NO PURCHASE OR OBLIGATION NECESSARY TO ENTER

To enter, follow the directions published. If the Big Win Game Card is missing, hand-print your name and address on a 3″ ×5″ card and mail to either: Silhouette Big Win, 3010 Walden Ave., P.O. Box 1867, Buffalo, NY 14269-1867, or Silhouette Big Win, P.O. Box 609, Fort Erie, Ontario L2A 5X3, and we will assign your Sweepstakes numbers (Limit: one entry per envelope). For eligibility, entries must be received no later than March 31, 1994 and be sent via 1st-class mail. No liability is assumed for printing errors or lost, late or misdirected entries.

To determine winners, the sweepstakes numbers on submitted entries will be compared against a list of randomly preselected prizewinning numbers. In the event all prizes are not claimed via the return of prizewinning numbers, random drawings will be held from among all other entries received to award unclaimed prizes.

Prizewinners will be determined no later than May 30, 1994. Selection of winning numbers and random drawings are under the supervision of D.L. Blair, Inc., an independent judging organization whose decisions are final. One prize to a family or organization. No substitution will be made for any prize, except as offered. Taxes and duties on all prizes are the sole responsibility of winners. Winners will be notified by mail. Chances of winning are determined by the number of entries distributed and received.

Sweepstakes open to persons 18 years of age or older, except employees and immediate family members of Torstar Corporation, D.L. Blair, Inc., their affiliates, subsidiaries and all other agencies, entities and persons connected with the use, marketing or conduct of this Sweepstakes. All applicable laws and regulations apply. Sweepstakes offer void wherever prohibited by law. Any litigation within the province of Quebec respecting the conduct and awarding of a prize in this Sweepstakes must be submitted to the Régies des Loteries et Courses du Quebec. In order to win a prize, residents of Canada will be required to correctly answer a time-limited arithmetical skill-testing question. Values of all prizes are in U.S. currency.

Winners of major prizes will be obligated to sign and return an affidavit of eligibility and release of liability within 30 days of notification. In the event of non-compliance within this time period, prize may be awarded to an alternate winner. Any prize or prize notification returned as undeliverable will result in the awarding of the prize to an alternate winner. By acceptance of their prize, winners consent to use of their names, photographs or other likenesses for purposes of advertising, trade and promotion on behalf of Torstar Corporation without further compensation, unless prohibited by law.

This Sweepstakes is presented by Torstar Corporation, its subsidiaries and affiliates in conjunction with book, merchandise and/or product offerings. Prizes are as follows: Grand Prize—$1,000,000 (payable at $33,333.33 a year for 30 years). First through Sixth Prizes may be presented in different creative executions, each with the following approximate values: First Prize—$35,000; Second Prize—$10,000; 2 Third Prizes—$5,000 each; 5 Fourth Prizes—$1,000 each; 10 Fifth Prizes—$250 each; 1,000 Sixth Prizes—$100 each. Prizewinners will have the opportunity of selecting any prize offered for that level. A travel-prize option if offered and selected by winner, must be completed within 12 months of selection and is subject to hotel and flight accommodations availability. Torstar Corporation may present this sweepstakes utilizing names other than Million Dollar Sweepstakes. For a current list of all prize options offered within prize levels and all names the Sweepstakes may utilize, send a self-addressed stamped envelope (WA residents need not affix return postage) to: Million Dollar Sweepstakes Prize Options/Names, P.O. Box 7410, Blair, NE 68009.

For a list of prizewinners (available after July 31, 1994) send a separate, stamped self-addressed envelope to: Million Dollar Sweepstakes Winners, P.O. Box 4728, Blair NE 68009.

BWS792